The Visco Scandalous Affair

A Steamy Historical Romance

Book 1
THE STANTON LEGACY

M.M. Wakeford

First edition.
978-1-7395071-1-4

Cover designed by Sweet 'N Spicy Designs

www.mw-author.com

Table of Contents

Dedication 5

Chapter 1 6

Chapter 2 18

Chapter 3 22

Chapter 4 35

Chapter 5 39

Chapter 6 44

Chapter 7 49

Chapter 8 56

Chapter 9 60

Chapter 10 65

Chapter 11 71

Chapter 12 81

Chapter 13 84

Chapter 14 91

Chapter 15 98

Chapter 16 103

Chapter 17 107

Chapter 18 115

Chapter 19 120

Chapter 20 128

Chapter 21 145

Chapter 22 157

Chapter 23 162

Chapter 24 167

Chapter 25...173

Chapter 26...182

Chapter 27...190

Chapter 28...194

Chapter 29...200

Chapter 30...205

Chapter 31...216

Chapter 32...220

Chapter 33...231

Chapter 34...240

Chapter 35...253

Chapter 36...259

Chapter 37...263

Letters dispatched on 7th June, 1835....................................268

Epilogue..272

Afterword 284

About the author 285

The Vixen's Unlikely Marriage...286

Chapter 1..287

Chapter 2..292

Chapter 3..296

Also by this author 300

Dedication

This book goes out to all the Charlottes of this world—forgotten, ignored, sidelined—but still determined to make their lives matter. I salute each and every one of you.

March 1835

In the branches overhead, birds chirped, signalling their arrival on England's shores after a long journey over land and sea. The branches wore little green stubs that would soon turn into leaves and thereafter sprout pink and white blossoms. Charlotte Harding smiled to herself as she walked the familiar path to her friend Ruth's house. Despite the freshness of the breeze and the dampness of the grass beneath her shoes, spring had most definitely arrived.

Her quiet life in the small Gloucestershire village of Alstone was marked by the passing of each season. Of these, spring was her favourite. It meant an end to being closeted indoors in the stifling company of her stepmother, and the beginning of pleasurable daily walks in which to witness the wonders of nature's re-awakening after a long winter's slumber. Spring heralded the start of longer days and more light by which to read, and therefore an end to the prolonged hours spent poring over books in the dim glow of a candle.

"Every new beginning comes from some other beginning's end," she reflected as she walked the well-trodden path. Having grown surrounded by the works of classical philosophers in her father's library, she had a tendency to punctuate random moments of her life with a corresponding proverb from these ancient giants. Such was the life of a bookish country girl with little other means of entertainment.

Charlotte reached a bend in the path and caught her first glimpse of the little farmhouse where her dearest and oldest friend resided. She hurried her footsteps, eager to discuss the latest village gossip over a pot of tea, and perhaps also a generous slice of seed cake. Unlatching the gate, she made her way to the sturdy oak door and pulled at the bell. In only a few instants, the door opened wide to reveal the amiable figure of Ruth Ellis.

"Charlotte, how delightful to see you. Come on inside."

"I do not interrupt, I hope."

"Not at all. It is dreary work mending my brother's shirts, and I would love some company. You come in good time too, for I have just put a pot of tea to brew."

Charlotte followed her friend through the short hallway and into a snug but cheery parlour. Unbuttoning her plain brown pelisse, she carefully placed it on a hook by the door and settled herself on a comfortably frayed armchair in the corner of the room. Shortly afterwards, her friend bustled in, bearing a tray with the tea and a slice of cake for each of them. Ruth carefully placed the tray on a side table and busied herself pouring a cup for her guest.

"How goes it with you, dear friend?" she enquired.

Charlotte accepted the beverage gratefully, taking a sip with a happy sigh.

"I am well thank you, and glad to be welcoming in the spring. You talk of dreary work, Ruth, but that is not a patch on the wearisome time I have spent these past weeks listening to Sylvia prattle on about the merits of a match with George Finch."

Sylvia Gibbs, now Harding, was the good lady that her father had married eighteen months prior to his passing in February of last year. In her most private of thoughts, Charlotte sometimes wondered if perhaps it had been this lady's incessant inane chatter that had driven her poor father to his grave.

It had come as a surprise to everyone when that esteemed gentleman, widowed for many a year, had returned home from his annual visit to his man of business in London, engaged to be married. Having loved and mourned his first wife deeply, Hugh Harding had seemingly settled into a quiet life in the country with his only daughter for companionship, showing no desire to re-enter the state of matrimony. What then could have induced him to change course?

This question had taxed Charlotte greatly. Was it the need, in his later years, for the creature comforts that only a female could bring? Was it this lady's undeniable physical charms? In discourse with her father, he had indicated that one of his primary desires in re-marrying was to provide his daughter with the care and direction of a new mama.

"You have grown almost heathenish in your ways, dear child," he had said. "The fault for this is mine, for you have too long been used to the company of elderly males such as myself and not had the chance to develop those social graces that are required if you are to find yourself a good husband. Let Sylvia guide you in the ways of refined women, Charlotte. You must know that I cannot settle much of a fortune on you. That, and the fact that your mother was a foreigner, and not from a landed family, will set you back I fear. However, I am hopeful that with Sylvia's tender care, you may ultimately find yourself a match with a doctor or lawyer of good character, or perhaps even some country squire."

In the year since his passing, Ruth had often told her friend that it was a good thing he had remarried. "Else you would have been cast adrift, Charlotte. Where and with whom would you have lived? Your relatives on your father's side have all but turned their backs on you. It would have been unimaginable for a single young lady as yourself to live alone. In marrying, your father ensured you had the protection and guidance of a mama, and for that you must be thankful."

Charlotte had reluctantly acknowledged the truth of this, though with the observation that this new mama had come at a cost, both monetary and otherwise. Hugh Harding's modest estate of Alstone Grange, comprising the manor house and the surrounding five hundred acres of farmland, had been bequeathed entirely to his widow, with the exception of a lump sum invested in the funds which would provide Charlotte with a meagre income of £100 a year.

And notwithstanding the loss of the small but much loved estate, Charlotte had also been saddled with a mama of trivial understanding whose company she now had to endure day in and day out. At times, Charlotte could not help but wish that her father had chosen his second bride more wisely, for no two ladies could be further apart in looks, character and disposition than his first and second wives.

Her late mother, Juana, had been the beautiful and wilful daughter of a Spanish merchant whom Hugh Harding had met and fallen in love with while stationed in Spain during the Peninsular War. Juana had been a petite, exotic flower of a woman, with a surfeit of passion, courage and intelligence. She had loved her English husband and followed him devotedly to every one of his postings during the war, uncomplaining of the often spartan conditions, even when burdened with the care of their infant daughter. Upon the conclusion of hostilities, they had returned to England and settled in Alstone.

Juana, with her charming broken English and easy smile, had soon melted all but the hardest of hearts in their small rural community. She had raised her only daughter with a gentle but firm hand, instilling in her those true Christian values which taught that all persons, regardless of their social standing, were creatures of God, equally deserving of love and kindness.

It was in this spirit that Juana had befriended Mary, the wife of their tenant farmer, Robert Ellis, whose daughter Ruth soon became firm friends with her own Charlotte. When Juana passed away a dozen years ago, that kindly female had repaid the debt of friendship by bestowing love and care on the young, motherless girl, allowing the grieving Hugh to retreat into his study and lose himself in his books. In turn, Mary had been laid to rest some years later, and Charlotte had mourned her loss as keenly as if she had been her own mother.

Then, along came Sylvia. A handsome woman with a shapely figure and a trilling laugh, she had attracted Hugh Harding's attention at a dinner party held by an acquaintance of his in London. Upon further investigation, he had found out she was the widow of a country rector, in town visiting her married sister. A conversation had been struck up, followed by a hasty courtship. By the end of his week in London, Hugh had proposed and had been accepted. A month later, the two had quietly married in the village church of Alstone, and thus had begun Charlotte's life with a new stepmama.

Sylvia had eagerly taken on the role of mentor and guide into the ways of fashionable society. Charlotte's dark brows were too thick and had to be plucked daily. Her straight brown hair had been cut in what Sylvia assured her was the latest fashion and styled into artful ringlets around her face. Her skin had been deemed too tanned and consequently a regimen of daily washing with talc water instituted. She had been banned from venturing out without a bonnet and veil in order to protect her delicate complexion. And worst of all, her figure had been judged a little too busty and round. The cure? A tight corset to hold in the excess flesh, and a moratorium on the consumption of cakes, biscuits and cheese.

For the most part, Charlotte had suffered through these injunctions uncomplainingly. *"Patience is bitter, but its fruit is sweet,"* she had told herself, quoting yet another of her beloved philosophers. In truth, Charlotte was as keen as any other young, unattached lady of her age to find a good husband. Much as she had loved her father and his books, she had also yearned for romance and the elevated status that marriage would bring. Who could blame her? So, she had endured each tribulation imposed upon her by her new stepmama with as good a grace as she could.

In time, her figure had indeed slimmed down to much more pleasing proportions. Her complexion had improved, and with a few judicious additions to her wardrobe, she had been deemed ready to venture forth into society. Her stepmama had accompanied her to dances at assembly rooms and to social gatherings in the homes of the local gentry, all in hopes that she would catch some eligible bachelor's eye. Here it was, unfortunately, that aspiration had collided with reality.

For despite all the efforts expended into improving her appearance, it was impossible to transform her into a beauty. At best, what had been achieved was passable good looks. Her lips were a little too plump to conform to the beauty ideals of the time; her nose a little too long. Teamed with a lack of dowry and questionable Spanish antecedents, such looks were hardly likely to make a splash in local society. Perhaps had she been possessed of scintillating conversation or a beautiful singing voice, events might have taken a different turn. Be that as it may, the year following Charlotte's launch into local society had produced no offers of marriage and no prospect of any. None that is, until George Finch had come along.

Charlotte had just that fortnight celebrated—or should we say bemoaned—her twenty-fourth birthday. Cast into despondency at reaching such an advanced age without finding love, and chafing at the constant restrictions to her natural enjoyment of life, she had rebelled. Eyeing the refreshments on offer at a local country dance, she had helped herself to a large slice of cake and ignored the scandalised gaze of her stepmama. She had taken her first bite of cake and sighed in pleasure. The crumb was moist and beautifully spiced, and wonderfully, gloriously sweet. Uncaring of the world around her, she had taken a second ecstatic bite.

"Awfully good, isn't it?"

She had looked up in surprise. Beside her was a stout looking young gentleman, himself also bearing a plate with a slice of cake.

"Indeed it is."

"Forgive my poor manners. We have not been introduced. I am George Finch, of Endsleigh Court, at your service ma'am."

11

Charlotte had executed a little curtsy while still holding on to her plate of cake. "Charlotte Harding, of Alstone Grange. I have not had the privilege, sir, of seeing you before at these gatherings."

With a smile, he had responded, "That is because I have been away at Oxford and only recently returned."

They had both paused the conversation then to take another delicious bite of cake. The rush of sugar must have liberated her usually stilted tongue, for she had then exclaimed, "I do believe eating cake to be one of the greatest pleasures to be had in life! Or perhaps it is so because I have denied myself this pleasure these past many months."

"Why so, if I may be so bold as to ask?"

She had blushed prettily then. "It is only so as to maintain a pleasing figure, or so says my stepmama."

He had looked her up and down and exclaimed, "And such a pleasing figure it is!" Then it had been his turn to blush at the forward manner of his speech. Putting down his plate of cake, he had stuttered, "P—pardon my manners, ma'am. I say, would you do me the honour of a dance with me?"

Thus had begun George Finch's courtship of Charlotte Harding. At first, she had been flattered by the attention of an obviously enamoured male, her first experience of such a thing. Sylvia had been elated. Finally, an eligible prospect. George Finch was the only son of a local gentleman and heir to his not inconsiderable estate. A catch! True, he was not prepossessing in appearance. He lacked height and stature. His eyes were a watery blue in colour and there was a definite overbite to his lips. But looks were not everything, and Charlotte had been perfectly willing—alright, not perfectly, but willing—to overlook such deficiencies and focus on the other advantages of such a match.

In due course, however, two things had made her wary of George's courtship. The first was the rude manner he displayed in his dealings with servants. A groom that failed to catch the reins thrown carelessly at him was berated loudly and called a half-wit. A housemaid that brought him the wrong drink was disparaged for being a fool. Charlotte, who still lived by Juana's faithfully imparted teachings on treating all humans with love and kindness, had revolted at such treatment of others, especially those of inferior social standing, and was reminded of Cicero's famous maxim, "The higher we are placed, the more humbly we should walk."

The second thing that had given her pause was the discovery that George's knowledge of the classics was sadly deficient despite several years of study at Oxford. On a walk together one day, she had been silent for a considerable time, unable to find any mutually interesting topic of conversation, and he had teasingly quipped, "Silence is one of the great arts of conversation, is it not?" then made the monstrous mistake of attributing this to Virgil. Surely any classicist worth his salt should have known this was Cicero, not Virgil. In further discourse, it had become increasingly clear that George was not a man of great or even passable intellect. At times, she suspected him of being the half-wit he so loudly proclaimed his groom to be.

These two things had made her begin to doubt George's suitability as a husband, notwithstanding the £3,000 a year that her stepmama was wont to exclaim over. When it had looked like George was about to propose, she had been saved from having to refuse him by her father's sudden grave illness. After Hugh's passing, she had of course gone into mourning, which had made any romantic overtures inappropriate. In time, she had hoped that George would forget about her and move on to greener pastures. She had not banked on his surprising constancy.

Last month had marked a year since her beloved father had been laid to rest, and Sylvia had judged it proper to end their official state of mourning. The black garments were put away in favour of grey ones. And George had once again begun to call upon them. "Mark my words," Sylvia had said, "he will make an offer very soon."

Charlotte had hesitantly murmured, "What if I were to refuse him?"

Her stepmama had stared at her in shock and horror. "But of course you cannot do such a vile, terrible thing!"

"I—I do not believe we would suit."

"You shall have to suit, missy, for such an offer will not come your way again."

From thence had begun a month-long, tiresome campaign by Sylvia to induce her stepdaughter to accept George's unwanted advances. Stuck inside the house during the cold, wet and windy days of February, Charlotte had had to endure one harangue after another. So it was with a hopeful lift of her spirits that she had woken this morning to bright, sunny skies and decided to walk over to pay her old friend a visit.

Now, Ruth gently put to her, "Would it really be impossible for you to find happiness in a union with George?"

"You know it would!"

"You have reached this conclusion after calmly weighing all the advantages and disadvantages?"

"Believe me Ruth, I have thought of little else. I cannot marry a man who is both cruel and stupid, and frankly has little to recommend him apart from his wealth."

Ruth took another sip of her tea then put her cup down. "Has he ever shown cruelty to you?"

"No, but of course he would not do so when courting."

"What I mean to say," continued Ruth, "is that if he is favourably disposed towards you and holds you in high regard, then you may have the opportunity to guide him in altering his ways."

Charlotte cast her a doubtful look. "I do not have it in my power to change someone's nature."

14

"Perhaps not, but have you considered that his behaviour towards servants is not merely the result of a faulty nature but of his upbringing? A son will often follow in the footsteps of a father."

"All the more reason, surely, to not join such a family."

Ruth regarded her friend steadily. "It will not be without challenges, I agree. But Charlotte, consider the consequences of your actions. What will happen if you refuse George's offer of marriage?"

"I have no means of knowing he will make an offer," Charlotte said wryly.

"Let us assume he will. What then?"

Charlotte frowned. "I know Sylvia will be horribly upset and take it out on me. I shall simply have to bear it with fortitude until her anger has passed."

"Is that all she will do? I very much fear, that after the time and effort she has put into the project of marrying you off, she may, in her disappointment at such an objective failing, decide to make your life very difficult indeed."

"As to that, she already does!"

"Do not forget that she is now the proprietor of Alstone Grange. It is her home, not yours."

Charlotte made a little moue of distaste at this. "I am well aware, but she made a promise to father that she would always care for me as if I were her own."

"Promises can be broken, Charlotte," reminded Ruth gently.

"I do not think even she would sink so low."

Ruth was quiet, not answering. Eventually, she behoved herself to speak. "There is a matter I have been hesitant to bring up with you. As you know, when father passed away, my brother, Robert, took over the running of the farm from him and was assured that the terms of the tenancy would continue as before. However, two weeks ago, Mr Longley came to see him about raising the rent from sixteen to eighteen shillings per acre as of next month—and this after the rent was raised from fifteen shillings not a half year ago. Of course, Robert remonstrated with him about this, and he was told that it was your stepmother's firm instruction that the rents be raised again."

Charlotte regarded her in consternation. "Why did you not tell me of this before?"

"I did not want to bother you in your time of grief. Besides, what could you have done about it? Do not take offence my dear, but I doubt very much that your word has much clout with your stepmother."

Having consumed her slice of cake, Charlotte returned her now empty plate to the tray in chagrin. "No, perhaps not. However, I do wish you had not kept this from me, Ruth. Will you be able to afford this new rent?"

"We will manage. Robert and I live frugally, and we are fortunate enough to have put away savings over the years. Our main concern is if your stepmother decides to put the rents up yet again in another six months' time. Such rises are not sustainable in the long run."

Sitting back down in her armchair, Charlotte sighed in commiseration. "I am sorry Ruth. What a sad state of affairs for the both of us!"

Ruth smiled ruefully. "I did not tell you this to lower your spirits, only as a way to warn you that perhaps your stepmother's word is not to be trusted. The roof over your head is hers, and with her lies the power to make your life infinitely miserable. With this in mind, will you not reconsider George's suit? You say all that he has to recommend him is his wealth. From where I am sitting, dear friend, that is a great deal. Imagine having the security of being lady of your own fine home, with no need to ever count the pennies. It is not a prospect to be sneered at."

Charlotte stared pensively at the rhythmic rise and fall of the needle as her friend sewed the hem of one of her brother's shirts. Finally, she said, "I will think on it. Now let us talk of other matters. Is it true what they say about Lizzie Trent snubbing Fanny Chalmers at church last Sunday?"

And so the two friends spent another hour in convivial conversation about the goings on in their small rural village, which despite its modest size, nevertheless provided a great deal of delightful gossip.

Chapter 2

Upon Charlotte's return home, she was accosted by her agitated stepmama. Before even she had the chance to remove her pelisse, Sylvia was addressing her in aggrieved tones. "George Finch came by to see you, Charlotte, and waited over half an hour for you. Poor man was in such a tizzy. I do believe he had come to make you an offer, and where were you missy? Nowhere in sight, that's what!"

"I am sorry to hear that," Charlotte replied placatingly. "I had no idea he planned on visiting, for we have not seen him in over a week."

"Well, he shall be calling again tomorrow, and you will be sure to be here, looking your best."

"Yes of course," murmured Charlotte before slipping away to hide herself in the library. There was no escaping the coming encounter with George. She was almost entirely sure that, should he make an offer of marriage, she would refuse it. A tiny niggling voice in her head argued against such a course of action. *What if life for you here were to become intolerable after your refusal of George's offer? Where would you go? How would you live?*

To these questions, she had no answers. There was only one minor possibility. She could appeal to her father's family—that very same family that had disowned him, cut him out of their lives entirely, upon knowledge of his marriage to a Spanish tradesman's daughter. Hugh Harding had renounced a considerable fortune and position in society in order to marry his Spanish bride. The only material thing left to him after shipping out from the army and selling his commission was a legacy from a bachelor great-uncle, a small estate known as Alstone Grange. No matter to Juana. After the privations of life on the road in wartime Spain, her new home in England felt positively palatial to her. As for Hugh, the loss of a fortune was not such a hardship when balanced with the loss of tiresome interfering relatives. The rupture had proved to be a permanent one. No efforts at a rapprochement were made in the ensuing years, even after the death of Sir Edward Harding, the patriarch of the family.

Would the passage of time have softened their attitude? Admittedly, it was an unlikely possibility. As far as she knew, there had been no communication between the estranged branches of the family until she had written to her uncle and aunt to inform them of her father's passing. No response had been forthcoming from her uncle. Her aunt, however, had sent her son, a gentleman by the name of Frederick Morton, to attend the funeral in lieu of her ailing self. He had been correct and punctilious in his condolences, but Charlotte remembered little else of him, such had been the depth of her grief.

Mayhap she should write to her aunt explaining her situation and ask—ask for what exactly? To be taken in, given home and hearth? Charlotte's instincts rebelled against such an action. Bundled in her favourite armchair by the fireplace, she closed her eyes and reflected on the matter. After a time, she pulled herself upright and went to sit at the desk in the middle of the room. Removing a blank sheet of paper from the drawer and sharpening the nib of her pen, she then began to write.

•————————————•

Later that evening, Charlotte prepared herself for bed in her usual way. Dressed in her night rail, she sat at her dresser and combed out the tangles from her thick brown hair. Then, she rolled individual strands around a rag, tying it up neatly so as to ensure perfect curls the following day. She had dispensed with many parts of Sylvia's beauty regimen, such as the unbearably tight corset and the daily facewash in talc water, but this particular habit she had kept on. That and the occasional

19

pluck of her eyebrows. She had enough vanity to want to appear to the best possible advantage.

Her business complete, she stood and carried the candle to her bedside cabinet. Kneeling, she said her nightly prayer, adding an extra line or two of supplication for help and guidance in the matter of George Finch. Satisfied that there was nothing further to do, she climbed into bed, blew out the candle and nestled under the blanket. The house was quiet and the darkness impenetrable. Usually, she drifted into sleep effortlessly, but not on this night. There were too many thoughts pressing in on her. Ruth's words rang in her ears. *Promises can be broken, Charlotte.*

With her future looking so uncertain, the surest way forward was to accept George's suit. That was the most sensible course of action. Yet Charlotte had developed such a disgust of him that the mere thought of sharing intimacies with this gentleman had her feeling distinctly unwell. *"What is to become of me?"* she wondered. *"If I accept George, I shall be constrained to share my days and evenings with a man repugnant to me. If I do not accept him, my stepmama will undoubtedly find ways to render my living under her roof intolerable."*

She took a deep breath, trying and failing to quell those worrisome thoughts. At times such as these, there was one thing she had discovered — by sheer accident — that could bring her release from the cares and worries. It was not something she allowed herself to do often. Indeed, it was a most wicked thing to do, but just this once, she hoped God would forgive the depravity. She let her fingers trail down under the comforter to reach the hem of her night rail and pull it up to her waist. Then, the very same fingers sought a point at the juncture of her thighs. Burrowing into the wisps of hair, they found the moist, soft flesh she was looking for. Charlotte began to rub that sensitive flesh gently with two fingers, feeling her body fire up with delicious excitement.

Soon, her fingers were coated with a thick and sticky substance which seemingly flowed from her body the more she touched herself in that secret spot. With a gentle sigh, she increased the speed of her roving fingers, rubbing herself fiercely until she felt a wave of pleasurable contractions sweep through her body. "Ah," she cried, before muffling the sound by the expedient method of thrusting the wet and sticky fingers into her mouth, then sucking them clean. Her shallow breaths slowly returned to a normal, even rhythm as she savoured the strangely pleasing taste of herself. Eventually, when there was nothing more to taste, she withdrew the fingers, adjusted her night rail and fell into a deep dreamless sleep.

Chapter 3

At the very same instant that Charlotte was achieving this wicked sensual release in her bed, another person some hundreds of miles away was reaching a similar precipice of pleasure. Francis James Stanton, Viscount Stanton, or simply Frank to his good friends, was in the bed of his current mistress, Lady Caroline Drake, thrusting his erect member into her welcoming heat. Feeling the unmistakable contractions around his shaft that signalled the lady's pleasure, he allowed himself to reach his own peak of bliss, remembering just in time to withdraw from her body and spurt his seed over her soft belly.

"By jove that was good!" he cried.

The lady showed her agreement to this statement by emitting a long, joyful sigh. Stretching her arms above her head, she finally murmured, "What a clever boy you are."

Frank grinned and gave her a mock bow. "At your service, my lady." Getting to his feet, he strode to the jug on a nearby table and poured a little water onto a muslin cloth, bringing it over to Lady Caroline to clean up the mess he had made of her.

"Such a gentleman," she mocked gently, submitting to his ministrations.

He smiled as he threw the soiled cloth carelessly to the floor and lightly kissed her lips. "Anything for you, my heart," he replied. The endearment slipped easily from his tongue, more out of habit than out of true sentiment. His liaison with Lady Caroline was not an *affaire de coeur*, but more of an *affaire de corps*. He enjoyed immensely the fleshly delights of their union, with the welcome addition of her ready wit and excellence as a hostess of card parties.

In his youth, like many other young men of his class, he had indulged in the usual round of debauchery with ladies of the night. That had come to an abrupt halt when his good friend, Thomas Marchand, had contracted a virulent case of syphilis, the symptoms of which were enough to sow permanent fear and distaste for such pastimes in Frank's heart. Instead, he had decided to seek pleasure with ladies of his own class, preferably widows of a certain age—no despoiler of innocent misses was he. With such ladies, he conducted discreet and exclusive liaisons that ended amicably once the initial burst of passion ran its course.

This approach had served him well so far, and he saw no reason not to continue with such habits. He had no plans to fall in love nor to get married, at least not in the immediate future—perhaps not ever if he could help it. Let his younger brother take on the mantle of siring an heir to the title and estates. His observation of people was that happiest were those that were free of the shackles of matrimony.

The lady sprawled contentedly on the bed before him was a prime exhibit. Married at eighteen to a much older and extremely wealthy peer of the realm, she had done her duty for ten arduous years and produced two requisite children. Upon Lord Drake's demise, and after a suitable period of mourning, she had commenced a life of gaiety in the bosom of polite society while merrily indulging in discreet dalliances with gentlemen of the ton. The jaunty state of her current life could not compare with the dullness of her staid married existence.

Frank picked up the discarded items of his clothing from the floor and began to dress. Seeing this, Lady Caroline sat up in bed, not bothering to cover her nude form, and rang the bell for her maid. Frank observed the lady's voluptuous figure with an appreciative gleam in his eyes. "Damn, Caro, if I could paint, I'd put down on canvas the way you look right now."

She laughed delightedly, "It has been done already, my lord. Remember my little escapade with John Lancing two summers ago?"

"Oh yes. Where is this masterwork? I have not seen it."

23

"It is not for prying eyes to see. I have it hanging in my dressing room." She nodded her head in the direction of the room in question.

"May I see it?"

"Of course, my love."

Picking up a candle, Frank opened the door leading to the good lady's dressing room and walked in. He stood for several beats gazing at the painting, then returned to the bedroom chuckling. "If ever you tire of it, Caro, I'd be more than happy to take if off your hands."

Before the lady could make a reply, there was a quick knock on the door and in entered her maid. The poor girl nearly jumped in fright at the sight of Frank in a state of deshabille, for he had only managed by this point to pull up his pantaloons, of which the buttons were still undone. As the maid bobbed a curtsy, Lady Caroline spoke in a firm but pleasant tone. "Bridget, ask Drummond to call a hackney-carriage for the viscount, and let it wait a little further down the street."

"Yes ma'am," mumbled Bridget and hurried off to do her mistress's bidding.

Frank watched her depart with a wry smile. "We have shocked the poor girl. I do hope she does not have a loose tongue."

"She is paid far too well to ever loosen that tongue. It is an essential in my style of living to maintain efficient and loyal servants. One cannot do so without paying them well."

"You run a tight ship, Caro. My hat off to you."

"I do my best. Frank dear, when am I to see you next?"

Frank paused in the act of pulling on his boots. "Will you be at the Wilton ball?"

"The premier event of the season? Naturally."

"Then I shall see you there. Perhaps we can conclude the evening together?"

"Perhaps," agreed Lady Caroline with a saucy smile.

Some minutes later, Viscount Stanton slipped out of Lady Caroline's house and walked a few paces down the street to climb into the waiting hackney-carriage. The hour was late but not so late as to be close to the breaking of dawn. The viscount yawned, eager to make it to bed after the evening's pleasant exertions. He was six weeks into his liaison with Lady Caroline, and the novelty of her company had not yet worn off. *"Give it another six weeks and it will,"* said a cynical voice in his head. And then it will be time to search for his next conquest.

In the six-and-twenty years of his life, he had lived by the maxim, "Sameness is the mother of disgust, variety the cure." Whether it was women, horses, fashion, poets, card games or even the food he ate, boredom set in quickly and nothing fixed his interest for very long. So he flitted to the next thing and then the next.

He was self-aware enough to realise that this inability to stave off boredom was a defect in his own character and undoubtedly the result of having been blessed with everything he could possibly want in life — social standing, wealth, looks, charm and wit. The ease with which things came to him inevitably made him less appreciative of them. He knew he should be grateful for the good fortune that had blessed him, and of course he was. But still on occasion, he could not help feeling a certain restlessness of spirit.

All this is not to say that his life was a perfect canvas, unblemished by adversity. His one misfortune was the possession of a cold and exacting parent in his father, the Earl of Stanton. The earl had immutable ideas about the direction his son's life should take.

He would of course follow in his footsteps and enter the political sphere. In preparation for this, he was to serve in the House of Lords and ally himself with the Tories, naturally. He was to mingle in the highest echelons of society and make valuable connections, then seek advancement through positions in the civil service, and perhaps in time achieve a cabinet position in government or even reach the pinnacle of power in becoming prime minister. In due course, he would marry a girl of impeccable character and breeding, and sire the Stantons of future generations. The design of Frank's life had been written well before he even had the privilege of being born. It was no wonder then that he was bored.

From early childhood, he had been primed, groomed and educated for the life that had been mapped for him. Every Sunday, young Frank would be summoned to his father's study and made to repeat the substance of that day's church sermon. He was expected to memorise and recite, accurately and without fault, Cicero's Orations and Plato's Dialogues. As a young student at Oxford, he had been told in no uncertain terms by his parent that nothing less than a first class degree would do. Since the earl controlled his purse strings, Frank thought it prudent to heed that advice. Accordingly, he had distinguished himself with such a degree.

This state of affairs would have continued indefinitely had not Frank, upon entering his majority, come into possession of a small estate in Wiltshire which had been settled in a trust on his mother upon her marriage and then bequeathed to him. Judicious improvements to the running of the estate, and the investment of his small funds in various profitable ventures, had enabled him within a few short years to achieve an independent income of £2,000 a year—much to the surprise and discomfiture of his father.

It was not a fortune, and only a drop in the ocean compared to the vast Stanton patrimony, but now that he had enough means of his own to live in modest comfort, he was able, if not to cut the paternal strings entirely, at least to loosen them considerably. Such was the power and influence of the earl, who was one of the ten richest men in the country, that it was unwise to be openly at odds with him. Frank had no desire to cross that cold, unbending personage. Nevertheless, he was keen to remove himself as far as possible from the earl's orbit of influence. The first order of business had been for him to change living arrangements and reside in his own bachelor lodgings on Wimpole Street rather than in the grand family townhouse on St James's Square where every move he made was observed and conveyed to his father by the servants in his pay.

This address on Wimpole Street is where the hackney-carriage now drew up. Tossing the driver a few coins, the viscount emerged from the vehicle and leapt up the steps to his home. Upon entering his abode, he was greeted by Hudson, his valet, with a missive that had arrived in his absence. The viscount took it with a frown, seeing from the franking that it had come from his father. Nothing good was ever relayed in such communications. Opening the missive, he scanned it quickly and remarked, "It seems my presence is required urgently. Prepare a bag, Hudson, we leave for Stanton Hall in the morning."

"Yes sir. Will we be away long?"

"No more than a few days at most, I hope."

"Very well, sir," replied Hudson, and withdrew to begin preparations for the morrow.

At nine o'clock the following morning, revived after a night's rest, the viscount set out in his carriage for the family seat in Stanton Harcourt, an Oxfordshire village some sixty miles' distance from London. With several stops along the way to refresh the horses, it was early evening by the time the carriage finally drew up in front of the viscount's ancestral home. The building, surrounded by thirty acres of rolling parkland, was a curious mixture of old and new. The eastern flank of the house, which dated as far back as the fifteenth century, comprised an uneven stone façade with mullion windows. Over the generations, the house had been expanded and improved upon, with the latest additions overseen by the present earl himself. These were in the classical style, with symmetrical lines and Corinthian columns rising majestically on either side of the main entrance.

In the dim light of the evening, very little of this magnificence was readily visible, but the building was so etched in the viscount's mind that he unerringly bounded up the front steps, eager to stretch his legs after being confined in the carriage for so many hours. The door was opened to him by a lugubrious looking butler named Webster.

"Good evening, my lord," said he.

"Evening Webster, I trust you are well."

"As well as can be expected, my lord."

"Am I arrived too late for dinner?" Frank had stopped for lunch at a posting inn halfway along his journey, but that was hours ago, and he was now feeling decidedly famished.

"No sir. His lordship requested it be held back until your arrival. If I may be so bold as to say, it would be wise not to keep his lordship waiting for very much longer."

Frank laughed, "Of course. I shall be down in a thrice." And with this, he hurried away to his rooms. He was as good as his word, emerging some minutes later dressed in cream-coloured knee breeches that fitted closely over his muscular thighs, stockings, a crisp new shirt and an elegantly tied neck cloth. Over this he wore a double-breasted claret tailcoat made of superfine. His dark wavy hair, which was cut short à la Titus, had been lovingly brushed by his valet, and now, striding down to the drawing room, he looked in all ways the fashionably turned out gentleman.

Upon entrance to that room, he found himself the object of scrutiny of seven pairs of eyes. Frank recognised some of the faces in the room, but others not. In pride of place on his favourite armchair by the fireplace, sat his father, looking decidedly disgruntled. Having his dinner postponed evidently did not agree with his lordship. Opposite his father sat Frederick Morton, a gentleman with substantial landholdings a few miles south of Stanton Hall. Frank knew Frederick well since both their mamas had been close friends. A few years older than Frank, Frederick was a tall, stocky gentleman with a pleasant countenance and easy manners. Beside him sat an unknown older gentleman, and in the corner of the room four ladies played a game of whist at a small card table.

Frank bowed to his father. "Sir, I apologise humbly for having kept you from your dinner."

The earl gazed at him irritably. "Had you left London an hour earlier, Francis, I would not have had to wait."

"My mistake, sir. I trust you are in good health."

His father's tone was cold. "I am always in good health. I do not believe in getting sick, as you well know. Come now, and say your hellos to everyone so we may proceed to dine. Frederick Morton, you know of course."

Frank smiled and bowed to Frederick. "Evening Morton, a pleasant surprise to see you here."

"And this is Sir Horace Powell, of the Wiltshire Powells," continued the earl, not giving Frederick a chance to reply.

Again, Frank bowed. "A pleasure to make your acquaintance, Sir Horace."

The earl nodded his head towards the ladies at the card table. "Mrs Morton and Mrs Frederick Morton need no introduction. With them are Lady Powell and her eldest daughter."

Frank approached the card table and greeted the ladies punctiliously. No sooner had he done so than the earl stood, indicating they should proceed to the dining room, and held out his arm to Mrs Morton. The two of them walked out of the drawing room, followed by Sir Horace and Lady Powell, and then by Mr and Mrs Frederick Morton. This left only Miss Powell. Frank bowed to her politely and held out his arm. With a rosy flush to her cheeks, she placed her hand on his arm and walked with him to the dining room where she took a seat facing him.

Dinner was a tedious affair, but such was his breeding that Frank showed no trace of *ennui* in his demeanour. It was clear the urgent matter on which he had been summoned would have to wait until an opportunity came for a private audience with his father. He therefore conversed amiably with Mrs Morton, his mother's old friend, finding out from her that the Powells were relations of her late husband stopping over to visit on their way to London for the season, where Miss Powell was due to make her debut. The Mortons, too, would soon be decamping to the great metropolis, having stayed in the country through the winter for Mrs Frederick Morton's confinement. Much was made of little Edwin Morton, the new addition to the family, with exclamations of what a sturdy little fellow he was and what excellent temperament he had. Frank bore with this good naturedly though he had not the least interest in children, be they young or older.

Miss Powell answered enquiries prettily but did not otherwise contribute very much to the conversation. She was a fine-figured young lady with a healthy bloom in her complexion and delicately drawn, pleasing features. Given the extent of the Powell landholdings and the family's connections, Frank had no doubt that she would end the season with an eligible match.

Dinner was followed by an interminable round of port with the gentlemen, in which his father quizzed him on the latest happenings in the House of Lords. The earl made the journey to Westminster infrequently, claiming the London air to be toxic to the healthful functioning of his lungs. He preferred to rely on his son for the latest *on-dits*, and Frank dutifully obliged, recounting the most recent debate he had attended in the House, where Lord Teynham had unsuccessfully argued for the repeal of malt duties.

"Quite rightly so," opined the earl. "A repeal would bankrupt the country. Why I have it on reliable sources that malt duties brought in close to £4 million to the exchequer last year. A loss of this revenue, given the demands on the public purse, would be disastrous."

"I do not necessarily disagree," responded Frank, "however, it is indisputable also that the duty imposes intolerable hardships on labourers, farmers and even on landlords in procuring rents."

"What alternative is there?" wondered Frederick Morton.

"As to that, I cannot say. Perhaps, rather than to repeal, one should be looking at a gradual reduction in the duties, allowing for the public purse to make adjustments over time. Merely continuing as before is imprudent, in my view, for these duties are having a profound effect, not only on the farmers but on the production of malt in the country. To give an example, my own tenant farmers have switched crops away from barley to wheat for that very reason."

The earl nodded. "What you say makes sense, Francis. Perhaps you should be setting out such arguments next time the subject is raised in the House."

Frank smiled, "Perhaps." Truth be told, he had no intention whatsoever of doing so. The last thing he wanted was to further his political career, despite his father's long stated ambitions in that regard. Frank's interests lay far more in managing his estates as profitably and responsibly as possible, as well as in the seeking of new investments in modern manufacture and transportation—not in seeking glory through political office.

That his son did not intend to pursue a political career was something the earl had yet to discover. It would have been little use for Frank to disclose this, since the earl did not take kindly to having his plans overturned. Navigating the disappointment of such a demanding parent required care and consideration. As with all delicate negotiations, Frank was aware that he would need to accede to his father's wishes in some things in order to dissent from them in others—the question was where to draw the line between such demands he was able to come to terms with and demands he was not. As the evening drew to a close, he wondered inwardly whether the reason behind this latest summons to Stanton Hall would prove to be one of those things where disagreement between himself and his father would arise.

He had to wait until the following morning to find out. Once their houseguests had departed, Frank was bade to go see the earl in his study. Upon his knock, he was greeted with a gruff, "Enter!"

"You wanted to see me sir?"

"Come in boy and sit yourself down."

Frank did as he was bid, saying, "You spoke of some urgent matter in your letter. May I know what it is?"

The earl eyed his son sternly. "Francis, it is time for you to marry. I have thought long on this and made many enquiries on your behalf. I believe the charming Miss Powell would make an excellent viscountess."

Frank stared at his father, taken aback. "Marriage? I had no thought of it, at least not for a very long time!"

"And why not? You are at the customary age for it. I myself was a year younger than you when I married your mother."

"I–I… times have changed," spluttered Frank.

"Our good friend Frederick Morton was six-and-twenty at his nuptials. And Viscount Cranford entered into the state of matrimony only this past month at the age of four-and-twenty. Times changed? Pray disabuse yourself of that notion."

"I would wish, sir, to enter into that state at a time and with a lady of my choosing."

"I am a reasonable man, Francis. Should you have taken a dislike to the lady in question, then naturally, we would seek out other matches."

"I have nothing against the good lady; I barely know her."

"Then make it your business to get to know her."

"I would, if my object were to marry. However, that is not the case."

The earl looked askance at his errant son. "What earthly reasons do you have for not wanting to marry?"

"It has been my observation, sir, that being married is not a felicitous state of affairs for many of our estate in life."

"And you think it felicitous to end your days a bachelor, with no heir to pass your name and title to?"

"There is always Jasper," said Frank hopefully of his younger brother.

At this, his father exclaimed in irritation, "That rapscallion!"

"He is young, granted, but in time he will come into his own."

"Do you in all seriousness want to place the great responsibility for this title and estate on your brother's shoulders? Do you jest Francis? If so, let me assure you I am not much amused."

Seeing himself at an impasse, Francis decided to play for time. "Very well sir, if marry I must, then I will do so, but at a time of my choosing."

"There is no reason to delay, and there is no finer prospect than the young lady you met last evening."

"As to that, sir, I do not know. I would have to become greater acquainted with her and to cultivate other acquaintances too before I could be sure of it."

His father regarded him in silence for several moments before stating, "Francis, tomorrow you will call on the Mortons and spend some time getting to know Miss Powell. Take her out for a stroll in the gardens perhaps, or read some poetry with her—whatever it is that you young men do these days to woo a lady. If you feel strongly then that she is unsuited to you, you will start seeking out other prospective matches once you are back in London. In either case, I want you married by the year end."

Frank sat stiffly in his chair, contemplating his options. He could refuse, but to do so would cause the earl great anger and distress. He was not so hard-hearted as to ever wish to inflict such feelings on his father. Moreover, would marriage be so very bad if he picked a sensible, well-bred lady for his wife? They could reach an accommodation on how to spend their time as husband and wife. He would not necessarily become shackled to the lady day and night. Certainly, marriage was a lesser evil than having to pursue those political aspirations his father had for him. Giving in on this matter would place him more strongly to resist on the other.

Finally, he nodded his head. "As you wish, sir."

Chapter 4

Mrs Morton put the letter down with an exclamation of dismay, "Well, I never!"

"Whatever is the matter?" asked Lady Powell, about to take a sip of her tea.

"A letter from Charlotte Harding, my brother Hugh's daughter."

"Hugh? Is not your brother named William?"

"You are thinking of my eldest brother," Mrs Morton replied. "I had another brother called Hugh, laid to rest this last year."

Lady Powell put down her cup, looking mortified. "My dear Margaret, my deepest condolences! I was not aware of this else I would of course have written. How is it I did not know?"

Mrs Morton let out a long sigh. "Hugh was cast out of the family long ago for a very imprudent marriage. Father broke all ties with him and insisted his name never be spoken again. And so, it never has. Not until this Charlotte Harding wrote informing us of his passing."

"An imprudent marriage? I cannot recall any such scandal. When was this?"

"Oh, a good twenty-five or twenty-six years ago. You were not yet out, Julia, which explains why you did not hear of it. My brother was serving in the war against that upstart Bonaparte in Spain. There, he met some local tradesman's daughter, fell madly in love and married her."

"Oh my good Lord! Imprudent is the least of it. To align a great and noble family such as the Hardings with a foreign nobody. Why there have been Hardings at Longborough Manor since the time of the Conqueror—were they not named in the Domesday Book? I can well imagine the late Sir Edward's horror and disgust at such a thing." Lady Powell wrinkled her nose in distaste. "And this Charlotte is the product of that union?"

"Yes, as far as I know, they only had the one child."

"Why is she writing to you now? To ask for alms for herself and her Spanish mother?"

"Not quite. Her mother, it seems, passed some years ago, and Hugh remarried a gentlewoman, some rector's widow by the name of Sylvia Gibbs. He left her a small estate in Gloucestershire."

"I see. And Charlotte?"

"Frederick went to see them after the funeral. He assured me Mrs Harding and her stepdaughter lived comfortably, if modestly. Had the girl been in dire straits, something would have been done; you may be sure of that. My conscience would not have allowed me to see Hugh's child reduced to penury."

"Quite right," nodded Lady Powell. "And she writes to you now, why? Has there been a change in her circumstance?"

Mrs Morton raised her spectacles to peruse the letter once more. "She writes that her stepmama has arranged a match for her with a most unsuitable person. She fears that her refusal of this man's suit will cause great discord between herself and her stepmama, and she wonders if she might visit here for a time to get away from the lady's displeasure."

"Indeed! What manner of a man is this unsuitable match?"

"She does not say. It is highly irregular." Mrs Morton sighed. "What to do? We leave for London in another week, so it is no good inviting her to stay here."

"Raised by such a mother, it is anyone's guess what manner of a person she is." Lady Powell shuddered. "What if you were to bring into your home a girl of poor breeding who does not know how to comport herself in gentle society? Unimaginable! I do not advise it, my dear."

36

Mrs Morton looked troubled. "And yet, if the situation is genuinely as she describes, I would not like to turn my back on such distress."

"Ever the kind hearted you are, Margaret. Perhaps you should consult with Frederick. He did after all meet this Charlotte. Count on it, he will know what is to be done."

Thus it was that Mrs Morton sought out her son the following morning, before he was due to take a ride around his estate. Upon reading Charlotte's letter, he frowned. "This is indeed troubling," he said.

"What do you propose we should do?" asked his mother.

"There is nothing else for it. Charlotte must come and stay with us for however long is necessary."

"I wonder, will it be appropriate to have her with us, mingling with our acquaintances?"

Frederick stared at her, puzzled. "Whyever not?"

"Well, Frederick, her mother was by all accounts a Spanish tradesman's daughter. Having been raised by such a woman, her breeding may not be all that it should."

"Nonsense! She is a gentlewoman, and from what I saw, extremely well mannered. The language in this letter speaks to the young lady's education. Rid yourself of the notion, mother, that your niece lacks breeding. One should not speak ill of the dead, but I have always thought my grandfather's decision to cast out his son as he did was poorly done. Perhaps this is a chance for us to atone for the sins of the past."

"Atone?" demanded his mother, much aggrieved. "You think I have need to atone?"

He laid a placating hand on her arm. "Dear mother, calm yourself. You did what you thought was right in following your late father's injunctions. However, even you must see that casting a son out of the family was an unduly harsh penalty for having made an unfavourable marriage. If it had been me done this, would you have cast me out, never to speak my name again?"

Mrs Morton gave a weak smile. "No, my dear, of course not. It is true that over the years, I have often wondered about Hugh and hoped for a reconciliation. I waited for him to write me, intent on healing the breach, but he never did."

"Such is the price for pride, mother. Neither of you was willing to make the first move, and now the opportunity has been lost. All the more reason not to forego this chance we have now to make things right."

His mother nodded in acquiescence. "As ever, Frederick, you are quite right. But what is to be done? We leave for London in a week's time."

Frederick pondered the question. "A young lady ought not to travel alone. I will need to go fetch her—it is an easy day's ride from here. Then we shall all set out for London together. I will write to her now, informing her of this. If you write too, our letters can go out at once in today's post."

"Yes dear, of course."

Accordingly, the letters were sent out, arriving at their destination not two days later. And no person could have felt such relief as Charlotte did upon reading those two missives.

Chapter 5

Mr George Finch puffed up his chest and prepared to make his much practised discourse. Seeing this, Charlotte tried one last time to dissuade him from this endeavour.

"It is with much surprise that I heard you called yesterday, Mr Finch," she said in a cool but cordial tone, "and that you waited some time for my return. A man such as yourself must surely have more pressing matters to attend to, and I am sure I would not want to keep you from them. If you are come to enquire after my health—for I was a trifle unwell the last time we met—then I can assure you I am back to full health and thank you for your concern."

"Ah, well that is to say, I am glad to hear that you are in full health again," George mumbled.

Charlotte continued, "I am of course exceedingly gratified and conscious of the honour you do me by so graciously coming to enquire after my health. I trust your esteemed parents are well, sir?"

"Yes, they are thank you. Erm, although of course I am glad to see you in the full bloom of health, Miss Harding, that is not the main purpose of my visit today."

"Indeed?" Charlotte tried to infuse a cold hauteur into her tone. Would that he read these subtle signals and realised the futility of his mission. Unfortunately, the young gentleman was too much in the thrall of passion to notice the lady's coolness.

"Miss Harding, please allow me to tell you how ardently I admire and love you. It would make me the happiest man in England if you would consent to be my wife." With a flourish, he took hold of Charlotte's hand and planted on it a fervent kiss.

Charlotte disengaged her hand gently. "Sir, you do me a great honour. I am exceedingly flattered by your offer of marriage. However, much as I hold yourself and your family in great esteem, I do not return the sentiments you have just expressed, and I am therefore unable to accept your proposal of marriage."

George stared at her dumbfounded. "Unable to accept? You mean you're turning me down?" His face began to take on a darkened hue.

Charlotte nodded. "I am sorry but I must decline your most gracious offer."

"But that is preposterous!"

"Sir?"

"Miss Harding, I am not unaware of the straightened circumstances you find yourself in after your father's passing. Then there is also the matter of your questionable antecedents on your mother's side. All this, I was willing to overlook, a fact most other gentlemen might not. And in light of this, you decline my offer? Have you taken leave of your senses?"

"Sir, I would appreciate if you would maintain a courteous tone when addressing me. I am aware of the honour you do me, however I cannot and will not be your wife. I think we have spoken enough on the matter and should say no more."

"And that is your last word on the matter?"

"It is."

George seized his hat, nodded curtly and turned to go. Such was his haste in opening the door, that there was not enough time for Sylvia to move away from where she had been furtively trying to eavesdrop on the conversation. George took one startled look at her and nodded briskly. "Good day, madam." Then he stormed out of the house.

Sylvia turned to face her stepdaughter. "What is the meaning of this?" she demanded.

"Mr Finch made me an offer of marriage, which I most graciously declined."

"Most graciously declined?" Sylvia's voice rose. "Why you ungrateful hussy! What can have possessed you to do such a thing?"

Charlotte's voice wavered as she spoke, "I cannot marry him. We would not suit."

"Have you a long list of suitors at your beck and call that you can afford to turn down an eligible offer?"

"No ma'am, I do not. Yet still, I cannot marry him."

"You will live to regret this, Charlotte. You mark my words. Now take yourself from my presence, for I cannot abide to look into your disgraceful countenance a minute longer. Go!"

Not needing to be bid twice, Charlotte hurried away to put on her pelisse and bonnet. A few moments later, she was outside, walking briskly with no destination in mind, in a state of turmoil. She had walked as far as the neighbouring village of Alderton before she regained a measure of equanimity. Deciding to make use of the journey, she went into the village shop and bought herself a length of pale blue ribbon to trim her bonnet with. She spoke cordially with acquaintances she met there, giving no indication of the dramatic events of the morning. Her purchases complete, she made her way back home, her spirits revived, for she was not a lady prone to bouts of melancholy. "*Come what may, all bad fortune is to be conquered by endurance,*" she said to herself, quoting another well-loved philosopher. "*I will endure.*"

Her resolve would be put to the test upon her arrival back home. No sooner had she stepped inside the house and made her way up the stairs, than she noticed two housemaids emerging from her bedchamber, carrying a large box. "What is the meaning of this?" she asked.

The housemaids put down the box and curtseyed. "We have been instructed to move your belongings, miss, up to the attic room."

"Instructed? By whom!"

"If you pardon me miss, it was Mrs Harding that bade us do this."

Charlotte felt a wave of anger sweep through her body. "And where, pray tell, is Mrs Harding?"

"In the main parlour, miss."

Charlotte nodded curtly and rushed back down the stairs to the parlour. There, she found her stepmama settled comfortably by the fireplace, engaged in needlework. She hurried over to her. "Why is it that my belongings are being moved to the attic?"

Sylvia continued with her needlework, not looking up at her stepdaughter. "Thinking that you would shortly be married, I invited my dear sister Rose to come and stay at Alstone Grange to keep me company. I had plans to put her up in your room and her boy in the small room next to it. Now that you are no longer set to marry, naturally I cannot rescind the invitation, so I have decided it best if you move to the spare attic room and make way for my guests. They shall be arriving within the month."

Charlotte felt her spirits sink. This bedchamber had been hers ever since she had been old enough to have a room of her own. To be stripped of that space and moreover made to occupy a small room in the attic, on the same floor where the house servants slept, was an act of blatant contempt.

She began to shake, both in anger and anguish. "You would do this, Sylvia? Relegate the daughter of the house to sleep in the attic with the servants?"

Sylvia eyed her coolly. "You are no daughter to me, Charlotte. Certainly not after your antics this morning."

Charlotte continued to stare, unable to believe the length to which her stepmama was willing to go in humiliating her. Then, she swivelled on her feet and exited the room. "*I will endure*," she chanted to herself.

Over the next few days, she tried to make herself as comfortable as possible in her cramped new space. Every so often, she caught an inadvertent look of pity on the faces of the house servants, quickly disguised. Even worse, she noticed a change in their behaviour towards her. They were not quite disrespectful, but in subtle ways, they made it clear that they knew she was no longer mistress of them. They would keep her waiting much longer than before when she pulled the bell for hot water or asked for tea. To fall so far down the social order in her own home was an intolerable state of affairs. And so, when four days after George Finch's proposal, she received a letter both from her aunt and her cousin inviting her to stay with them in London, the relief she felt was not inconsiderable.

Chapter 6

As instructed by his father, Frank paid a visit to the Mortons and their guests, the Powells. He took Miss Powell for a perambulation around the gardens and engaged her in polite conversation. In the bright light of the sunny spring morning, her looks withstood a second inspection remarkably well. Miss Powell was exceptionally lovely to behold. She answered Frank's questions quietly and thoughtfully, demonstrating the most refined of manners. Frank could well see why she had made such a favourable impression on his father. He was himself not immune to her charms.

"I look forward to furthering my acquaintance with you in London, Miss Powell," he now said as they made their way back to the house.

"You do me a great honour, my lord," she replied demurely.

"When do you leave for London?"

"At the week's end, my lord."

"Then you will, I hope, be attending the Wilton ball?"

"I believe so. Invitations will have been delivered to our town house. I will be presented at court the day before the ball."

"Ah yes, of course, and I take it you will be seeking vouchers for Almack's?"

"Mother is good friends with Lady Sefton, who has promised to procure us the vouchers. I hope to attend a dance there very soon."

The viscount smiled, "Almack's is not, in truth, a favourite haunt of mine. However, I may be tempted to pay it a visit."

They had by now rejoined the others in the party. Soon after, the viscount took his leave. Riding back to Stanton Hall, he reflected on this latest encounter with Miss Powell. Throughout their brief promenade in the gardens, he had observed her keenly, wanting to find fault with her but finding none. Her expressive eyes gave hint of a vivacious spirit. They had shone with humour and wit as he told some amusing anecdote. Her figure was trim and elegant, showing off the well-cut gown she wore to perfection. And as for those pretty rosebud lips of hers—they were such as to inspire a poetic verse or two, had he the inclination for such things.

A lady such as she was sure to be in high demand, with ardent suitors flocking to her like bees to honey. Should he count himself as one? There was no great harm in it, as long as his attentions did not become too marked. Much as he was delighted by the beauty, he was not yet ready to contemplate a marriage to her or anyone else. There was no violent stirring of his heart at the thought of Miss Powell, but there again this was no bad thing. Love was not a desirable emotion when it came to choosing a bride. Esteem was a much better basis for a successful union, not that he had seen many examples of this in the society he frequented. Most of the married couples he knew, after the first flush of passion had dissipated, engaged in discreet—and in some cases not so discreet—affairs outside the marital bed. This was particularly the case when the wife was charming, rich and beautiful, as Miss Powell undoubtedly was.

He still could not envisage himself a married man, but more so, he could not envisage himself one of these cuckolded husbands who turned a blind eye to the romantic adventures of their wives while seeking escapades of their own. If he were to marry, then he would expect fidelity from his spouse, and it was only fair that he should offer it himself in return. Yet the idea of being bound to the same female in perpetuity felt like a noose around his neck. Damnation! Why could not his father leave him in peace?

Upon his return to London a day later, he decided to dine at White's, hoping to run into Rupert Weston, his good friend since the time they had studied together at Oxford. He was sitting at a table, savouring a particularly fine sherry when that very person sauntered into the elegant dining room. Rupert glanced around the room, spied his friend, and came over to him, sliding into the seat opposite. "So you are back," said he. "My sources tell me you have been out of town. Did your journey prosper?"

"If by a prosperous journey you mean being summoned urgently by one's father to be told one must wed before the year is out, then indeed it was."

Rupert sat up straight. "You are to wed?"

"My father even went so far as to find me the perfect bride and make the introductions."

"Indeed? And who pray is this paragon of virtue?"

Frank waved a dismissive hand. "No matter. The salient point is that father insists I must marry and do so by the end of the year."

His friend regarded him shrewdly. "You know full well, Frank, that he cannot compel you to do so. If it is not your wish, then do not marry."

Frank grimaced. "Much as I despise his interference in my affairs, I do hold the old goat in high regard. I do not like to cross him."

"Oh the weight of parental expectation! I should know, for I have to suffer much the same from mother dearest."

This time it was Frank's turn to regard his friend keenly. "What has she asked for now?"

Rupert let out a long sigh. "She wishes me to purchase a commission in the Dragoon Guards for Anthony. I suppose it would be possible for me to scrape together the sum needed if I were to mortgage some of the land. Yet it pains me to do so. You know full well how long it has taken me to clear the estate from the debts my father incurred. It would be like taking a step backwards to secure a new debt on that land."

"Cannot your brother wait another year or two? He is not yet eighteen."

"That is what I told her, but he is impatient, and mother is powerless to resist his urging."

"You are head of the family now, Rupert. They cannot compel you to purchase the commission."

"Just as your father cannot compel you to marry…"

Frank winced. "Touché, my friend."

They were silent as they both partook of the excellent sherry on offer. Finally, Rupert asked, "So, you still have not told me. Who is the lady your father wishes you to marry?"

"Miss Helena Powell, daughter of Sir Horace Powell of the Wiltshire Powells. She is set to make her debut next week."

"And what think you of the lady?"

"You shall meet her soon and so you will see that she is beautiful, charming and well bred."

"Aha! Indeed a paragon!"

Frank smiled wryly, "A diamond of the first water."

"And yet I sense your hesitation."

"Our society is full of beautiful and charming, but faithless wives. One need only look at the great patronesses of Almack's, those doyennes of the ton, for an example—Lady Cowper's long love affair with Lord Palmerston, Lady Jersey's many loves; the list goes on. Do you know, when asked why he had never fought a duel to preserve his wife's reputation, Lord Jersey replied that this would require him to fight every man in London." Frank shook his head in disgust.

"It matters to you that your wife be a lady of virtue?"

Frank nodded gloomily. "It may seem odd coming from me, who can hardly make any claims to virtue. What I have seen of marriage does not predispose me favourably towards the institution."

"Not all marriages are as you describe, you know. For every faithless wife, you will also find a virtuous one. You need only look to your friend Frederick Morton for proof."

"Frederick is the exception that proves the rule."

"And if we are to talk of the great patronesses of Almack's, I put to you that no wife was as devoted as Lady Castlereagh was to her husband."

"All this does is prove that marriage is a risky enterprise which one enters at one's peril. Success is as likely as failure."

Rupert nodded sagely. "One must choose wisely."

"I have until the end of the year to do so."

"How do you propose to go about this?"

"I suppose I must venture into that marriage mart called Almack's. I go there Wednesday next week, and you shall come with me too to provide moral support."

At this, Rupert blanched. "No, really Frank. That is too much. No friendship can withstand the sacrifice you ask of me."

Frank arched a brow. "Rupert!" he said severely.

"Oh very well, but I am doing this under duress."

"Noted. Now how about a game of hazard to clear our minds of all these troubles?"

"A splendid idea."

Chapter 7

Charlotte folded the letter with hands that shook. Her cousin, Frederick Morton, would be here in two days to escort her to his home, and thence on to London. London! The furthest she had ever ventured was to the neighbouring town of Tewkesbury. That had been the most exciting journey of her life so far. And now she was to go to the great city of London. What an extraordinary turn of events! Cast so low one minute, and the next filled with hope and anticipation. There was so much that needed to be done in preparation. Trunks to be packed; gowns to be altered and mended; a new bonnet to be purchased. But first, she needed to see her friend and share the good news.

Hastily, she put on her pelisse and bonnet, tucking the two letters into her reticule. On her way through the main hallway of the house, she encountered her stepmama. "Going out again Charlotte?" the lady asked.

Pausing in her steps, Charlotte turned to Sylvia with a sweet smile. "Seeing as my presence offends you, madam, I think it best to be out as often as possible, do you not?"

"Just as long as you do not set tongues wagging. That would not do at all."

"You may ease your mind on this matter. I am merely paying a duty call on our tenant, Miss Ellis."

Sylvia observed her coolly. "Very well."

With a little curtsy, Charlotte hurried out of the house. The walk to Ruth and Robert Ellis's farmhouse was not long, a matter of fifteen minutes at most. Rounding the bend in the path towards the house, she saw a burly figure approaching. Once he was close enough for speech, he doffed his hat respectfully. "Good morning, Miss Harding," he said in a deep voice.

"Good morning, Mr Ellis. I trust you are well."

He grimaced. "As well as can be expected, miss. If you are paying a call on Ruth, I am sure she will be happy to see you."

"I am. Good day to you, Mr Ellis."

"Good day, Miss Harding."

As Charlotte took a step to walk past him, he spoke again, "Miss Harding."

"Yes?" Charlotte paused and looked enquiringly at him.

He hesitated, then said, "I hope I am not speaking out of turn, Miss Harding, when I say I am most sorry to hear about recent events up at the main house."

Charlotte cast her eyes down, heat surging in her cheeks. Robert Ellis continued hurriedly, "What I wish to say, miss, is that I am at your service should you ever need assistance in any way. I am a humble tenant farmer, and perhaps it is not my place to speak so, but Miss Harding, I do not like to see what is being done to one whose family I hold in such high regard. It is not right."

Charlotte spoke softly in reply, "I thank you for your concern, Mr Ellis. It warms my heart to know I have such good friends."

He nodded brusquely. "I will let you be on your way, Miss Harding. Good day."

"Good day."

Charlotte watched Robert Ellis go for a few moments before turning around and resuming her journey. She had known him all of her life. Only a year older than Ruth, he had joined in with their childhood games. Back then, he had been "Robbie" to her. Then as they grew, so too did the formality between them. Robert Ellis had been careful to maintain the proper respectful distance required between a gently bred lady and her tenant farmer. Very rarely did he address more than a word or two of polite greeting to her. Yet it was impossible to erase entirely the memories and familiarity of a childhood playmate. Robert's words to her just now had moved Charlotte immensely. Irrespective of the difference in their stations in life, it was warming to her heart to know that she was not alone and friendless.

With a lighter step, she walked up to the front door of the farmhouse and pulled the bell. In a moment or two, it opened. Ruth stood in the doorway with a pleased smile. "Charlotte, how lovely to see you. Do come in."

"I come bearing news," Charlotte said, unable to contain herself, as she stepped over the threshold.

"And by the looks of you, it is good news."

Charlotte stood, unbuttoning her pelisse with careless fingers. "I have received word from my aunt, and also from my cousin."

Ruth took the pelisse and bonnet from her and went to put them on a hook by the parlour door. "Come and sit yourself down, Charlotte, and you can tell me all about it."

Charlotte threw herself on the nearest chair and took the letters out of her reticule. Waving them about excitedly, she said, "My aunt writes to invite me to stay with them and to accompany them to London. London, Ruth, can you imagine!"

"Oh my, that is good news, and coming at just the right time too."

"Yes! I can admit to you, Ruth, that I have been cast so low these past few days, not knowing what was to become of me. And now this!"

"I am so happy for you, my dear. When do you leave?"

Charlotte held up her cousin's letter. "My cousin Frederick also writes to say he will come to fetch me in his carriage. He arrives the day after tomorrow, so there is no time to be lost. I have so much to do, but first I had to come and tell you my news."

"I am so very glad for you, although I will be sad to say goodbye to a dear friend. Once you leave Alstone, it is quite possible you may not return."

Charlotte's smile fell. "I had not thought so far."

"Nay, Charlotte, do not fret. I do believe this is God's plan and things will work out for the best. Perhaps now is a good time to tell you that I too have news."

Now Charlotte looked askance at her friend. "And what news would that be?"

"You know of course that I have an older brother, Joseph, from my mother's first marriage, and that some years ago, he left to seek his fortune in America."

"Yes, you have told me of this."

"We had not heard from him since he left until yesterday that is, when we received a letter. It has taken a very long time to reach us, but in it he says he is well established and prospering. He invites us to join him, saying there is plenty of good land to claim with honest toil if we can but save enough for our passage and a little more to invest."

Charlotte's eyes widened in surprise and dismay. "Oh," she said. "You are leaving?"

Ruth touched her friend's hand gently. "It has not yet been decided, but we are thinking of it, especially after your stepmother put up our rent again. We have savings enough to make the journey, should we decide to. In all honesty, I have been hesitant to leave the familiarity of our home here, but if you are going away, then perhaps I too should be brave and look for a fresh start in the new world."

"Such a journey is not without danger," Charlotte spoke, casting a worried glance at her friend.

"Have you not often told me that fortune favours the brave?"

Charlotte was forced to smile at this. "That is true." After a little while, she continued, "It seems both our lives are about to change. Let us hope it is for the better."

"As I said, it is not yet decided, but if you furnish me with an address, I will write and let you know in the eventuality we do leave for America. It may take some time to make all the arrangements, so I do not foresee that this will happen for several weeks at least."

Charlotte nodded. "Yes, we will write to each other, though the Lord knows how quickly letters will reach you once you are on the other side of the world."

"Put your trust in God, dear Charlotte, and keep your wits about you."

"I will." Charlotte stood and embraced her friend. "I must go. There is much to do."

●————————————————————●

The day for Charlotte's departure duly came, a bright crisp morning at the tail end of March. Sylvia had received the news that Charlotte was to leave with a raise of her brow and the remark, "Well missy, it seems you have landed on your feet. Do not squander yet another good offer of marriage, should you receive one." To this, Charlotte had made no reply.

Now, standing in the parlour was her cousin Frederick, bowing over her hand. "Cousin, it is good to see you looking so well," he said earnestly.

"Thank you, Mr Morton. I am most grateful to you for everything you have done."

He smiled, "It is the least I can do. Since we are family, will you not address me by my given name?"

"I would be honoured to, and please do call me Charlotte."

"Then Charlotte, let us be on our way. Your trunks have been loaded on the coach. It is time to say your goodbyes." At this, he nodded coolly towards Sylvia.

The lady had been all obsequiousness since his arrival a few minutes before. Now she came forward, clasping Charlotte to her powdered bosom. "My dearest Charlotte, how I will miss you! Please do not forget to write and tell me how you are."

Charlotte played along with the farcical farewell. "Of course dear stepmama. God be with you."

"And you my dear." Sylvia wiped a lone tear and sniffed into her handkerchief. "God be with you dear child."

Frederick bowed to Sylvia. "Good day, madam." Then, he held out a hand to Charlotte. "Come Charlotte, we must not tarry if we are to reach our destination before dark."

Taking his hand, Charlotte walked out to the waiting closed carriage and allowed him to help her into it. It was a large, elegantly appointed vehicle, with well-sprung plum coloured seats and clear glass windows. Charlotte settled herself comfortably, her heart beating fast with excitement at this new adventure, though she tried to maintain an air of nonchalant calm. Frederick climbed aboard and sat across from her, then tapped peremptorily on the wooden board above him to instruct the coachman to start the journey.

Charlotte watched through the window in silence as the coach moved slowly down the gravelled lane that led to Alstone Grange, then picked up speed once it reached the main road. Frederick observed her quietly, letting a distance separate them from her old home before speaking, "So, Charlotte, now that we are on our way, will you tell me what has happened since I saw you last? What was this unsuitable match you talked of in your letter?"

Charlotte hesitated, not wanting to speak ill of others. He waited patiently for a response, his expression kindly. It was this that finally decided Charlotte to tell her tale. She recounted the events of the past year in a clear and forthright manner while Frederick listened attentively. When she came to the end of her speech, he said, "You did right Charlotte, in refusing Mr Finch's suit, especially in light of his ungallant words to you after you turned him down. Those were not the words of a true gentleman. Now that we go to London, you will, I hope, get the chance to meet other prospective suitors and make a better match. In any event, you have a home with us for as long as you should wish."

Charlotte felt her lips tremble, but managed to say, "I thank you, Frederick. No words can express how grateful to you I am."

"There is no need for thanks. This is your due as a member of our family. The estrangement that occurred between your late father and the rest of us should never have been allowed to continue for so long without steps taken to bridge the differences. I very much regret that it has taken until now to welcome you back into the fold."

Charlotte nodded, too choked with emotion to speak. Frederick patted her hand gently then sat back and was silent for some time. Eventually, she composed herself enough to converse with her cousin, and they continued on their journey in amiable companionship. By the time they arrived at their destination late in the afternoon, Charlotte was certain that she and Frederick were to become firm friends, and reassured as to the shape her future might take.

Chapter 8

A few days later, a magnificent equipage set out from Stanbourne, Mr Morton's country seat, heading for London. In the front coach sat Mr Morton, his wife holding their infant son and Charlotte. The second coach was occupied by Sir Horace and Lady Powell, their daughter and Mrs Morton. The ladies conversed desultorily while Sir Horace grunted every so often in response. A half hour into this conversation, the subject of Charlotte Harding was brought up.

"What are your thoughts on Miss Harding, Margaret, now that you have had an opportunity to get acquainted with her?" asked Lady Powell.

Mrs Morton sighed volubly, "I had hopes that the daughter of a great beauty, as her Spanish mother was reputed to be, would also turn out to be a beauty herself. Alas, my hopes have been dashed, Julia."

"Yes, it is a great pity. She is not quite what one would call *laide*, for I noticed her eyes are remarkably fine, but certainly her looks will not attract much in the way of attention."

"She has my brother's square jaw and his nose, poor dear. On a man, the features are distinguished, but not so on a woman, I'm afraid. She has such a look of him though, it is extraordinary. Why last night, as she was speaking I very nearly imagined Hugh was sitting opposite me. She has his manner of speech and even cites the same philosophers he did." Mrs Morton smiled wistfully, "It quite took me back."

"On this point at least, you may set your mind at rest. The girl shows good signs of breeding and education. I found her manners unexceptional."

"Yes, that is a relief. I did worry about her comportment not being up to the standards required in our social circles, but I needn't have done so. She is a sweet young thing."

"Think you that she can make a match in London?" asked Miss Powell.

"It is hard to say. What are your thoughts on this, Julia?"

Lady Powell's expression turned grim. "As I said, she is not quite plain but very nearly so—the square jaw, long nose and lips that are far too plump for fashionable tastes. And as for her figure. It is not quite as trim as one would like and much too full in the bust. With her lack of fortune and questionable antecedents, I do not hold out much hope for her, Margaret. Perhaps some old widower of modest means might make her an offer. Otherwise, I do believe that sadly, she is destined for spinsterhood."

Mrs Morton nodded sorrowfully. "It is as I thought too. Poor child."

"Looking on the bright side," said Miss Powell, "she now has the comfort of being back in the bosom of her family, which must be a heartening thought."

"Yes indeed," smiled Mrs Morton.

"Fine filly of a girl," grunted Sir Horace. "I liked her spirit."

"Yes dear," concurred his lady.

"Shall she accompany you to Almack's for the dance on Wednesday?" asked Miss Powell.

Mrs Morton gazed back at her in consternation. "Oh my, I had not thought of that. We would need to procure her a voucher. Would Lady Sefton be agreeable to that?"

Lady Powell looked doubtful. "It is unlikely, given she hails from Spanish trade."

"Oh dear," cried Mrs Morton. "I fear she will have to be left behind whenever we go to Almack's."

Lady Powell patted her hand. "Console yourself, Margaret. It is only one evening in the week, if that, when go to Almack's.

She can accompany you the rest of the time, and I am sure she will enjoy her stay in London immensely."

"I do hope so," said Mrs Morton, and the subject was closed.

●————————————●

In the front coach, at that very moment, the young lady in question was conversing animatedly with Harriet Morton, Mr Frederick Morton's lady. The two young women were of the same age and—happy discovery—the same disposition. Before her marriage to Frederick Morton, Harriet had been a quiet, reclusive young woman with bookish pursuits. And in point of fact, books was the current topic of this animated discussion.

"First thing we need to do in London, Charlotte, is to sign you up with a circulating library. Do you not agree, Frederick?"

Frederick looked affectionately at his wife. "Most ladies would commonly have said the first thing to do in London is to go see the modiste."

Harriet laughed delightedly, "Well, that too."

"Oh no, that will not be necessary," demurred Charlotte.

"But of course. You will need a gown for the Wilton ball at the end of the week and also something new to wear at Almack's."

"Almack's?" repeated Charlotte in alarm.

"Darling," Harriet asked of her spouse, "can we not procure a voucher for Charlotte?"

"I do not see why not," he replied. "I will send a note to Lady Cowper this evening to kindly ask for one."

"There. You see?" Harriet beamed a smile at Charlotte. "And so you will need some new gowns."

Charlotte worried her plump bottom lip. She had not dipped very heavily into her £100 a year, so she could, if need be, rustle together the funds required to purchase new gowns, though she very much feared that London prices for such things far exceeded what one would pay in the country.

"This is what I propose," said Frederick with an air of authority. "Tomorrow morning, I shall walk the two of you to the modiste and leave you there while I attend to my business. Then I shall treat you both to a fine lunch at Simpson's, after which we shall all go to Lackington and Allen to get books and Charlotte a subscription with the circulating library."

"I—er, I do not like to bring up such an indelicate matter, but my funds are limited," said Charlotte diffidently. "Perhaps, I could buy some lace to make a few alterations to my best gowns instead of having a new one."

"Frederick!" Harriet looked on at her husband expectantly, and he did not disappoint her.

"Rid yourself of these concerns, Charlotte. Send all the bills to me, and I will take care of them."

Charlotte flushed a fulsome pink. "That is very kind of you Frederick, but I could not accept such generosity."

"Oh fiddlesticks! Of course you will because it is not generosity on my part, but simply your due as a member of this family." Seeing her unconvinced expression, he went on, "When your father was cut out from grandfather's will, his portion of the inheritance was split equally between my uncle William and my mother. We have been enriched by Uncle Hugh's dispossession, and let me assure you, any bills I may pay will be a fraction of what we received."

"I had not thought of that," said Charlotte slowly, thinking the matter through.

"So let that be the end of any argument."

"I would not want to feel beholden," began Charlotte.

"You are not!" answered Frederick with asperity. "Believe me Charlotte, I can well afford to buy you whatever fripperies you need. Let us cease this conversation now, for it is giving me a headache."

And so for now, the matter was settled.

Chapter 9

Viscount Stanton adjusted his cravat one final time as Hudson brought out his morning coat and helped him into it. The reflection staring back at him through the looking glass was that of a tall, well-formed gentleman. Dark locks, cut fashionably short, framed a masculinely carved face distinguished by deep-set, penetrating brown eyes. Dangerous eyes, one female admirer had once said of them.

"Mr Weston awaits in the drawing room, sir," said Hudson, brushing a little lint from the viscount's tailcoat.

"Splendid!" replied Frank. He strode out of his bedchamber and down the corridor of his bachelor apartment to the drawing room where his friend sat on the settee, reading a newspaper. "Morning Rupert," he called out jovially.

Rupert put down the paper and stood to greet his friend. "Good morning to you, Frank."

"Have you breakfasted?"

"Of course, Mrs Evans makes the finest scrambled eggs this side of London. They are not to be missed."

"Ah yes, the delights of living in a boarding house. Well then, if you are ready, let us be on our way."

Rupert picked up his hat and gloves. "Perhaps you might enlighten me as to where we are going?"

"Perhaps," smiled the viscount mysteriously. Then he relented. "First we shall be calling on family friends just arrived in London. You know the Mortons of course."

"Indeed."

"After which, we shall call on the Powells and pay our respects. I am sure you will want to count yourself as one of the first to set eyes on the incomparable Miss Powell."

"I cannot wait."

"How is the weather out there? Does it rain?"

"No. It is cloudy but dry, with only a light breeze."

"Well in that case, I will forego wearing a greatcoat. Come along, Rupert."

The two friends went merrily on their way, deciding to walk the half-mile journey to Grosvenor Street rather than take a cab. They arrived some minutes later and were shown into the Mortons' drawing room, where Mrs Morton sat together with her son, daughter-in-law and niece.

Frank bowed to Mrs Morton, enquiring, "I trust I find you well, Mrs Morton, and that the journey from Oxfordshire did not tire you unduly?"

Mrs Morton smiled fondly at him, "At my age dear Francis, everything is fatiguing. However, I am fully rested now and fit as a fiddle."

"I am glad," Frank smiled back, then bowed to Frederick Morton and Mrs Frederick Morton. His attention was drawn to the fourth occupant of the room, and Frederick was quick to make the introductions.

"This is my cousin, Miss Harding. Charlotte, I am pleased to make known to you a very old family friend, Viscount Stanton, and with him is Mr Rupert Weston."

Charlotte curtsied prettily as the viscount bowed and said in a polite tone, "At your service, ma'am." He gave her a cursory perusal and made his own private judgement—unprepossessing looking girl, a little shabby in her dress, probably some obscure poor relation. Having catalogued her in his mind to his satisfaction, he turned his attention to Frederick and engaged him in conversation.

The two friends lingered at the Mortons for another quarter of an hour. They accepted an invitation to dine there the following week. Then they stood and made their farewells. It only took a few minutes' walk to reach the Powells' Berkeley Square townhouse. There they were ushered in and welcomed by Sir Horace, Lady Powell and Miss Powell. Having made the proper greetings and introductions, Frank settled himself on a chair beside the young beauty.

"It is a pleasure to see you looking so well, Miss Powell. London society is much improved by the addition of your fair presence."

"You flatter me, my lord."

"Not flattery I assure you, merely a statement of truth."

Miss Powell acknowledged this with a most becoming rose tinge to her complexion. "I am looking forward to making my own, modest, entrance into London society and of course to explore the sights and wonders of this great city. What would you recommend I visit first, Viscount Stanton?"

He gave her a warm smile. "There are so many things to see that it is difficult to choose just one. You must of course visit the theatre at Drury Lane or Covent Garden. I would also suggest a visit to the Royal Academy to view the latest works of masters such as Turner and Constable. Not to mention taking a promenade in Hyde Park. In fact, seeing as we are on the subject, I would very much be honoured if you could all accompany me on a ride in the park tomorrow afternoon."

Miss Powell quite rightly and properly deferred this matter to her mother. Lady Powell smiled her approval, "Thank you, my lord, we would be pleased to do so."

"Well that's settled then. We shall take a ride tomorrow afternoon in the Stanton barouche."

"I look forward to it," replied Miss Powell.

Conversation flowed for a few more minutes before Frank and Rupert rose to their feet, careful not to overstay their welcome. Farewells made, they left the Powells' house and decided to walk along to Hatchards to have a browse through the books. As they began their stroll, Frank asked, "So, Rupert, what did you think of Miss Powell?"

Rupert clutched his heart. "I am in love!"

"Did I not tell you she was of incomparable beauty?"

"Not just beauty Frank, but delightful wit and such charming manners."

Frank eyed him quizzically. "So you think I should court Miss Powell?"

"You would be a fool not to." Rupert paused, then added, "But I see where your worries might also not be unfounded. A lady such as she is bound to be chased and hounded and courted, even after marriage."

"I must think with my head, Rupert. Marriage is something that will last far longer than the first bloom of passion. Would I find felicity long term with such a person as she?"

Rupert frowned. "As to that, it is impossible to say. It is much too soon to make any judgement on the matter. Certainly, pay court to the incomparable—for if you do not, I guarantee she will slip through your fingers—but also keep an eye out for other matches that may stand an equal if not better chance of bringing you felicity."

"That is why we are going to Almack's on Wednesday, you and I."

Rupert sighed, "Must we really?"

"Yes, we must. You have given me your word and cannot bow out now. I shall want your views on the ladies we meet for I value your opinion and cannot do this alone." An idea came to the viscount, and he smiled brilliantly, "In fact, Rupert, I do believe you should join me in the pursuit of a bride. I am sure it would gladden the heart of your dear mama. Why should I be the only one to get shackled? We should enter into the state of matrimony together. A capital idea, now I come to think of it."

Rupert shuddered. "You are overstretching the boundaries of friendship, Frank. Accompany you to Almack's I will, if I must, but rid your mind of the notion I should marry."

"And why not? If it is incumbent on me to do so, then the same applies to you. We are of the same age. We are both well-born and in possession of substantial estates. In fact, you outrank me as you are already the head of your family. Of course you must marry too. Whyever did I not think of it?"

"Frank, I am failing to be amused by your latest jest."

"I do not jest, I assure you. It is a shocking idea at first, I acknowledge. It took me a full day or two to recover from it when father first made his demand. Immersed as we are in the bachelor life, it is hard to imagine our lives as married men. But now that I have had time to adjust my perspective, I am not so disgusted at the prospect of matrimony. I expect it will be the same with you."

Rupert shook his head in distaste. "I am not so sure of that. And besides, my estates may be vast, but they have been encumbered for many years and only recently out of debt. Impoverished as I am, I can hardly be considered an eligible suitor by the ladies of high society."

"I disagree. You are a good-looking enough fellow with a charming turn of phrase, and while your income may have been diminished as you very honourably paid off the mortgages on your land, you stand to make a good living in years to come. That is what I call an eligible prospect."

"And I still have to provide for my brother and sister, do not forget."

"Even so, I call you eligible. Now are we agreed? We both find ourselves a bride before the year is out."

"You may speak for yourself on this one, Frank. I own, if I were ever to meet a young lady that beckoned to my heart, I would not discount the idea of paying court to her. However, I will not tie myself down with any promises to wed by the year out."

Frank grinned, more than satisfied with this answer. "That, my friend, is good enough for me."

At this, they both entered the bookshop in fine spirits.

Chapter 10

Charlotte's first day in London was as magical as she could have imagined, perhaps even more so. As promised, Harriet Morton took her to be fitted for new gowns at Madame Elise, a modiste known for her elegant and stylish creations. Measurements were taken, designs were discussed and fabrics chosen—a fine silk of the palest blue for the Wilton ballgown, and white satin with blue ribbon trim for Almack's. Madame Elise tutted upon being asked to have them ready within such a short time, but agreed to the matter eventually, not wanting to lose the custom of such fine a lady as Mrs Frederick Morton.

Overwhelmed at the expense, Charlotte once again raised objections to such extravagance but these were firmly dismissed by her new friend. "Enough, Charlotte. Frederick has already agreed to this. Let us talk of it not more." And so Charlotte relented and let herself succumb to the joy of acquiring new gowns of the latest fashion, as any young lady would.

Once they were done, Frederick came by to take his wife and cousin to a fine lunch at Simpson's, where Charlotte consumed the tenderest roast beef. But even more enchanting than all these experiences was their visit to the temple of the muses, also known as the fine establishment of Lackington, Allen and Company, the most wondrous bookshop Charlotte had ever set foot inside. She ambled through this shop, which was reminiscent of a large and opulent temple, travelling up winding staircases and exploring galleries filled with endless row upon row of books. *"Is this heaven?"* she wondered to herself. *"As near as,"* she concluded.

The ladies and Mr Frederick Morton returned from their expedition laden with parcels and glowing with the happy satisfaction of a journey well accomplished. They elected to have a quiet dinner at home that evening, needing to rest—and in Charlotte's case—to read from her treasure trove of new books.

The following morning brought the first wave of visitors calling. Charlotte was reading quietly in the drawing room when Viscount Stanton and Mr Rupert Weston were announced. She stood with the others and waited to be introduced to these two fine gentlemen.

Frederick duly did so. "This is my cousin, Miss Harding. Charlotte, I am pleased to make known to you a very old family friend, Viscount Stanton, and with him is Mr Rupert Weston."

The viscount stepped towards her and bowed. "At your service, ma'am," he said.

It was as if time stood still. Charlotte had read about such moments in the racy and less than literary novels she sometimes liked to devour, though she had never truly believed in such things until now. In that instant when he stood before her, a tall, imposing and exquisitely dressed figure, and she breathed in a new and intoxicating scent of expensive cologne combined with a wonderfully masculine fragrance that was entirely his own, Charlotte felt as if she could swoon. Ever so minutely, she swayed towards him, then righted herself at once, executing a curtsy to mask her faux pas.

She need not have worried about humiliating herself, for the viscount's attention promptly turned to her cousin, with whom he began to converse in seemingly absolute ignorance of the tumultuous feelings raging inside her breast.

It was Mr Weston's turn next to make his bow. He did so, giving Charlotte a cordial smile. "I am honoured to make your acquaintance, Miss Harding."

A hammer pounded in Charlotte's head, yet she managed to compose herself enough to respond, "The honour is mine, Mr Weston."

With relief, as she did not know if her limbs would continue to support her, they all sat, and Charlotte looked down at her clasped hands, frantic to slow her racing pulse. Realisation came quickly that the gentleman who had caused this mad response from her was not someone for whom she should entertain any sort of sentimental feelings. If what she had heard from Mrs Morton was correct, the gentleman in question was much taken with the lovely Miss Powell. And why wouldn't he be? Miss Powell was blessed with looks, wit, wealth and connections. Certainly Charlotte could never compete with such a paragon nor hope to attract the attention of the rich and handsome Viscount Stanton. The fact that he was turned away from her, not showing an ounce of interest, was proof enough.

Common sense began slowly to reassert itself. There was no point in wallowing in a bout of unrequited love. Her head had been turned at meeting such a fine looking person. Having lived a sheltered life in the country, she was unused to personages of such stature and refined good looks. Reassured that she had not quite lost all her wits, Charlotte was able to raise her eyes again.

"Is this your first visit to London, Miss Harding?" asked Mr Weston.

She smiled, "Yes, indeed this is the first time I have been further than a few miles from my home village of Alstone, in Gloucestershire. It is all very new and exciting to me."

Mr Weston laughed amiably, "You remind me of how I felt when I first came here as a young man. Tell me, what has been the most exciting thing so far?"

"I do not even need to think about the answer. It was our visit today to the bookshop of Lackington and Allen."

Mr Weston drew his chair a little closer to Charlotte. "I take it you have a love of books."

"It is said that reading is to the mind what exercise is to the body. In my view, it is more. Reading is an unparalleled journey into distant worlds and great minds that can never be achieved in the physical realm, only through the pages of a book. That is especially true for someone such as myself, who has travelled so little."

"I agree wholeheartedly. Reading opens the mind to infinite possibilities. Tell me, what book is it that you are reading at this time?"

Charlotte reached to the side table where she had put it down when their visitors had arrived. "It is 'Travels in North America' by Basil Hall," she said, handing the book to him.

Surprised, he leafed through it then looked at her again. "I must confess to some astonishment, Miss Harding. I had not thought this to be the kind of book to interest a gentle young lady such as yourself."

"Whyever not? Did I not say that reading is a journey to distant worlds that can never be achieved in the physical realm? America is such a distant world as I could never hope to visit in my life, so visit it through the pages of a book I must."

"I would dispute your claim to the impossibility of such a journey. Why packet ships leave daily for America, though I do agree it is unlikely that you would travel on one. What, may I ask, interests you about America in particular?"

"I am interested in all parts of the world. However, it is true that I have a special interest in America since a friend of mine is considering emigrating there. She and her brother are tenants on our estate. They hope to build a more prosperous life for themselves. Wild and untamed land in America is there for the taking by anyone with the will to clear it and cultivate it."

"Yes indeed, I have heard tales of English farmers going to seek their fortune in the new world."

Charlotte opened the book to a page she had marked earlier. "The author writes about one such person here," she said, then read on,

"A large and handsome farmhouse, near Canandaigua, was pointed out to me one day, the owner of which had come to that part of the country between twenty and thirty years before, at which period it was pretty nearly an unbroken forest. He commenced with

very slender means; but persevered in clearing away the woods, and ploughing up the ground, till he came at last to accumulate a considerable fortune. He then built a large brick house, married, brought up sons and daughters, and having retained his health and spirits entire to the age of sixty, had the prospect of a quiet, hearty, green old age before him."

Mr Weston laughed, "A pioneer indeed! And is this a prospect that your friends hope to emulate?"

"I believe so. There is very little hope, at any rate, for them but to continue as they are should they remain in England. America offers them the possibility of raising their state from tenants to landowners."

Mr Weston nodded. "Yes, but such fortune does not come without considerable risk. I would hazard a guess that for every three persons that go on such a quest, only one of them does succeed."

That was something that had been worrying Charlotte too, for she could not view her friends' prospective journey with any degree of equanimity. Something in her face must have betrayed her concern, for Mr Weston said quickly, "I am sorry to have distressed you, Miss Harding. Please disregard what I have just said. I am sure that if your friends have the courage and grit to undertake this journey, then their chances of success are high."

"I pray it is so," murmured Charlotte.

"Now that you have whetted my appetite, I would very much like to read this travel book. Would it be an imposition if I were to borrow it after you have finished reading?"

"Not at all," Charlotte smiled. "It would give me great pleasure to lend it to you."

"Thank you, Miss Harding. I see the viscount getting ready to make his farewells, so our time today is cut short, but I hope to have an opportunity to further my acquaintance with you on another occasion." He stood and bowed. "Good day, Miss Harding."

69

"Good day, Mr Weston."

Charlotte kept busy the rest of the day with more visitors calling, a promenade in Hyde Park with the Mortons, followed by a small card party at Mrs Hurst's, another family friend. Throughout the day and evening, however, she could not help the warm glow that came with the hope that she had made a new friend in Mr Weston. Could it possibly lead to more? Of Viscount Stanton, she resolutely refused to think, though perhaps she did dwell briefly on the perfection of his figure and the strength of his features.

That night, as she put out her candle, she wondered not for the first time when next she would meet the charming and kind Mr Weston. Perhaps at Almack's tomorrow evening? Her perturbation was such that she could not sink into slumber. There was nothing for it therefore, but to lift her night rail and touch that special place between her legs. She was sure her last thought had been of Mr Weston. So why was it that at the peak of her pleasure, she saw instead Viscount Stanton's smouldering dark eyes looking back at her?

Chapter 11

Charlotte stood nervously as their names were announced at the doors of Almack's, that haven of exclusivity, and their vouchers checked. Tonight, she was in her new ballgown, a beautiful creation of white satin silk and blue ribbon trim. The gown was cut low off the shoulder in a style that flattered her fuller figure, and laced tightly at the waist. To complete the look were voluminous layers of skirt and puffed sleeves embellished with pretty blue bows. It was the finest gown she had ever worn in her life.

Harriet had insisted her hair for this occasion be styled by Jenny, her maid. The result was an elaborate top knot with delicate ringlets falling at either side of her face. Jenny had also applied a little rouge to add colour to Charlotte's cheeks, saying it was perfectly respectable. Glancing at her reflection in the mirror, Charlotte saw a fashionable-looking lady with fine eyes and a healthy bloom to her cheeks. The gown exposed the elegant slope of her shoulders and for the first time, Charlotte felt almost pretty.

As they entered the crowded ballroom, they were greeted by Lady Sefton, one of the patronesses of this fine establishment. "My dear Margaret," the lady now said. "How good it is to see you."

"And you, Maria. I must say you are looking well," replied Mrs Morton.

Lady Sefton's eyes twinkled. "As well as can be expected in our advanced years." She addressed the other members of the party. "Mr Morton, Mrs Frederick Morton, a pleasure to see you here tonight. And who have we here?"

"Lady Sefton, may I introduce you to my niece, Miss Charlotte Harding. She is my late brother Hugh's daughter."

Lady Sefton raised her lorgnette to inspect Charlotte from head to toe. "Indeed."

Charlotte curtsied. "It is an honour to make your acquaintance, my lady," she said in a soft, cultured voice.

Lady Sefton inclined her head regally. "Welcome to Almack's, Miss Harding."

The introductions over, the Mortons and Charlotte moved into the ballroom, the ladies procuring dance cards from the master of ceremonies. "Put my name down for the first dance with you, Harriet, and the waltz," said Frederick. Turning to Charlotte, he added, "And put me down for a country dance with you, Charlotte. I think with that, one should consider my duty done, and you will not mind, I hope, if I then find my way to the card room for a game or two."

Harriet observed him in amusement. "I am honoured then to merit two dances with you, my dearest, seeing how little you enjoy it."

"Well dear, I could not allow any other gentleman but myself to waltz with you."

The two exchanged a tender look, which filled Charlotte with gladness and, truth be told, a little envy. Would that one day someone looked at her that way. Mr Weston perhaps? Despite her less than successful foray into Gloucestershire society, Charlotte was still at this time hopeful of finding love. She had not yet lived long enough to have such sweet dreams dashed, and so she allowed herself the luxury of dreaming a future with Rupert Weston. It is true that they had only had one short meeting, but to her inexperienced romantic mind, she felt the weight of its significance. He had paid her special attention, drawing his chair closer so they could talk about her favourite thing, books, and asking to borrow her copy of 'Travels in North America'.

Charlotte cast a furtive glance around her, hoping to catch sight of this fine gentleman, but could not find him in the crowd. They spent the next half hour circulating the room with introductions being made and more dances being requested. Charlotte was surprised to see even her own card begin to fill up, though there were still several dances she would need to sit out with Mrs Morton and Lady Powell, who had joined them.

Towards the end of that time, she finally perceived across the room Viscount Stanton and with him, Mr Rupert Weston. Both gentlemen cut a fine figure, the one tall and dashingly handsome, the other, elegantly turned out. Could one blame Charlotte for the sudden mad pounding of her foolish young heart? It was not surprising therefore, that having spied their presence, she continued to observe — very discreetly of course — their progress around the room.

She saw Viscount Stanton bow and extend his hand to an elegant looking lady dressed in a mint green gown. Something in his smile made her curious. "Who is that lady stepping onto the dance floor with Viscount Stanton?" she asked her aunt.

Mrs Morton glanced in their direction. "That, my dear, is Lady Caroline Drake, the widow of Sir Giles Drake, an extremely wealthy baronet."

"The viscount seems very taken with her."

Lady Powell sniffed. "And so is every other man in London. The lady is known to run in quite racy circles. I do not advise you, Charlotte, to have anything to do with her if you can help it."

"Does that mean the viscount also runs in such circles?" asked Charlotte innocently.

"My dear, a gentleman may frequent insalubrious establishments with no fear as to his reputation. The same cannot be said for a lady."

This exchange only served to increase Charlotte's curiosity. She studied the viscount and the lady in question as they danced a quadrille. Both were quite correct and proper in their manner, yet Charlotte discerned the occasional warm glance between them. What could that signify? Was there some close but hidden relationship between the viscount and Lady

73

Caroline? Was he—here Charlotte's imagination ran riot as she remembered gossip she had heard about such things—was he her lover? The thought shocked her to the core. This was the man who was paying court to Helena Powell while at the same time entertaining the company of a mistress. Her upright principles could not conceive of such abominable behaviour. Along with the shock and revulsion was another uncomfortable feeling. Charlotte's poor heart was hurting just a little that her unattainable hero, the gentleman who had very nearly caused her to swoon on their first meeting, had in fact feet of clay.

It was best to put the viscount out of her mind. His sort and hers did not mix; this much was clear. Was Mr Weston, his good friend, of the same ilk? Surely not. She turned her attention to this second gentleman, who was also on the dance floor with some stylish looking lady. As with the viscount, Mr Weston's manner was most proper and correct. Charlotte looked in vain for secretive warm glances between himself and the lady, but did not see any. This reassured her to an extent, though she could not help but compare her own looks unfavourably with those of the lady. Would she ever be able to win his affections when there were so many other prettier, wealthier and better connected ladies for him to choose from?

Her heart sank, then she reminded herself of his marked attention to her during their meeting, when they had discussed books. Perhaps she would win his affection in that manner, through her mind rather than her looks. Was it not better this way? Looks could fade and any attraction based on appearances alone was guaranteed to be short-lived. But the attraction of like minds? That was the long-lasting kind.

All these musings flitted through Charlotte's head as she watched the dancers from the side of the ballroom where she sat with the older matrons who were not dancing. Such was the lot of a wallflower, but she would not complain. Even this was far more exciting than anything that had happened in her quiet country life so far.

The dance came to an end, the gentlemen bowed to the ladies and escorted them back to their seats. Harriet and Miss Powell returned, looking a trifle flushed from their exertions, and were glad to sip from the lemonade which Frederick kindly procured for them. He now extended a hand to Charlotte. "May I have the pleasure of this dance, Miss Harding?" he asked most correctly.

Charlotte curtsied prettily and took his hand. "You may, kind sir," she answered.

With a smile, Frederick escorted her to the dance floor where they took their places for a rendition of "Hole in the Wall", a favourite country dance of hers. Standing at the other end of the long line of dancers, she spied Mr Weston and Viscount Stanton, both now with different partners. The music began and she followed the stately, elegant movements of the dance, curtsying and twirling around, swishing past Frederick with a demure smile to exchange places with him, moving along to the next place in the line, then forming a circle of four with another couple on the dance floor.

Charlotte had danced this many a time before, but in the dazzling setting of Almack's ballroom, dressed in exquisite finery, it felt wonderfully new and exciting. Smiling delightedly as she exchanged partners and moved gracefully along the line, Charlotte lost herself in the pleasure of the dance.

At last she came to stand across from the viscount, who bowed solemnly showing no sign of recognition as he took her hand briefly in the dance. They completed a circle of four, then twirled along to their next partners. Now it was that she faced Mr Weston, whose pleased smile set her heart aflutter. He took her hand and murmured, "Miss Harding, a pleasure to see you tonight."

She curtsied and mumbled, "The pleasure is mine, sir," then moved along to her next place in the dance, eventually making her way back to Frederick. Soon after, the dance came to an end. Frederick bowed and walked Charlotte back towards their

75

seats. He stayed long enough to ensure all the ladies were comfortable, then excused himself to go to the card room.

"How did you like your first dance at Almack's?" asked Harriet.

"It was everything I had imagined and more," stated Charlotte.

"I am glad to hear," smiled her friend.

Mrs Morton looked approvingly at her niece. "You were very elegant on the dance floor, my dear."

Lady Powell nodded her agreement. "Yes indeed, Charlotte, you have excellent deportment. Margaret, I see Mr Bertram Hodge approaching. Do you not think he would make a good partner for Charlotte in this next dance?"

Mrs Morton fanned herself as she replied, "Mr Hodge? Is he in town? I have not seen him since his sad bereavement two summers ago."

"He is. The poor man has a young son and two daughters to care for. I have heard it from good sources that he is in town on the lookout for a gentle lady to be a wife to him and mother to his children. I think it would be a marvellous idea to introduce him to Charlotte."

"Indeed!" agreed Mrs Morton. "Let us catch his attention."

The two ladies looked in the direction of a portly gentleman of around forty, who was at this time walking nearby. They nodded to him, and this was encouragement enough for him to come over, executing a bow. "Lady Powell, Mrs Morton, a pleasure."

"Mr Hodge," said Lady Powell. "It is good to see you looking so well. May I introduce you to my daughter, Miss Powell, to Mrs Frederick Morton and to Miss Harding, Mrs Morton's niece."

Mr Hodge executed a bow to the ladies. "Charmed, I'm sure," he said.

"Mr Hodge, if you do not have a partner for the next dance, may I suggest my lovely niece," said Mrs Morton smoothly. "She is new in town and this is her first ball. I am sure she would be delighted to step on the dance floor with you."

Charlotte was less than delighted. Mr Hodge's thick jowls, small beady eyes and perspiring forehead were hardly a captivating proposition for a young, romantic soul as she. However, she could not voice her disagreement without sounding rude, so she smiled and curtsied when Mr Hodge responded, "Of course. I would be delighted. Miss Harding, will you do me the honour of this next dance?"

"I thank you, sir," she murmured, and walked with him towards the dance floor just as her party was joined by none other than Viscount Stanton and Mr Weston. She saw the viscount bow to Miss Powell, asking her to dance and Mr Weston likewise asking Harriet for a dance. *"What poor luck!"* she thought. *"Had it not been for Mr Hodge, Mr Weston would surely have asked me for that dance."*

There was nothing for it but to accept her lot with as good a grace as possible, going through the motions of the dance, an old-fashioned gavotte, with Mr Hodge for a partner. After a while, she began to enjoy herself, her naturally sunny disposition reasserting itself. She smiled gaily as she executed the steps of the dance with deft elegance. From the corner of her eye, she glimpsed Helena Powell dancing with the viscount and dimpling prettily at him. The sight caused an unpleasant tightness in Charlotte's chest. Had she not told herself already that the viscount was not only out of her reach but also most probably a shocking reprobate? With determination, she turned her attention back to her elderly partner and did not look towards either the viscount or Mr Weston again.

When the dance ended, Mr Hodge bowed punctiliously, took out a handkerchief to mop his sweating brow and offered her his arm to escort her back to her seat. "This has been a pleasure, Miss Harding. Will you do me the honour of a second dance later this evening?"

Charlotte did not know what to say. She had not yet mastered the art of the polite refusal. Instead, she murmured, "Of course, sir." By now, they had reached Mrs Morton and Lady Powell. Mr Hodge bowed again and took his leave. A moment later, Harriet and Miss Powell were returned by their partners. The gentlemen bowed and walked away, disappointing Charlotte yet again. It seemed she would never have the chance to dance with Mr Weston.

The evening progressed and Charlotte stood for two more dances. One with Mr Hurst, Mrs Hurst's son, a young man of twenty-three or twenty-four years, whom she had met at the previous evening's card party. The other was with Colonel Huxley, another acquaintance from that card party, a jovial man in his late thirties. Both dances she enjoyed immensely, though neither partner caused any stirring in her heart.

The final dance of the evening was to be a waltz. She was prepared to sit it out, unless Mr Hodge asserted a claim to it, which she rather hoped he would not. As Colonel Huxley returned Charlotte to her seat, she saw that Frederick had rejoined the group. He smiled kindly at her. "How has it been, Charlotte?" he asked.

"Tremendous!" she replied happily. She would not let her disappointment at not having danced with Mr Weston cloud what was otherwise a joyful and exciting evening. In that same instant, she saw a sight that both raised and sunk her spirits, for coming towards them from two different directions in the ballroom were Mr Hodge and Mr Weston, accompanied by Viscount Stanton. It was anybody's guess which of the gentlemen would reach them first. Lady Powell also perceived Mr Hodge, and an expression of smug satisfaction came over her face at the apparent success of her matchmaking efforts.

In the event, it was Mr Hodge who got to them first. He bowed to Charlotte, then took out his handkerchief to mop his brow. That small pause was enough time for Mr Weston and Viscount Stanton to catch up with them. Mr Hodge began to speak, "Miss Harding, will you do me the—"

He was interrupted by a cheerful, booming voice. "Miss Harding, I believe this is our dance." Mr Weston bowed and held out his hand.

"Excuse me," she said to Mr Hodge, then took Mr Weston's extended hand and let him lead her onto the dance floor. "Mr Weston, you hold me in your debt," she breathed.

"Not at all, Miss Harding. I had come to ask you for a dance, but I may have overstretched my claim to it a little."

"Well, I thank you."

They had reached the dance floor by now, and as the music started, Mr Weston took her hand and placed his other around her waist. Charlotte was unused to being held so closely by a gentleman. When the waltz had first graced the ballrooms of London, many had deemed it a scandalous dance, but that was several years ago and now, it was considered perfectly respectable. However, the small assembly dances that she had attended thus far in her life tended not to have the waltz, so although she had learned the steps, this was her very first time dancing it at a ball. Standing so close to Mr Weston, she was struck down by momentary shyness which caused her to stumble and miss her step.

That gentleman very smoothly righted Charlotte and guided her in the dance. Over the next minute or two, she concentrated on getting the steps right, staring intently at his cravat. After a while, Mr Weston spoke. "It is a finely knotted cravat, I do admit, but surely not worthy of such interest, Miss Harding?"

She looked up into his eyes then. "I am sorry. I was trying to count the steps. This is my first time dancing the waltz."

"And you are doing it marvellously well. Put yourself at ease, Miss Harding, and let me lead you."

So Charlotte did, and soon she was twirling around the ballroom in Mr Weston's arms, staring dazedly into his kind grey eyes and fancying herself in love. The dance came to an end, as did their evening at Almack's, but as the Mortons and Charlotte were driven away in their carriage, she still felt a warm glimmer of happiness, for there was nothing more romantic than dancing a waltz with a handsome single gentleman.

Chapter 12

Viscount Stanton turned to his friend as they left Almack's. "The night is still young. Shall we go to White's?"

"I don't see why not," replied Rupert. "The air is wonderfully fresh after the heat of the ballroom. Let us walk."

"Yes, let's."

Side by side, the gentlemen strolled, enjoying a convivial silence, each thinking about the evening just passed.

"Why on earth did you ask Miss Harding for a waltz?" asked Frank suddenly.

"I had not meant to. It was a spur of the moment decision when I saw that frightful old bore about to ask her for a dance. I had to ride in chivalrously to the rescue."

"Careful Rupert, or you will give the poor girl ideas."

Rupert huffed, "Hardly! She struck me as an eminently sensible girl on first acquaintance."

"I saw her make dreamy eyes at you."

"Oh," replied Rupert, a little deflated. "Then perhaps I should have more care."

"Yes, perhaps you should. On to other matters. What did you think of Miss Pemberton?"

Rupert frowned in concentration. "Nice-looking girl. Know her brother. Boxed with him a few times. Pleasant chap but a little dull."

"D'you think it would be worth calling on her?"

"There is no great opportunity for conversing to be had at a ball. If you were to call on her, you would be able to figure out if she's as dull as her brother or not."

"Very well," agreed Frank. "We'll add her to the list of ladies we call on tomorrow."

"We?"

"Well of course," said Frank. "You don't want to miss out on the fun surely?"

Rupert sniffed but did not deign to respond.

"And what about Miss Fortescue?" continued Frank.

"Which one do you mean? Miss Marianne or Miss Hester Fortescue?"

"Miss Marianne."

"Pretty thing. She titters when she laughs. Mighty irritating."

"Really?" Frank frowned. "I had not noticed."

"Believe me, if you were to spend anything more than a half hour in her company, you would."

Frank quirked his lips. "I stand corrected." After a pause, he went on, "Well in that case, for the moment it's Miss Powell or Miss Pemberton." He sighed, "Can you see me shackled to either of them, Rupert?"

"It's hard to say."

Frank looked at his friend in disgust. "You're no help at all!"

Rupert laughed, "Well it would not be me marrying them, so it is hard to say. You ought to know better than me how you feel about them."

"Right now, I feel nothing more than admiration. They are both fine looking and well-bred ladies."

"It is early days yet. We are in April now, and the season still has a good three or four months to go. Give yourself time to get to know them better."

"I suppose so," answered the viscount morosely. "I had hopes to get the matter dispensed with quickly and to move on to other pursuits."

Rupert burst out laughing. "It is a marriage we are talking about, is it not? A lifelong partnership is hardly something than can be dispensed with quickly."

"All I meant to say was that once an engagement was announced and the banns called, I would be free to return to my usual pursuits and would no longer need to put quite so much time and effort into courtship. Look at me now, having to make morning calls, go out on afternoon expeditions in the park, attend balls and soirées. It is quite tiresome! Once engaged, I could reduce such activities to maybe taking the good lady out for a ride in the park once a week or so."

"I think you would find that once engaged, you would be honour bound to take the good lady out to the theatre, to Vauxhall Gardens, to balls and soirées, and so on—no, Frank, you would not be able to return to your usual pursuits quite as easily as you think. That is why I have no plans to marry for a very long time."

"Botheration!" cried the viscount in frustration.

They walked on quietly for some minutes.

"Do I take it then," asked Rupert, "that you have changed your mind about getting married?"

They had by now arrived at White's. Frank let out a long-drawn sigh. "No, I have not. I know father. Once he has the bit between his teeth, he will not let it go. Marry I must." With that sobering thought, he stepped through the doors of his club.

Chapter 13

Charlotte lingered in bed the morning after her debut at Almack's, thinking back dreamily over the events of the previous evening. For a first waltz, that waltz with Mr Weston had been marvellously wonderful. Could she think of any more superlatives? Suffice it to say that this one dance, where Mr Weston had held her closely in his arms, looking into her eyes as he twirled her around the ballroom, would forever more be etched into her memory. And as for the way he had gallantly claimed a dance with her over Mr Hodge's feeble attempts. So romantic!

When her daydreams reached the feverish point at which she began to practise a new name for herself, Charlotte Weston, even she knew it was time to put a stop to the fancifulness and rise from her bed. She dressed and went down to breakfast in the sunniest of spirits. "Good morning Harriet," she said, waltzing over to her seat.

Harriet smiled back weakly, "Good morning Charlotte. I see you are well rested after last night's exertions."

"Yes thank you, I am. However, I cannot say the same for you."

"Little Edwin would not settle all night. I wonder you did not hear him, so loud were his cries."

"I am a sound sleeper," replied Charlotte. "The loudest of thunderstorms will not keep me from my slumber."

"You are fortunate."

Charlotte helped herself to some eggs and slices of cold beef. "Have Frederick and Aunt Margaret breakfasted already?" she asked.

"Yes, long ago," replied Harriet, stifling a yawn.

Looking at her friend, Charlotte said gently, "We had better stay in today and forget about our planned expedition to the Royal Academy. We can go there another time. You look like you should be abed."

"I think you are right, though I hate to ruin your plans, Charlotte," Harriet said a little guiltily.

"You have not ruined them at all," Charlotte replied truthfully. "I shall simply stay home and settle myself comfortably with a good book." Her breakfast finished, she fetched the latest tome she was reading, a popular gothic romance by the name of Rookwood, and went to settle in her favourite nook in the drawing room, a comfortable chaise longue set by the window, giving plenty of good light for her to read by.

There it was that Mrs Morton found her a few minutes later. "Charlotte my dear, there you are."

Charlotte put down her book and went to greet her aunt. "Good morning Aunt Margaret. I'm sorry I missed you at breakfast. I'm unused to being up so late and must have slept in."

Mrs Morton smiled kindly, "I fully expected you to. I am sure it took you a time to get to sleep after the excitement of your first London ball."

"A little," admitted Charlotte, "though not very long, for it seems I slept through Edwin's cries in the night."

"Poor Harriet. She did look quite pale and wan this morning."

"I told her we should postpone our visit to the Royal Academy."

"Quite right, my dear. I think it best we all rest at home today, for we have the Wilton ball tomorrow to look forward to—" Mrs Morton paused in her speech as they heard the sound of the front doorbell being pulled. "This must be Lady Powell," she said. A minute later, that lady was indeed announced.

"Margaret dear," Lady Powell said, walking into the drawing room. "I hope last night's exertions did not overtire you."

Mrs Morton stood and greeted her friend with a light kiss on the cheek. "Not at all," she said. "Helena does not accompany you today?"

"She woke this morning feeling not quite well. I am sure it is nothing serious, but we thought it best for her to stay abed and rest," replied Lady Powell. "Miss Harding, good day."

"Good day," curtsied Charlotte, who then reclined back onto the chaise longue with her book. The two older ladies settled themselves on the settee by the fireplace, and began to enjoy a pleasant gossip about last night's ball.

"Helena was quite the success last night," said Mrs Morton, "and it did not escape my notice that Viscount Stanton asked her to dance twice, one of them being a waltz!"

"Yes," said Lady Powell. "His attention to her was all that it should be. I am hopeful, dear Margaret, but it is early days yet. Onto other matters, what did you think of Lady Baxter's lilac monstrosity of a gown?"

"That it was quite monstrous," laughed Mrs Morton. And the two ladies continued with their reminiscences of the previous evening. Charlotte read, not paying them much heed until the name "Weston" in the conversation had her pause and prick up her ears.

"Sophia Weston writes that she is anxious for Anthony, her youngest, to get a commission in the Dragoon Guards, but Rupert is reluctant to approve the expense. She wonders if Frederick could have a word with him to help change his mind. Well," chuckled Mrs Morton, "she certainly does not know Frederick if she thinks he'll interfere in such matters."

"Anthony is very young still, is he not? Why I believe he is no more than a year older than my Henry; that would make him seventeen or so. Rupert is quite right to wait until he is older."

"Yes, most probably. In any event, it is not for us to opine on the matter. And then Julia, can you believe it, in her postscript, she writes to say it is high time Rupert got married and asks if I know of any eligible young lady I could introduce him to."

"Hmm, that may be harder than she thinks. Did not Rupert Weston inherit a ton of debt from that wastrel of a father of his?"

"That is the rumour, though I have heard he has made great economies these past two years to try to settle these debts. I believe that is why Emily did not have her come out this season. They are rusticating in the country to save on expenses."

"Well," said Lady Powell, "that hardly puts him in a good position to pay court to a lady."

"That may be true, but the Weston estates are vast, and likely to turn in a tidy income in time under Rupert's sound stewardship. There must be some young ladies, perhaps with small portions, that would welcome his suit."

"Do you have anyone in mind?" wondered Lady Powell.

Over on the chaise longue, Charlotte waited with baited breath. Unfortunately, her aunt's mind did not fix on her. After thinking long and hard on the matter, Mrs Morton speculated, "Perhaps Eliza Herbert?"

"Perhaps, and how about Horatia Colborne?"

"Of course! Why did I not think of her? I could invite the Colbornes and Herberts to our dinner party next week and arrange the introductions. What do you think, Julia? I could seat Viscount Stanton next to Helena, and make sure Eliza and Horatia are on either side of Rupert Weston."

"My dear, I think that is a marvellous idea." Lady Powell paused, then a big smile spread over her face as another thought came to her. "And Margaret, you could also invite Mr Hodge," said she, raising her brow meaningfully.

Charlotte kept her gaze on her book, pretending not to listen to the two ladies as they broke her spirit, without even knowing it. The words swam in front of her eyes. All her happy dreams from this morning had collapsed in one fell swoop of her aunt's tongue. She was not considered eligible enough for Rupert Weston—even impoverished as he was. No, all that she was good for was an elderly widower with no looks to recommend him, who needed a new mother to care for his children. Oh why did she think things would be any different for her here in London than they had been in Gloucestershire? Why had she fooled herself into thinking she might find love? It seemed once again, her choices were stark. Marry someone she did not care for, or live the life of a spinster dependent on the charity of others. The gallant but impecunious Mr Weston appeared to be out of her reach.

These painful thoughts crossed Charlotte's mind in a flash like sharp needles piercing the inside her head. Her fingers, grasping the pages of her book, trembled. With great effort, she stilled them and tried to compose herself. She would not let her aunt or Lady Powell see her distress. Her pride would not allow it. She cast about in her mind for a suitable proverb to help lift her spirits. *Endure and persist; this pain will turn to good by and by.*

"Yes," she thought, "*it will not always hurt so.*" Deliberately, she turned the page of her book, appearing to be engrossed in the story while she sought comfort from her great philosophers. *Human misery must somewhere have a stop; there is no wind that always blows a storm.*

On and on she read, without taking in a single word. She thought of one final uplifting proverb. *The greatest wealth is to live content with little.* How could she complain when she already had so much? She had been welcomed by Frederick and Harriet, and even Aunt Margaret, into their home. Frederick had told her that she could stay with them for as long as she wished, and he was a man of his word. She lived in great luxury. Every night, she slept on soft, fragrant sheets and woke to a tray of fresh tea by her bedside. She had beautiful gowns and access to the finest entertainment that London had to offer.

And most of all, she had books to lose herself in. Was this really so bad?

"I am blessed, truly I am," she reminded herself. If it was not in God's plan that she marry, then she would seek a new purpose in life. She would devote herself to her family and find a way to do good, engaging in charitable work. She could even try her hand at writing a novel. Her earlier compositions had lacked substance, but already since arriving in London, she had a wealth of experiences to draw upon in her writing. She could continue to observe the goings on of London society and be inspired to write more. Yes truly, she was blessed.

Slowly, she felt herself regain her equanimity. In the midst of this flurry of positive thoughts, she did take a moment to regret the fact she might never get to experience the intimacies of a man and wife, or even have a first kiss. But it was only a moment, for she pushed the thought firmly away. She would be grateful with her lot and not ask for more. Therein lay her happiness.

And thus it was that when her aunt called out to her, she was able to respond with a genuine smile. "Charlotte, would you be a dear and run up to see if Harriet would like to join us for a ride in Hyde Park? I believe the fresh air would do us all a world of good."

"Yes of course, Aunt Margaret," she replied, and stood to do her bidding. On nimble feet, she ran up to Harriet's chamber, knocking softly on the door. On entering, she saw that Harriet was sound asleep, and so she backed quietly out of the room, returning swiftly to the drawing room. She was about to step into that room when she overheard her name spoken by Lady Powell. Not meaning to eavesdrop, she nevertheless paused to listen.

"I was wondering, Margaret, if you would let Charlotte accompany Helena on promenades and other outings with the viscount. I do feel that he would be more encouraged to court Helena without my presence obstructing his romantic

89

inclinations. Perhaps Charlotte could act as a less intimidating chaperone than me. And there could be no fear that she would distract the viscount's attention, for she is a quiet little thing, and my Helena's good looks will be all the more striking when set in contrast with hers. What do you think?"

Mrs Morton hesitated. "She is young to be considered a chaperone. Will it not occasion gossip?"

"Rest assured on this matter," said Lady Powell. "No one would ever entertain the idea that she is there other than as a chaperone. I do not believe it would occasion any undue risk to her reputation."

"Well in that case, of course I have no objection."

Charlotte stood frozen in the doorway, another little dagger piercing her heart. She took a deep calming breath. *Endure and persist; this pain will turn to good by and by.* She turned and retraced her footsteps up the stairs, then made her way down again, this time making sure to announce her presence more loudly. With a bright smile, she entered the drawing room. "I'm afraid Harriet will not be joining you for a ride, for she is still sound asleep," she told her aunt.

"Oh, that is a shame," said Mrs Morton. "Will you be coming out with us dear?"

Charlotte doubted she could take any more of the two ladies' chatter today. "If you do not mind, Aunt Margaret, I would prefer to stay home and continue with my book."

Mrs Morton gazed at her fondly. "Always buried in a book, just like your father. In that case my dear, we shall be on our way."

Charlotte smiled breezily, "I am sure the fresh air will do you good, Aunt Margaret. Do have a pleasant ride. Good day to you, Lady Powell."

"Good day, Miss Harding."

Chapter 14

The following evening, the Mortons' carriage drew up in front of the magnificent entrance to Lord and Lady Wilton's Palladian mansion set in large parkland on the northern outskirts of London. Frederick jumped down and helped the ladies alight. Behind him, the mansion was lit by dozens of small oil lamps, casting a gilded glow over the frontage of the house. Through the open doors, the sounds of music drifted out. The Wilton ball was the pre-eminent event of the season. Everyone that mattered in London society would be here tonight, and so would she, Charlotte Harding.

She picked her way up the front steps carefully and followed the Mortons into the house where Frederick presented their invitation cards for inspection. Before entering the ballroom, the ladies visited a powder room to straighten their gowns and check their appearance. Looking at herself in the mirror, Charlotte could not help but be pleased. Madame Elise had outdone herself.

The gown she wore hugged her figure in all the right places and fell in a deceptively simple swish of pale blue silk that complemented her complexion. Jenny had styled her hair again, this time sweeping it into a curtain over her brow, then looping it around her head in artfully braided tresses. Even if Charlotte had no prospect of a decent suitor, she was here in her finest gown looking her best and was determined to enjoy herself. Perhaps Mr Weston would ask her to dance again; maybe he would prove her aunt and Lady Powell wrong.

Once preened to their satisfaction, the ladies emerged from the powder room and rejoined Frederick, who awaited them patiently. Then their names were announced, and they entered the busy ballroom. Their first half hour at the ball was spent in greeting their hosts and other acquaintances, and the ladies filling out their dance cards. As before, Frederick claimed two dances with his wife and one with Charlotte.

Such was the throng of people that even Charlotte's card began to fill up, though to her disappointment, Mr Weston did not come to claim a dance from her. She had glimpsed him in the busy ballroom, bowing and smiling at other young ladies. He had had many opportunities to catch sight of her and approach, but he had not. Her spirits took a dive. It had been foolish of her to read anything but common courtesy into the attention he had paid her previously. She should cure herself of any romantic notions in his regard.

Her first dance partner, a slightly wet-behind the ears young dandy by the name of Eugene Barton, came to escort her onto the ballroom floor. She accepted his hand, and they took their positions for a quadrille. He was not the partner of her romantic dreams, but no matter. Tonight, she was determined to enjoy herself. She skipped and laughed gaily to the steps of the dance, so that by the time Mr Barton returned her to her aunt's side some minutes later, she was flushed and happy, with not a care in the world. Nothing becomes a lady more than happiness. It radiates from the eyes and brings a soft glow to the complexion, a fact that was noted by more than one gallant gentleman at the ball. More dances were claimed on Charlotte's card—tonight at least, she was not to be a wallflower.

In the pause between dances, Frederick suggested they help themselves to refreshments, which were more generous than the offerings to be had at Almack's. Charlotte accepted a glass of lemonade and nibbled on a slice of cake, appreciating the delicately spiced crumb. Looking across the ballroom, her eyes spied Mr Weston smiling mischievously down at a pretty young lady as he said something to her, and the lady flushing delicately in response.

Oh how foolish she had been to imagine anything between her and him. Disgusted with herself, she turned away abruptly.

Unfortunately, she did not look carefully enough at where she was stepping and collided with none other than Mr Hodge, holding out a glass of lemonade, the contents of which spilled all over the front of her gown. She looked down at herself in consternation; her lovely gown, ruined.

"Oh my, I am ever so sorry Miss Harding. Do forgive my carelessness," mumbled Mr Hodge, but she barely heard him.

Harriet came forward with a handkerchief and tried to mop the worst of the spillage. It was no good. "Come quick, Charlotte. Let us leave the ballroom and see what we can do about this." With military precision, she guided Charlotte out through a side door, which led to a small anteroom from whence a set of stairs took them to the floor above. They walked along the corridor and opened the door to the first bedroom. "In you go, Charlotte. I shall fetch a lady's maid to help you out of the gown so it can be cleaned and pressed. I shan't be long."

The moonlight and the decorative oil lamps outside cast a faint light into the room as Charlotte went and sat on the edge of the bed, still reeling in shock and looking down at her gown in desolation. Harriet was as good as her word, returning a minute later with a maid in tow and a lighted candle which she placed on a side table. Together they helped Charlotte out of her ballgown, leaving her in just a corset and petticoat over her stockings. "Don't worry madam," said the maid. "It is only lemonade and won't leave a stain if we give it a quick clean. I'll have it pressed and brought back to you as soon as I can."

"Thank you," said Charlotte gratefully. Feeling a little bare without her gown, she went to sit on a large bench that was positioned behind a four-panelled carved wooden screen. "I'll wait over here," she said to Harriet, then added as her friend made to come and sit beside her, "No Harriet, there is no need for you to stay and miss out on the ball. Do go back; I shall be just fine."

"Are you sure you wouldn't rather I wait with you?"

"I'm sure. Go on, go and enjoy yourself, and please give my excuses to my dance partners."

Harriet seemed to hesitate, then nodded. "Fine, but if you are not back in the ballroom within the next half hour, I shall come back and look for you."

Once Harriet had left, Charlotte sat quietly, going over the events of the past few minutes in her mind. How on earth did she not see Mr Hodge? Why did she have to turn so suddenly and be so careless? The recriminations continued for a little longer until she forced herself to stop. "*What is done is done,*" she thought. "*And if I can return to the ballroom within the half hour, I will have missed at most two or three dances. The evening has not been entirely ruined.*" With that, she had to be satisfied, and she waited with as much patience as she could muster for the maid to return.

A noise made her sit up eagerly. That was quick! The door opened, but it was not the maid that entered. Puzzled, and aware of her state of undress, Charlotte stayed hidden behind the screen. She heard an unknown female voice. "In here, darling." The door shut and for the next minute, all that could be heard was the faint rustling of silk.

Her curiosity aroused, Charlotte tiptoed silently towards the screen, putting her eye to one of the tiny carved holes in the wood. The sight she saw made her catch her breath. A gentleman and a lady were kissing passionately. She could not make out their identities in the dim light of the small candle.

Then the man spoke, "Getting impatient Caro. I thought we had agreed to conclude the evening together."

"I could not wait, Frank. I have missed you. It has been two long weeks since we last were together."

"Indeed? I could have sworn that we danced only three nights ago."

The lady rapped him on the top of his arm. "You know quite well what I meant. And now, enough talk, my lord, as we do not have much time."

Charlotte stood frozen behind the screen. That male voice she had recognised. It was Viscount Stanton! And the lady with him could be none other than Lady Caroline Drake. What was she to do now? She could hardly reveal her presence in her state of undress and especially not after having heard what had just been said. All she could hope was that they would leave after a few more rounds of kisses. But that is not what happened next.

"What is it you want?" grunted the viscount.

"I want your cock, and I want it inside me now!"

He growled in response, "Then show me that glorious cunt."

Charlotte put a hand to her mouth in shock. Never had she heard such filthy language. She watched with a mixture of outrage and disbelief as Lady Caroline lifted her gown and petticoat to her waist. Beneath, she was bare apart from her stockings which were tied with a garter just above the knee. Clearly visible at the apex of her legs, was a triangular patch of dark blonde hair.

The viscount fell to his knees and buried his face in that patch of hair, while the lady made gasping little breaths. "Open up!" he rasped. She spread her legs wider and Charlotte had a brief view of her soft pink folds before the viscount put his mouth to them. Unbelievable! He was kissing her in that same sensitive spot that Charlotte liked to rub alone in bed at night. Oh the wickedness! Charlotte watched in amazement as the viscount began to lick Lady Caroline in that private, intimate place. It was the most depraved thing she had ever seen. But at the same time, she wondered, *"What would it feel like to have a tongue there rather than my fingers?"* By the sounds of pleasure coming from Lady Caroline, it would seem she had her answer.

The lady's gasps were becoming louder and louder. She clutched his head to her mound as his tongue fluttered faster and faster. All of a sudden, she gave a loud moan, "Ah!" and Charlotte knew she had reached that point of pleasurable contractions. A moment later, the viscount was back on his feet, his face wet with the lady's sticky juices. Hastily, he unlaced his breeches and brought them down together with his drawers, revealing the perfect rounded globes of his buttocks to Charlotte's avid gaze. "Lie back and open your cunt to me," he growled.

He nudged Lady Caroline onto her back on the edge of the bed, and she obligingly spread her legs wide. Then the viscount began to thrust himself into her. Charlotte heard the lady's loud gasp. Was he hurting her? He continued to buck into her. From her vantage point behind the screen, all Charlotte could see was the flexing of the muscles in his buttocks. Lady Caroline gasped again, "Yes! Harder!" Perhaps she was not in pain after all.

The viscount picked up speed, plunging into the lady harder and faster until he gave a loud grunt and pulled away quickly. That is when Charlotte saw the most shocking sight of the evening. As the viscount pulled away from the lady, his body turned slightly so as to allow Charlotte to see his large male appendage jutting out thickly, an angry looking purplish red in colour. *Is that what he was thrusting into Lady Caroline? How did it fit inside her? It's so big!* These questions were set aside a moment later as the viscount circled his appendage with his hand, giving it a harsh tug and letting out a stream of pearly white liquid. He grunted again, his eyes shutting briefly in his pleasure.

Then he was striding in her direction, and Charlotte very nearly cried out in fear. Stopping at a table beside the wooden screen, he picked up a cloth and dipped it into the bowl of water, wringing the excess from it. He used the cloth first to clean himself up, wiping his hands and his appendage. He then wet the cloth again and handed it to Lady Caroline. She wiped herself clean while he readjusted his clothing. Once he was dressed, he murmured, "I'd better go out first." He gave her a light kiss then left the room. Lady Caroline stood, readjusting her clothes. She stepped to the mirror and glanced at herself from every angle, tidying her hair. Then, satisfied that all looked as it should, she also hurried out of the room.

Once the door closed behind her, Charlotte let out a long sigh of relief, collapsing onto the bench. *"What have I just witnessed?"* she thought. Her mind conjured visions of the viscount's buttocks tightening with each hard thrust of his appendage into Lady Caroline. She lifted her petticoat and put a hand to her private place. It was sticky and damp. What would it feel like to have a large hard appendage—a cock—ram into her? Her fingers rubbed her sticky nub, imagining the viscount touching her there, licking her, then thrusting himself into her. Her fingers picked up speed, rubbing frantically until she gasped her pleasure. And just then, the door opened once more.

Chapter 15

Viscount Stanton made his way back to the ballroom chuckling to himself. That was the very first time he had ever had a semi-public tryst of this kind with a mistress. It was a risky thing to do, but the element of danger had added a frisson of pleasure to their encounter. He was well satisfied with the outcome, doubly so as it meant he did not need to call on Lady Caroline tonight after the ball but could return straight home.

He reached into the pocket of his breeches for his snuff box. *Damnation*! It wasn't there. He must somehow have dropped it in that room upstairs. There was nothing for it but to go back and get it. Nodding at acquaintances here and there, he deftly wove his way through the crush of people back to that side door that led to the staircase. Quickly, he retraced his steps and opened the door of the bedchamber he had vacated not a few minutes before.

As he opened the door, he heard a distinct gasp come from the end of the room where there stood a wooden screen. He closed the door gently behind him and stood still, listening. All was quiet. His gaze tracked across the room, looking for his discarded snuff box. He spotted it at the foot of the bed and swiftly went to pick it up, slipping it into his pocket, then paused. Could he have imagined that sound? It was best to check. With quick steps, he darted towards the wooden screen, folding it back. Another gasp. There sat a lady in a state of undress, her face flushed.

"Miss Harding! Whatever are you doing skulking here, and what has happened to your gown?" He narrowed his eyes at her. "And just how long have you been here?" he demanded.

She stared at him in horror, unable to articulate speech, her mouth forming a wide O. There was his answer. She had been here, hidden behind the screen, while he and Caro had made love. His lips curled into a sneer. "Were you watching us, you prurient little girl?" He caught then an unmistakable whiff of her female sex. "And did you touch yourself to our lovemaking? My, what a dirty girl you are!"

"I—I didn't mean to," she finally whispered.

"Didn't mean to? And who is going to believe that a gently bred girl would simply sit and watch while two people copulated in front of her eyes?" Those very eyes widened, so he went on, "This will not reflect well on you should you dare speak of it to anyone. You had best keep your mouth firmly shut, Miss Harding."

"I wouldn't dream—"

"You had better not." The viscount edged closer, grasping Charlotte's chin in one hand. "I am making myself clear, am I not? A word of this to anyone and I will make it my personal business to destroy you."

Her lips trembled drawing his gaze to them. Plump. Delicately pink. A devilish idea occurred to him. His voice turned to a warm purr as he said, "In any case, why would anyone believe your tales when we all know what you really want is this." And he captured those plump lips with his. He felt her freeze in shock beneath him but carried on kissing her, bringing the tip of his tongue to the seam of her lips. She gasped, the little movement allowing him to dart his tongue into the soft cavern of her mouth. Her shocked breaths told him with a deep certainty that this was the first time she had ever been kissed. She stood still in his embrace, not knowing what to do. He pulled her to him and deepened the kiss, weaving his tongue with hers. He felt her shiver. It only increased his ardour.

He knew the exact moment when she melted against him and began, diffidently at first, to respond. Her hands slid up to rest against his chest and her tongue came out to play with his so innocently it made him burn. He renewed his onslaught of

99

kisses, holding her firmly to him. She kissed him back with increasing fervour. Her lips felt so soft, so gently inviting, that he lost himself in their embrace. In time, he pulled away, only to return, raining kisses along the line of her neck and down to her collar bone. One hand came down to clasp her breast over the firm material of her corset, then to delve inside, freeing the lush flesh from its constraints. He held the soft, full breast in his large hand, marvelling at how it filled his palm and admiring the rosebud pink of her delicate nipple. He could not resist putting that nipple to his mouth and biting it gently. At this, Charlotte gasped and finally pushed him away, her breaths coming out in shallow pants. "We must not!" she cried.

Common sense washed over him in an instant. What was he doing, seducing an innocent? He cast one last longing look at her luscious breast, still peeking out of her corset, then he straightened and forced an expression of contempt on his face. "No indeed, Miss Harding, no one would ever believe your tales of Caroline and me, not when your own desires are plainly evident." He tapped her lips with the tip of his finger. "Keep them shut, or you will answer to me." With that, he swivelled and strode from the room.

⸻

Charlotte stood, her pulse racing, unable to believe what had just transpired. After a moment, she bethought herself to re-arrange her corset and tidy up her appearance.

She sat down on the bench once more, her thoughts churning. The viscount had kissed her. He had held and bitten her breast. The cad! Even worse, she had loved every moment of it. Oh what a mess! That wicked reprobate had seduced her, fresh off having made love to another woman. Though he needn't have bothered with the threats. There was no possible way she could ever tell anyone about what she had seen or what had happened next. Her lips were tightly sealed. And that should be the end of it. Neither she nor the viscount would ever speak of this again. She would put it out of her mind—except that was an impossibility. Hadn't she been regretting that she would end her days a spinster, never knowing what it would be like to be kissed? Well, at least now she knew.

The door opened and the maid bustled in, carrying her gown. "Here we are miss, as good as new." Charlotte smiled and allowed the maid to dress her. She examined her reflection in the mirror, studying her face. Was there any indication in her countenance that not long ago, she had acted like a brazen hussy? No, she looked the same as ever. Maybe her lips were a little swollen, but surely no one would notice? Thanking the maid for her kind efforts, Charlotte left the bedchamber and made her way back to the ballroom. She rejoined her aunt and Harriet just as a gentleman came to claim her hand for the next dance.

As she took her place for the cotillion, she caught sight of the viscount at the other end of the ballroom, smiling blithely down at his dance partner. How could that man do the things he did up in that room and then pay his addresses to another lady without a seeming care in the world? Charlotte was troubled. This world of sexual frolics behind closed doors was new to her. She could never have imagined that such things took place. Now that she knew, she was forever changed, forever tainted. She tried to shake these thoughts away and to keep her mind on the dance. For a while, she succeeded in doing so, laughing gaily as she danced in a circle and executed nimble footwork.

It was towards the end of the dance that she happened to glance to her left and to meet the viscount's eyes very briefly. His gaze was expressionless, showing complete disinterest. In an instant, it was over. Charlotte inhaled sharply, unaccountably pained. That she meant little to the man that had given her an unforgettable kiss and made her swoon was plain to see. She should not start to fancy herself in love with him like she had Mr Weston. She would be wise and sensible, and put the entire incident behind her.

The dance came to an end, and she curtsied to her partner. Back at her aunt's side, Charlotte fanned herself briskly to try to cool her flushed cheeks. "I am glad to see your gown was not irreparably damaged," said Mrs Morton, "but please do try to have more care in future, Charlotte. Mr Hodge was most distressed and promises to call on you tomorrow to convey his fulsome apologies."

"There is no need," protested Charlotte. "The fault, indeed, was mine."

"Nevertheless, he feels duty bound to call, and I daresay he will want to remedy things with you. I need hardly tell you, Charlotte, that eligible prospects for you are thin on the ground, and that you should make the most of the marked attention Mr Hodge is paying you."

"Yes, Aunt Margaret, I do understand." This was not the time or place to voice her disagreement. She had no intention of encouraging Mr Hodge's advances and receiving yet another unwanted offer of marriage. Her experience with Mr Finch had convinced her more than ever that, if she could not marry a person she had regard for, then she would not marry at all.

The evening progressed with more dancing and gaiety, and Charlotte tried her best to put these cares from her mind and to enjoy herself as she had intended. At last, it was time to go home. Charlotte rode in the carriage with the Mortons, tired and pensive. Her last thought as she laid her head on the soft pillow of her bed and drifted off to sleep, was that now she knew what it was like to be kissed, she was very much afraid that one kiss would not be enough.

Chapter 16

It was few days later that Charlotte arrived at the Powells' townhouse to accompany Helena Powell on a promenade in the park with the viscount. The expedition had been justified to Charlotte in the following manner.

"My dear," Mrs Morton had said. "I have just received a note from Lady Powell to say she is feeling a trifle indisposed and will not be able to accompany Helena on her afternoon ride with Viscount Stanton. Would you be a dear and go in her stead? Helena is so dreading having to turn the viscount down, for of course she cannot be going on her own."

Charlotte was deeply suspicious of this sudden indisposition, given the conversation she had overheard between her aunt and Lady Powell, but agreed nonetheless. Now, dressed in her drab brown pelisse and a plain bonnet, she looked every inch the spinster chaperone. None observing her in this garb would ever believe that she had once been in a mad, passionate embrace with the viscount.

Truth be told, Charlotte had thought of little else but him since the Wilton ball. No matter how many times she told herself to put that wicked episode behind her, she could not forget about it. His scent was imprinted on her memory, as was the feel of his lips against hers. It was no use reminding herself that he was a rake and a libertine conducting an illicit affair with Lady Drake while also courting Helena Powell, not to mention the liberties he had taken with her. She could not put him out of her mind.

That is not to say that she indulged in romantic dreams where he was concerned. That was not possible, even with her fanciful nature. No, her thoughts were of the carnal variety, much to her shame. She remembered his every touch and yearned to experience his kisses again. Even worse, she recalled what he had done with Lady Drake and wondered what it would be like to feel him rut into her with that great big appendage. Shameful thoughts! All the more important, therefore, to look as dowdy as possible and do everything in her power to ensure he forgot their sinful encounter at the Wilton ball. She would make sure to fade into the background and allow his attention to be entirely on the lovely Miss Powell.

Some minutes after her arrival at the Powells, the viscount came to collect them for their ride. He awaited outside by his open top barouche, looking fine and handsome in a many lapelled greatcoat. At catching sight of Charlotte, he frowned. "Miss Harding, I had not known you would be joining us today."

"Good day, Viscount Stanton. Lady Powell is a trifle indisposed and begged that I should come in her stead."

"I see." He bowed and assisted her into the carriage, then turned to greet Helena. "Miss Powell, may I compliment you on how delightful you look today."

Miss Powell blushed becomingly. "I thank you, my lord. What lovely weather we have. I own I am much looking forward to our ride."

"And I as well." He helped her into the carriage, then climbed on and sat beside her. The carriage began its slow perambulation down London streets on its way to Hyde Park. "Tell me Miss Powell," the viscount went on. "What sights of this great city have you enjoyed so far?"

"My lord, I took your advice and went to visit the Royal Academy this week. I enjoyed it immensely."

The viscount smiled charmingly at her. "And what paintings did you enjoy the most?"

"I thought John Constable's paintings were masterfully created—such wonderful detail he put into his pastoral landscapes. Though I must confess to also appreciating the fine portraits by Thomas Lawrence that were on display."

Miss Powell prattled on while the viscount paid her every pleasing attention, complimenting her good taste, vowing the fresh air much became her complexion and telling her how honoured he would be if she would accompany him on an outing to the theatre, duly chaperoned of course.

Charlotte listened to all this with half an ear, her eyes fixed firmly outside the carriage, giving the couple every opportunity for private discourse. She would only have been human though to have felt a little wistful that such attentions by a handsome gentleman were never, it seemed, to be paid to her. Glancing surreptitiously at the viscount, she admired his fine form, then remembered what she had seen of it from behind the wooden screen at the Wilton mansion—the powerful muscularity of his thighs and firm curve of his buttocks, his large male appendage that stood proudly against his groin, the pearly white fluid that came out of it as he reached physical ecstasy. Her cheeks bloomed at the memory.

Looking up, her gaze happened to cross paths with the viscount's. His look was far from friendly. She saw his eyes travel down her unbecoming get up then rise back to her face, unsmiling. Perhaps he was wondering how on earth he could have embraced such a plain and dowdy female. Brusquely, he addressed her. "And how about you, Miss Harding? Have you been to the Royal Academy yet?"

"Yes, my lord. I was there but a few days ago."

"What paintings most caught your eye?"

Charlotte was thoughtful. "It is true that the Constable landscapes were meticulously observed, but I marvelled most at the poetry and emotion expressed in Turner's work."

"Is that what you look for most, poetry and emotion?" he asked sardonically.

"If art does not make one feel an emotion, then of what use is it?"

"One can admire the beauty of perfectly executed brush strokes without getting poetic or emotional."

105

"That is true of course," she replied, "but what you describe is simply an aesthetic appreciation of an artwork. There are many artists that can produce pleasingly beautiful paintings, but few that can convey emotion with each brush stroke."

His lips lifted into a subtle sneer. "And I come back to my first point, Miss Harding, that it is not necessary to feel emotion when looking at a painting."

"On this point then, my lord, we are bound to disagree," retorted Charlotte.

He opened his mouth as if to speak, then thought better of it. Instead, he gave a brisk nod and turned his attention back to his lovely companion, not deigning to address Charlotte again. In due course, their ride came to an end. The viscount handed both ladies down from the carriage, and escorted them to their door.

"I thank you, Viscount Stanton, for a most agreeable excursion," smiled Miss Powell.

He bowed over her hand. "I should be the one thanking you, Miss Powell, for the delightful company. I trust we may do this again, perhaps next week?"

"I would be honoured," she responded sweetly.

The viscount bowed one more time, executed a quick bow in Charlotte's direction, then took his leave.

Walking back to the Mortons' townhouse a short time later, Charlotte could only conclude that her efforts to fade into the background had been successful. The viscount had evidently put her from his mind—that is, if she had ever occupied anything more than a fleeting position there in the first place. She should be glad of this. Yes, she should.

Chapter 17

Frank was in his study, poring over a set of documents laid out before him. They had come from his man of business and contained the details of an investment opportunity that might be of interest to him. He wasn't yet sure whether he would be purchasing shares in this overseas company that was proposing to invest in the construction of new canals and railways in America.

He picked up the papers and read through them again, then went to stand by a wall of his study on which hung a large and beautifully painted map of the world. With a finger, he traced the route of each canal and railway whose construction was being proposed. A trickle of excitement ran through him. A wise man would probably turn down such an investment. Too far away. Too many unknowns. Too ambitious a project. Frank was usually quite sensible and level-headed when it came to investing his funds, which was why he had accumulated a tidy sum over the last few years. So why was it that he was considering this one?

Usually, he conducted full investigations before investing in a project, talking to the people in charge and going to the places in question, then making a judgement on whether or not these were sound investments. However, this was not possible in this case, since the projects were all on the other side of the Atlantic Ocean. To make matters worse, the window of opportunity for this investment was closing. His man of business had written that investors needed to declare their intent by 1st May, two days hence. He huffed out a breath, deep in thought. If only he could find out a little more about these faraway places he had just traced on the map.

Five minutes later, he was striding out of his lodgings and hailing a hansom cab. "Take me to Lackington and Allen bookshop in Finsbury Square," he instructed the driver. On arrival there, he walked over to the large circular counter whereupon a shop assistant, seeing the expensive dress of the gentleman, came over quickly to assist him.

"I am looking for a travelogue or any sort of written work about North America. Would you have something of the sort?" asked the viscount.

"One moment sir, let me take a look at our catalogue." The shop assistant took out a large leather bound tome and flicked to a page entitled "Travel", running his finger down the list of travel books. "Ah," he said. "This may be what you are looking for. It is entitled 'Travels in North America' by Basil Hall, published in 1829."

"Recent enough. Is there a copy of the book in the shop?" asked the viscount.

"I will find out, sir." The shop assistant now took out a large ledger and spent a few moments searching for the book in question. He looked up at the viscount with an apologetic expression. "I am very much afraid, sir, that we sold our last copy of this book only two weeks ago. It may be possible to order another from the publisher, if you should wish?"

The viscount sighed in irritation. "No, that will be too late. Do you have a name for who it was that purchased this book?"

The shop assistant hesitated, but then seeing the undoubted quality of the gentleman, looked down again at the ledger. "The bill of purchase was made out to a Mr Frederick Morton of 10 Grosvenor Street."

The viscount began to laugh. "Well, what do you know?" He thanked the shop assistant and left, hailing another cab, this time to take him to Grosvenor Street, for he was sure Frederick would not mind his old family friend calling on him in the middle of the afternoon. He was shown in to the downstairs parlour while a footman went to inform Mr Morton of his arrival. A few minutes later, the footman returned and ushered him up to Mr Morton's study.

Frederick stood from his desk and came forward to greet him. "My dear Frank, this is a pleasant surprise. Do come in and have a seat. Would you like a glass of sherry?"

"Good day Frederick, and yes, thank you."

Frank waited while Frederick poured out the sherry and brought it over. They sat comfortably opposite one another, each taking a sip of the amber coloured drink. "I am sorry to intrude on you in such a cavalier fashion," he now said, "but there is a matter in which I am hoping you may assist me."

"Of course, anything within my power I will do. What is this matter?"

"I believe you are in possession of a book entitled 'Travels in North America' which I would very much like to borrow if I may?"

Frederick smiled, "If I had such a book, I would of course be happy to lend it to you."

"You do not have it?" Frank looked at him in confusion.

"I'm afraid not. Whyever did you think I did?"

"I was informed the last copy of the book was purchased by yourself just two weeks ago."

Frederick's expression cleared. "Ah, I believe I have the solution to this mystery." He rose and rang the bell. When the footman appeared a moment later, he asked, "Have the ladies returned from their expedition, Jones?"

"Yes, sir, they have been back this past quarter hour."

"Excellent. Jones, could you please have Miss Harding come here and ask her to bring along her book on travels in America."

The footman bowed and hurried to execute this instruction. Frank looked to Frederick in confusion. "Do you mean to say it is Miss Harding that is in possession of this book? It is not what I would expect a young lady to be reading."

"Ah," Frederick smiled fondly, "but Charlotte is not the usual kind of young lady."

"*No indeed,*" Frank reflected to himself. He had spared more than one thought for her soft lips and plump breasts, and the way she had artlessly responded to his kiss with a wanton innocence that had been hard to resist. It was all the more puzzling since she was undoubtedly plain-looking. His inspection of her during their carriage ride the other day had merely confirmed his original opinion—she was sadly unprepossessing.

He was brought back to the present by Frederick enquiring, "Why the interest in North America, if I may ask?"

"There is an investment my man of business has suggested to me. Shares are being offered in an American company that invests in the building of new canals and railways there. I am curious about it."

"If you are looking to invest in such things, there are several railway projects right here in England. Why look further afield?" wondered Frederick.

"Oh, I'm investing in a few railway projects here too. I'm not sure I can tell you why America holds such allure. Perhaps it is because everything there seems to be on a much grander scale than here. One of the canals the company proposes to build will be 460 miles long, linking the Great Lakes to the Ohio River. Can you imagine what kind of trade opportunities that could open up?"

"It could also be a highly risky investment," remarked Frederick shrewdly.

Frank chuckled. "Of that, I am very aware."

Just then, there was a knock on the door, and Charlotte walked in. "Hello Frederick! You wanted to see my book on America?"

"Not me, but Frank did."

She came to a sudden halt as she caught sight of the viscount, who rose to his feet and bowed. "Good day, Miss Harding."

"Good day, Viscount Stanton." A slight flush coloured her cheeks.

"Come and sit with us, Charlotte," said Frederick. "Would you like a drink of sherry?"

"No, thank you," Charlotte replied, settling herself down on the only unoccupied seat on the settee next to the viscount.

"Miss Harding," said he, "I understand you have a book named 'Travels in North America' which I would be very interested in borrowing from you, if you will allow me."

"I—I'm afraid that will not be possible, for I no longer have the book."

The viscount frowned. "Indeed! Where is it now?"

Charlotte smiled, "It seems the book is much in demand, for it is your good friend Mr Weston who asked to borrow it."

"You mean Rupert has it!" exclaimed the viscount.

"I'm afraid so."

Frederick chuckled. "It seems you have had a wasted journey, Frank, but at least you should be able to track Mr Weston down easily enough."

"May I ask why you wish to borrow this book, my lord?" Charlotte ventured to ask.

"I am considering an investment in American canals and railways, and I wanted to widen my knowledge of the country."

Charlotte nodded sagely. "Yes, ever since the completion of the Erie Canal, there have been many attempts to emulate its success. May I ask where the canals you propose to invest in will be built?"

"There are several. The first will run from Pennsylvania to the town of Akron in Ohio."

"And I take it from there it will link up with the Ohio and Erie Canal?"

"Yes, how did you know?" Frank asked, surprised.

Charlotte shrugged. "It would make sense to do so, as this would open up shipping lanes all the way from the eastern states to Lake Erie."

Frank stared at her, mystified. "Miss Harding, I am astounded at your grasp not only of American geography but of existing shipping routes. Please enlighten me as to how you have come by this knowledge."

"It is no great matter, my lord. A very close friend of mine and her brother are thinking of emigrating to America to claim land in the north east of Ohio, where their eldest brother has already established himself. I simply wanted to learn as much as I could about where she would be going. Ever since Joseph left for America two years ago, I have gotten into the habit of reading the business section of newspapers and scouring for news from that region. And of course, once I came to London, I was able to obtain 'Travels in North America' which I found most enlightening."

"What kind of friends do you have that they are considering such a journey in order to claim land?" demanded the viscount with a touch of hauteur.

At this, Charlotte laughed, "My lord, they are tenant farmers on my late father's estate. I have known them since I played with them as a child."

The viscount was shocked. "You were allowed to play with children outside your social station?"

"Why yes. My late mother, God rest her soul, believed very firmly in the Christian gospels which teach that we are all creatures of God, equally deserving of kindness and respect, regardless of social standing. She hailed from Salamanca and was the daughter of a grain merchant that helped procure supplies to the British army during the Peninsular War. That is how she met my father. She had no social pretentions, but a deep love of God and fellow man. She it was that befriended Mary Ellis, the wife of one of our tenant farmers, and she took

112

me to play with Mary's children, of whom Ruth, I now consider my truest and closest friend."

The viscount was dumbfounded. Having been raised in the most rarefied of circles and taught from a young age of everyone's proper place in the social order, he could not imagine ever being allowed, let alone encouraged, to fraternise with tenant farmers. His father would be scandalised by what Miss Harding had just revealed. That gave him pause. This was one young lady his father would definitely not approve of. Yet an innate sense of rebellion within him against his father's strictures celebrated Miss Harding's eccentricity, if one could call it that. What a delightfully interesting creature she was turning out to be.

Aloud, he said, "I should caution you, Miss Harding, against speaking openly about such a friendship in our social circles. It would not be considered *comme il faut*. Of course, you need not worry that anything said between us here will be repeated."

Frederick sighed his agreement. "I'm afraid Frank is right, Charlotte. While I do appreciate the noble sentiments that drove your late mother to befriend this farmer's wife, and I am sure your friendship with Ruth Ellis is true and worthy, I do not think you would wish it to be widely reported among the people of the ton."

Charlotte looked a little crestfallen, but then raised her head proudly. "I will of course be circumspect in my speech about this matter, but I will tell you now, Frederick, that I am not at all ashamed of my friendship with Ruth."

"Nor should you be, my dear. However, it would be wise to exercise a little caution. I do not want people to spread malicious talk about you."

Charlotte nodded. "I understand."

All the while, Frank had been studying her. There was fire in her eyes as she defended her friendship with this Ruth Ellis. He knew instinctively that she would be loyal to a fault when it came to the people she cared for. Different pieces of the puzzle that made Charlotte Harding were beginning to fall into place.

He decided to return to the initial subject at hand. "Miss Harding, seeing as you have far more knowledge than I on this matter, would you mind sharing your opinion on the other canal and railway projects proposed by this investment?"

"Of course, though please do not overestimate my knowledge of such matters."

"I assure you, it is far greater than mine."

It was almost an hour later when Frank rose to take his leave, saying, "Miss Harding, I thank you for broadening my knowledge of North America. I apologise for having taken so much of your time, and yours Frederick."

"Think nothing of it," replied Frederick. "Shall we see you for dinner tomorrow?"

"Of course, I look forward to it." Frank bowed to them both and departed, with much to ponder.

Chapter 18

The following afternoon saw Frank pay a visit to his mistress, Lady Caroline Drake, and spend a pleasurable few hours in her company. His body sated, he lay on her bed and idly kissed his way up her lusciously curved body, paying homage to the pleasing dimples on her lower back then finding his way to the soft skin of her graceful neck. She gave a delighted little shiver. Giving her one last kiss, the viscount murmured, "It is time I should get going."

"Must you?"

"I'm afraid so, my dear. I have a dinner engagement at the Mortons tonight."

She sniffed. "You seem to be spending an awful lot of time with them these days. Could it be to do with Margaret Morton's close friendship with a certain Lady Powell, and her young marriageable daughter?"

Frank gave his mistress a light spank on her ample backside. "Behave yourself Caro! These matters are none of your concern and well you know it."

She turned over to lie on her side, facing him. "So it's true what everyone is saying. You are courting the beautiful Miss Powell."

"Everyone should mind their own business and so should you, my dear."

"Funny, Frank, but I thought you were my business," she replied, a little stung.

Frank sat up and began to get himself dressed. "*Here we go,*" he thought. He entered into all his amorous liaisons with the clear understanding that they were to be casual and temporary dalliances—after all, his history with the ladies should speak for itself. Whenever a lover began to cling and presume more of the relationship than what had plainly been agreed at the start, he knew it was time to call an end to things.

Finished with dressing, he turned to gaze coolly at Lady Caroline, who sprawled in the nude, displaying her glorious body to his eyes. There was no doubt she was a beautiful woman. He had thoroughly enjoyed getting intimately acquainted with all her charms. Already, however, he could feel his interest wane, as it always did. Very gently now, he said, "I think, Caro, that it is time for us to part ways. This thing between us was always supposed to be a fun and light-hearted dalliance, nothing more." He took her hand and kissed it. "I wish you well, my dear."

She snatched it away. "Do you have the temerity to end things between us just like that? Know Frank, that I am not to be dismissed so easily."

His gaze hardened as he stood. "Caroline, you would be well served to remember that you do not have much choice in the matter. You have no hold over me and never had. Now, it is past time I should be going. Good day to you madam."

"Don't you dare to walk out of here!"

He saluted her. "Oh, but I do." He narrowly missed the ceramic pot that was flung at him as he reached the door of the lady's bedchamber. Turning back one last time, he chided, "Poorly done, Caro." Then, he left.

An hour later, he was presenting himself at the Mortons, his good friend Rupert Weston at his side.

●————————————●

Frank stood by the piano solicitously as Miss Powell played and sang that popular Irish ballad, "The Last Rose of Summer", turning the sheet music for her. She sang with a sweet, well-modulated voice, and it was a pleasure to listen to her. This was yet another of her many accomplishments. In all the weeks he had known her, she had not put a foot wrong, always looking beautiful and elegant, always showing excellent breeding and decorum. She had partnered him in a game of cards earlier in the evening and acquitted herself well. Now, here she was singing delightfully. Really, there was no end to her talents and nothing he could fault her with. She was an excellent choice for a wife. All he had to do was gird up his loins and propose.

He turned the page and stepped back again, and as he did so, his eyes happened to land on Miss Harding, sitting quietly in a corner of the room, listening to the music. The contrast between her and the angel by his side could not be greater. Where one was trim and in all ways pleasing to the eye, the other was dumpy and plain. His lips curled. Good lord, what could have ever possessed him to kiss her? And yet, as far as kisses went, it had been good, surprisingly so. She had responded with an innate sensuousness that had fired up his ardour. Her skin had been soft and fragrant, the taste and feel of her lips exquisite.

Just then, a gentleman sitting by Miss Harding leaned close and whispered something in her ear. She smiled and responded quietly. Frank furrowed his brow. He had a vague recollection of being introduced to that gentleman earlier, a Mr Hodge was it? He had not paid him much heed. He switched his attention back to the music, turning the sheet. Yes indeed, Miss Powell sang beautifully. He watched her in profile as she sang, admiring her slender, graceful neck and finely etched features. He could do a lot worse than to gaze upon such a countenance every morning at the breakfast table. His breath swelled in his chest as he came to a decision. He would wait a few more weeks, just to be sure, and then propose.

The song came to an end, and he joined everyone in polite applause. Mrs Morton approached the piano with a smile. "How beautifully you sing, Miss Powell. Thank you for gracing us with this song."

Miss Powell bowed her head. "I make no claims to perfection, but I am glad you enjoyed the song."

"Very much so, my dear. And now, let us adjourn to supper."

At the dinner table, Frank found himself seated beside Miss Powell—*quelle surprise*—and Mrs Frederick Morton to his left. He saw that his friend, Rupert, had been placed between two young ladies who had made their debut this season, Eliza Herbert and Horatia Colborne. "*Aha*," he thought. Mrs Morton was obviously up to her matchmaking tricks. Well, he would be glad to see Rupert shackled alongside him in matrimony. It was only fair!

Glancing around the table, he noticed that Miss Harding was once again seated next to Mr Hodge. Was this too an attempt at matchmaking? Surely not. The man was at least forty and with little in the way of looks to commend him. His holdings, up in Suffolk if he remembered correctly, were modest. Why in the world would Mrs Morton think him an eligible suitor for her niece? On a second glance, he thought he understood. The both of them were short and stout, with corresponding plain looks, and moreover, Miss Harding had no sizeable portion to bring as dowry. Mr Hodge, while not in the first flush of youth, was a gentleman of good standing. It would make eminent sense to match these two persons together. Having resolved the conundrum yet feeling unaccountably ill at ease, he brought his attention back to his fair neighbour.

"I look forward to our visit to the theatre next week," said Miss Powell. "I hear that Madame Malibran will be performing. I have heard much about her."

"She has an extraordinary voice and such dramatic flair. I am sure you will appreciate her performance."

"It is wonderfully kind of you to invite us, Viscount Stanton."

"You honour me with your presence, Miss Powell."

"Do you often go to the opera, viscount?"

Frank answered her absentmindedly, his attention once again commanded by Miss Harding and her suitor, Mr Hodge, who was leaning a little too close to her and saying something that caused her to flush. It took much effort for Frank to iron out the frown that appeared on his face.

And so the evening went, with light, uncomplicated chit chat with Miss Powell and Mrs Frederick Morton, while every so often he glimpsed Mr Hodge paying effusive compliments to Miss Harding. By the end of dinner, he could stand it no more. He lingered as little as possible over the port, and at the first opportunity, rose to his feet and made his excuses. On his journey home, he blamed the break-up with Lady Caroline for his dark mood. That and the forthcoming prospect of his marriage were enough to make any staunch bachelor feel decidedly morose. There could be no other earthly reason for his low spirits.

Chapter 19

For her part, Charlotte had been having a very trying evening too. It pained her to watch both Viscount Stanton and Rupert Weston flirt with the fashionable ladies at their side while she was relegated to sit with Mr Hodge. Further acquaintance with this gentleman had not endeared him to her. He was a dull conversationalist, and oh that sweaty brow that kept being mopped with his damp handkerchief!

To make matters worse, he was quite clearly paying court to her. Someone, perhaps Lady Powell, had sown the seeds of a potential match between them, and now they had taken root in his mind. He had a habit of leaning close to her when making his fulsome compliments, obliging her to draw in his less than fragrant breath. The flush that resulted on her cheeks was more from vexation than coyness. Was this then all she was deemed worthy of? Her mind rebelled at the idea.

She was more than just a plain, poor and slightly overweight female. If only people could see beyond the surface to who she really was—a person with a kind heart, sound intellect, an abundance of humour and good sense. The people who knew the real Charlotte had all valued her—her parents, Mrs Ellis, Ruth, her cousin Frederick. It was this conviction of her self-worth that had Charlotte determined to deflect Mr Hodge's advances. At the earliest opportunity, she would find a way to set him right, well before another unwanted proposal of marriage came her way.

For this reason, and only this reason, she accepted Mr Hodge's invitation to accompany her on a walk to the bookshop the following day. With the semi-privacy this afforded them, she would, as tactfully as possible, hint that she did not welcome his advances. And after that, she would make it her mission to evade any other future mismatches. She was beginning to come round to the idea that she might never marry—not unless she met someone who truly valued her for what she was and for whom she could reciprocate the sentiments.

The doorbell rang the following morning, signalling Mr Hodge's arrival. Charlotte took a deep breath and steadied her nerves with another of her well-loved proverbs. *The secret to happiness is freedom… And the secret to freedom is courage!*

She would not miss this opportunity to put an end to Mr Hodges importunities. When the footman informed her that Mr Hodge awaited her out front, she nodded, donned her bonnet and brown pelisse—alas she had not replaced this with a more fashionable garb—and headed out.

"Good morning, Mr Hodge."

"Good morning, Miss Harding. And may I say how well you look today."

As Charlotte had glanced at herself in the mirror a short while ago, she could only surmise that he needed his eyesight examined. They negotiated the steps down from the house and began to walk side by side.

"I gather you have a love of books, Miss Harding," began Mr Hodge. "It is a pleasing disposition to have, for with a book, one can never be bored."

"I agree, as long as there is a good supply and variety of books to be had, then it is difficult to imagine one being bored. I am very fortunate to have access to a wide range of books here in London, much more so than in the country."

Mr Hodge saw a chance to advance his suit. "Were you to visit my country seat, Frogley Court, you would be impressed, Miss Harding, at the great variety of good books to be found in the library."

"I am sure that may be the case, however I do not foresee that I shall visit."

"Forgive my forwardness, Miss Harding, but I very much hope that you shall."

"Forgive my forwardness, Mr Hodge, but I can assure you that I will not," responded Charlotte with perhaps more acerbity than good manners.

His face fell. They walked on for a few minutes in terse silence. Finally, he murmured, "Am I to take it, Miss Harding, that you do not welcome my suit?"

"I believe it is best to be forthright and avoid any possible miscommunication, Mr Hodge. If your intent is to pay your addresses to me, then I would earnestly discourage you from doing so."

"I see." More silence ensued. "I appreciate your forthrightness, Miss Harding. Let me assure you I shall cease all such addresses forthwith."

"Thank you, Mr Hodge."

They continued on, not saying anything further. As Hatchard's bookshop came into view, Mr Hodge bestirred himself to speak. "Miss Harding, I will not oblige you to suffer my company more than is required. Would you mind very much if I leave you here, now that we are arrived at the bookshop?"

"I—of course," she muttered.

Mr Hodge bowed and took his leave. With a sigh of relief, Charlotte entered the bookshop and soon forgot him as she lost herself in the pleasure of discovering new books.

On her return to Grosvenor Street, she worried what Mrs Morton would say on finding out that Mr Hodge was no longer with her. She need not have fretted, for once home, she found everything in an upheaval as trunks were brought down and loaded onto the Mortons' carriage. Charlotte spied Frederick amidst the commotion and went to him. "What is the matter?" she asked.

"Ah, Charlotte, you are back from your walk. I am glad to see you before we go. I am taking Harriet and Edwin back to Stanbourne, where I'm afraid we shall stay for the remainder of the season unless there is a marked change for the better with Edwin. He has not been well, and I feel the London air is not agreeing with him. I am hoping the country air and the care of my old nurse, Hobbs, will help him improve."

"Shall I come with you?" wondered Charlotte.

"No, there is no need. Stay here with mama. Once we are settled back home and I am assured that Edwin is on the mend, I will visit to check on you and conduct my business affairs."

Just then, Harriet came down, clutching her fractious son in her arms. She looked pale, a crease of worry etched into her forehead. "Charlotte," she said faintly. "I am sorry to leave you like this, but it cannot be helped."

"Do not worry about me," responded Charlotte. "I only pray for Edwin's recovery, as speedy as that can be."

"From your lips to God's ears. Goodbye Charlotte. I shall write and keep you apprised of our progress."

"God be with you," replied Charlotte. She stood and watched as Frederick helped his wife into the carriage and waved to them as they started on their journey. Going back into the house, Charlotte went upstairs to remove her outer garments and refresh herself, then went to look for her aunt. She found her in her private parlour, resting languidly on a chaise longue. "Aunt Margaret," she cried, going to kneel at her side. "Are you unwell too?"

Mrs Morton patted her hand. "Nothing that won't pass with a little rest. It is just worry about poor Edwin and Harriet that does this to me. I do pray that his condition improves soon."

"I believe Frederick made the right decision. The fumes in the London air cannot be conducive to a quick recovery."

"You are right, my dear. I have asked Frederick to write every day, or else I shall be sick with worry."

Charlotte gazed at her aunt in concern. "What can I do to help?"

Mrs Morton smiled, "Bless you child, there is nothing you can do except perhaps read to me a little and keep my mind from fretting."

"That I would be happy to do."

They spent a quiet day at home together, both electing not to go to the soirée at Lady Elvington's, for which they had received invitations.

Over the next week, Mrs Morton and Charlotte lived quietly, preferring to avoid the social whirl of the London season, waiting for the post each morning with baited breath. At first, the news from Stanbourne was not encouraging. Edwin was still poorly, running a fever and refusing his milk. On the eighth day after Frederick and Harriet's departure, Mrs Morton was at the breakfast table with her niece, debating whether they should pack up the house and return to the country. If things were to take a turn for the worse, Mrs Morton wanted to be home with her son and daughter-in-law. "I think," said she, "that I will ask Mrs Webster to start preparing for our departure," — Mrs Webster being the housekeeper.

"Yes of course," concurred Charlotte. "I am quite sick with worry and would prefer to be with them too."

"Then it is settled."

A footman entered then, bearing the morning post on a tray. Mrs Morton grabbed the latest missive from Frederick and handed it to Charlotte. "Your eyes are better than mine. Read it to me, dear."

Charlotte broke the letter's seal and began to read it aloud. It was short and to the point.

Dear Mama,

Thanks be to God! Edwin's fever has broken and he slept well last night after taking some milk from his mother. I believe he is finally on the mend. You can well believe how thankful Harriet and I are. If all goes well, I hope to return to London for a brief visit in a week's time. I trust you and Charlotte are keeping well. Please be assured of my best regards,

Your loving son,

Frederick

Mrs Morton dabbed at her eyes. "Oh thank goodness. Such a relief to know Edwin is better." She took a calming breath and rang the bell for a footman. "I do believe dear, that I will have a small glass of sherry to calm my nerves." When the footman entered the room, she bade him bring her this beverage to the drawing room. She was resting there a while later, Charlotte nearby reading a book, when the doorbell rang and Sir William Harding was announced.

Sir William strode into the room, his face set in stern lines. He kissed his sister lightly on one cheek and stepped back. "Margaret, I am glad to see you in good health. Tell me, what news of Frederick and his little one?"

Mrs Morton fluttered as she always did in the presence of her domineering older brother, especially when he entered in such a purposeful way. "Good news," she trilled. "We heard only today from Frederick that Edwin is on the mend."

He nodded gravely. "That is good news." His eyes strayed towards Charlotte, who was regarding him with curiosity. It fell to Mrs Morton to make the introductions.

"William, this is Charlotte, Hugh's daughter."

Sir William bowed curtly in her direction, then turned back to his sister. "Margaret, I would have a word in private with you if you please."

At this, Charlotte jumped to her feet. "Do excuse me," she said. "I have some letters to write." With a quick curtsy in the direction of her uncle and aunt, she left the room. She wished she could be a fly on the wall to hear what Sir William had to say. She suspected it had something to do with her.

In this estimate, she was not wrong. As soon as the door shut behind her, William turned to his sister and exclaimed, "What is the meaning of this, Margaret?"

Mrs Morton spluttered. "William, I fail to understand —"

"Why do you have this girl living with you?" he interrupted sharply.

"If by this girl you mean my niece, who had been left in the care of an unprincipled stepmother, then I hardly need to explain why she is here. I am doing my duty as is right and proper."

"Your duty," thundered Sir William, "is to your father, God rest his soul. He made it clear that Hugh was no longer a part of our family and had him shunned. Now you defile his memory by going against his express wishes."

"William," breathed Mrs Morton, her shaky voice betraying her nerves. "I have long thought that father was unduly harsh in the way he treated Hugh. I could not turn my back on his daughter when she needed my help. Besides, she is a sweet thing who has been a great comfort to me in these trying times."

Her brother glared at her contemptuously. "Mark my words, Margaret, you will rue the day you brought this wretched girl into your home. It is said that blood will out. Her wild and unsteady mother will have left an imprint on the child. It will all come out one day. I beg you to reconsider and send her back to her home with this stepmother, regardless of her principles, before she engulfs us in a scandal."

"William, I cannot do as you say." Mrs Morton's voice took on a firmer tone. "You have not had the opportunity to get to know Charlotte as I have the last few weeks. Like you, I was a little concerned about her breeding before I met her, but I assure you she is a perfectly respectable young woman."

"Blood will out, Margaret, blood will out."

"It is Hugh's blood too that flows through her veins, William. She is so like him. It is clear that his influence has been the strongest. I assure you, there is nothing to fear."

William regarded her with derision. "You are a fool if you believe this. Will you or will you not send her away?"

"I will not."

"Then there is nothing more to say. Good day, madam." And with a final look of disgust, Sir William stalked out of the room.

Chapter 20

Next day at breakfast brought two missives, though neither one came from Stanbourne. Mrs Morton perused hers, a small crease wrinkling her brow. "Charlotte dear," she said. "Lady Powell invites us to join them and Viscount Stanton for a picnic outing to Hampstead Heath tomorrow, seeing as the weather is so fine. What do you think? Should we go?"

Charlotte was keenly aware that such outings were orchestrated to throw Miss Powell and Viscount Stanton together, and that her presence was being requested so she could act as a foil for that beautiful young lady. She had no great wish to keep playing such a role, yet looking across at Mrs Morton's wan features, she made a quick decision. "I think it is a splendid idea," she replied. "It will do us both the world of good to be out in the fresh country air, and now that Edwin is recovering, there is no point in us moping at home."

Mrs Morton nodded her head. "You are quite right. I shall write back to say yes." She looked at the letter on the salver lying next to Charlotte. "You do not open your letter?"

"It is from my good friend Ruth. If you will excuse me, Aunt Margaret, I would prefer to take it upstairs and read it at my leisure. I am sure she has a great deal of news from home."

"Of course, my dear. Take all the time you need."

Charlotte stood with the letter in hand, gave a quick curtsy and hurried up to the privacy of Frederick's study. There, she broke the seal and read.

Dear Charlotte,

I hope this letter finds you well and that your stay in London has been agreeable. Over here, life goes on as before. Your stepmama is busy entertaining her sister and introducing her to local society, so I

128

hear. I do, however, have big news of my own for you. Robert and I have decided to leave the farm and go to America.

We plan to sail from Liverpool to New York on the Hibernia on 7th June. From there we will be taking a boat up the Hudson River to Albany, and then we shall be travelling on that Erie Canal you have told me about. Yet another ship journey awaits us after that, as we travel from Buffalo to Ashtabula. By the end of this, I will be heartily sick of being on the water! If things go to plan, we hope to arrive at Joseph's farmhouse by the end of summer, in time to help him with the autumn harvest before we get to work on claiming our own parcel of land. Now that the decision is made, I am both excited and anxious, but chiefly I am excited for this new chapter in our lives. My only regret is that I will not get to see you before I leave, but I am determined that come what may, we shall keep in touch.

Your loving friend,

Ruth

"*So it is happening,*" thought Charlotte. "*Ruth is really going to America.*" She could not find it in her heart to fault her friend. This journey represented an opportunity for Ruth and Robert to better their situation in life. She would miss them terribly of course, but there was also a small part of her that felt envious at their ability to take their destiny into their hands and forge a new path for themselves. In contrast, she was powerless to do much except endure and accept her lot in life. With prospects of a good marriage more and more unlikely, it seemed she was condemned to a life as the perpetual spinster poor relation. She would do her best to find a modicum of happiness in that life, but it was a far cry from the dreams and aspirations of her youth.

In bed, later that night, her thoughts returned to the forthcoming picnic outing with the Powells and Viscount Stanton. She longed to see him again, for she had missed him this past week. The sight of him—tall, ruggedly muscular, intensely male—always shot a thrill through her. And if she got near enough to scent his heavenly manly smell, that thrill multiplied threefold. Of course, she had not forgotten what a reprobate he was, but after the long conversation with him about America, when he had listened so respectfully and appreciated her knowledge, she could admit to herself, in the privacy of her own thoughts, that she liked him more than just a little. What she did not like, was to see him fawn over Helena Powell. Try as she might, she could not rid herself of the jealousy and envy whenever he paid court to that beauty. *"What would it be like to have that attention on me?"* she wondered wistfully.

And then, like clockwork, her mind conjured up memories of that unforgettable kiss at the Wilton mansion. What she would give to experience it again! Her hand drifted down to touch that special place, as it did most nights since she had met the viscount. Closing her eyes, she imagined his lips on hers as she rubbed herself to completion. With a sigh, she settled down to sleep.

●———————————————●

They left shortly after breakfast the following morning. Sir Horace and Lady Powell rode in the carriage together with Mrs Morton and Charlotte, while the viscount escorted Miss Powell in his curricle. Charlotte had only a brief glimpse of him as she climbed into the carriage, before they were on their way.

It was a dry, warm day, with not a cloud in the sky—perfect weather for a picnic—and the party set out in high spirits. The drive to Hampstead Heath was not long, a little under an hour. On arrival, they stretched their legs with a leisurely stroll through the woods, reaching an elevated spot from which to enjoy the views. Naturally, the viscount was attentive by Miss Powell's side, and it fell to Charlotte to walk arm in arm with her aunt at the back of the procession, behind Sir Horace and Lady Powell. She took comfort in the enjoyment of the picturesque landscape before her and in seeing a bloom of healthy colour return to her aunt's face. "This walk is doing you a great deal of good, Aunt Margaret," she said presently.

"It was an inspired suggestion to get out of London for a short while and enjoy the fresh country air," agreed Mrs Morton.

"Do let me know when you tire, and we can find ourselves a pleasant spot under a tree to sit and rest."

"Thank you dear, I will, but I am feeling quite strong and can go on a little more. Let us get to the top of that hill yonder, for I think the view from there will be magnificent."

They continued on their way, eventually catching up with the rest of the party at the top of the hill. Viscount Stanton pointed to a grassy patch and suggested they lay their rugs there for the picnic. So it was arranged. Within minutes, the ladies and gentlemen were comfortably perched on the large rug which had been carried by one of the grooms, and the contents of the picnic basket laid out. The viscount was all solicitous with Miss Powell, slicing a crisp apple for her, pouring her a glass of lemonade, and loading her plate with slices of ham and freshly buttered bread.

Charlotte was similarly engaged, putting the needs of her aunt before her own. She made sure Mrs Morton's plate was filled and her glass was full. Only when everyone else had been served did she venture to take a plate for herself. She took a bread roll and buttered it, then reached across to the plate of ham. Unfortunately, it had been moved just out of her reach. She sat back, not wanting to disturb Lady Powell, who was in the middle of a long discourse and was closest to the dish. Instead, she contented herself with a boiled egg, which she munched on hungrily, for the walk had stimulated her appetite.

Lost in thought, eyes fixed on the view over the hill, she did not at first notice the viscount pile slices of ham on her plate, followed by a generous wedge of pork pie. It was only as he poured her a glass of cold lemonade that she snapped out of her reverie and paid attention. The viscount handed her the drink, and startled, she murmured, "Thank you, my lord."

He then reached for a pear and quartered it with elegant precision. These pieces, he now placed on Charlotte's plate, all without a word. Then he turned back to the fair companion at his side and resumed his conversation with her as if it had never been interrupted. Charlotte ate her repast, immensely grateful for the viscount's thoughtful intervention. Her liking of him went up another notch—a dangerous thing, for she could not afford to like him too much.

At last, their luncheon over, the picnic things were put away and everyone stood. They walked the return journey to their carriage via a different route, circling one of the many ponds on the Heath. Charlotte's day had been pleasant, even though her time had been spent chiefly at her aunt's side and she had not had any opportunity to converse with the viscount. Nothing soothes the soul quite so much as a good walk in beautiful parkland on a warm, bright day. Now, a little pink-cheeked, she boarded the carriage and settled herself next to her elderly neighbours for the journey back home.

They had only been on the move for five minutes when the incident happened. The curricle, with the viscount and Miss Powell on board, was travelling in front of the carriage and going over a narrow part of the road. Without warning, another curricle came along from the opposite direction, travelling at high speed, its driver a reckless lone gentleman. The viscount reacted quickly, urging his horses to step aside, but he was unable to avoid a collision. His curricle was knocked to one side while the other vehicle flew past, not even stopping to acknowledge the accident it had caused. A loud shriek was heard.

Sir Horace's carriage pulled up instantly and that gentleman, displaying an unexpected agility, jumped down and rushed over to the upturned curricle. Charlotte followed at his heels, her heart pounding anxiously. It was with tremendous relief that she saw the viscount emerge from the wreckage of his curricle, relatively unscathed apart from a short scratch on one cheek. Miss Powell, however, was not so lucky, for it was she who had emitted the shriek. Her father and the viscount helped her regain her footing, her bonnet askew and her dress in disarray. She sobbed in shock and pain. A quick survey revealed the cause of her sobs. Her left arm was hanging at an awkward angle, obviously broken in the fall from the curricle.

"We must get her to a physician at once," cried Sir Horace.

With immense gentleness, he walked his daughter to the awaiting carriage and helped her into it, letting her occupy the seat recently vacated by Charlotte. Lady Powell and Mrs Morton fussed over Helena noisily with exclamations of "Oh you poor dear!" and "Oh great God, what has been done to you?"

While they did so, Sir Horace leaned his head out of the window and addressed the viscount, "Forgive me, but I'm afraid I shall have to leave you and Miss Harding here, as speed is of the essence. Helena must be seen by a physician as soon as possible. It should not be far to walk to the nearest village. It is at most two miles away. There is an inn there, and I'm sure you will be able to hire an alternative conveyance to get you home."

"Of course," responded the viscount. "Do not mind us. Please see to Miss Powell, and I will ensure Miss Harding is returned safely back home." No thought was given to the propriety of leaving Charlotte alone in the company of a gentleman, for who would ever believe that a woman as plain and dowdy as she would need to have her virtue protected?

In a minute, the carriage was gone, leaving Charlotte alone in the presence of the viscount. He glanced at her, then away to his horses which thankfully were unhurt. "If you will excuse me, Miss Harding, I will release the horses from the curricle and tether them to one of these trees, away from harm. Unfortunately, they are not saddled, else we could have ridden them to the next village. Are you alright to walk there?"

"Yes, of course."

He smiled approvingly, "Good, then give me a moment, and we shall be on our way." With swift, practised hands, he released the horses from the mangled curricle and led them away to a small clearing, tying them to a tree. He pushed the wreck of the curricle away from the road, frowning at it. It was clear that extensive repairs would be needed to bring it back to use. With that done, the viscount came back to Charlotte's side and offered her his arm. "Let us be on our way, Miss Harding."

Charlotte slipped her arm into his and began to walk with him, all in a tingle at his touch. She was alone with the viscount! After a few paces, he enquired, "I hope, Miss Harding, that despite this mishap you have enjoyed our outing today."

"Oh yes, thank you, my lord, it was a lovely picnic."

"Seeing as we are all alone, may we dispense with the formalities? Please do call me Frank."

Shyly, she replied, "Very well, Frank. And please do call me Charlotte."

He grinned, "That's much better! It would seem odd to be so formal given the intimacies we have shared."

Charlotte's eyes flew to his in shock. "My lord, I thought we were never to mention that wicked episode again!"

His arm tightened, drawing her a little closer. "It's Frank, not my lord. And I asked for no such promise, only that you were never to talk of it to anyone else."

"Oh."

"Oh indeed. Was that your first kiss, Charlotte?"

"Yes, of course it was."

"Did you like it?"

"My lord—Frank, you are making me blush."

He gazed down at her face which was indeed becomingly flushed. "There is no need to blush. It is quite natural to enjoy a kiss."

"Then I think you should be well aware that I enjoyed it and not put me to the blush by asking!"

"Good. I'll have you know I enjoyed it tremendously too."

Her heart leapt at that revelation, but she did not make a response. They walked on quietly for a few moments, then, taking her courage in her hands, Charlotte ventured to enquire, "Frank, given that we are speaking freely, may I ask about what I saw you doing with Lady Caroline? I have been so curious about it."

He laughed, "Ask away! I am not shy. What would you like to know?"

"I—I saw your thing and it was so big. I was not sure what you were doing with it when you were pushing against Lady Caroline. It seemed like you were causing her pain."

"Has no one ever told you about the facts of life, Charlotte?"

She shook her head. "My mother passed when I was only nine. Who else could have discussed such things with me?"

"I see. Well, that thing you talk about is the male organ, called a penis, or a cock. It grows and becomes hard when a man is aroused. And what I was doing was pushing it in and out of Caro's cunt—the aperture at the juncture of a woman's thighs. It has a tight, slippery passage that leads to a woman's womb. It is a very pleasurable sensation both for the man and the woman, and if done well, there is no pain. I believe it causes the woman some pain the very first time—though I cannot be sure for I have not ever made love to a virgin—but there is none after that, I assure you."

Charlotte frowned in concentration, taking in all this fascinating new information. "What about afterwards, when you pulled out? You touched your thing—your cock—and this pearly liquid came out of it."

"Ah, that is my cum, a substance with my seed which I emit at the height of my pleasure. I make sure to pull out of the lady before I shoot my cum, so that she does not become with child. Not that this is a foolproof method, mind you, though it has

135

worked for me so far. I have not fathered any children that I know of."

"So it is possible for a man and woman to have intimate relations without it resulting in a child?"

He chuckled. "Yes, Charlotte, quite possible. The whole ton and demi-monde are at it all the time, not just me you know. Although, having said that, the occasional accidents are unavoidable."

"What would happen if you got Lady Caroline accidentally with child?"

"I haven't thought about it much. I suppose Caro would go away somewhere discreet and have the child, then have it raised by some servant on the estate. It would be well provided for, not that it is likely to happen. Caroline and I are no longer together you know."

Charlotte's heartbeat quickened at this. "You have had a rupture?"

Frank snorted, "I wouldn't go as far as to call it a rupture. What Caroline and I had was never anything more than a light-hearted dalliance. It was time to put an end to it though. I do not like things to ever get too serious, for I'm afraid I am fickle by nature and cannot fix my interest in a person for more than a few weeks at most."

"What about when you marry? Will you continue to have these dalliances?"

Frank's face grew serious. "Many men in the ton continue to indulge in such dalliances even after marriage. However, I do not think I shall be one of them. Once I marry, I fully intend to be faithful to my wife."

Charlotte asked the question for which she did not really want to hear the answer. "Will you be marrying Miss Powell, do you think?"

"Is that any of your business, Charlotte?" Frank queried gently.

"No, I am sorry. Of course it is none of my business. I could not help being curious about it, that's all."

Frank sighed, "My father insists I marry by the year's end. He strongly suggests I should propose to Miss Powell."

"And will you?"

"I suppose I will in due course."

"Are you in love with her?"

Frank gave out a short, bitter laugh. "No, I am not in love with her, but that is not necessary. I have a great regard and admiration for her, and that should be enough for us to rub along as best we can."

"It would seem a pity to marry someone just on the off chance you might rub along with them as best you can."

Frank glanced down at her in amusement. "You are a romantic, Charlotte, are you not?"

"I suppose I am, but for good reason. I remember my father and mother being very much in love and happy together."

"They were very lucky in that case. From what I have seen, that is rare indeed. I have no great hopes it will happen to me."

"No, I quite understand. I do not believe it will ever happen to me either."

"So I take it, you are not about to accept Mr Hodge's addresses anytime soon."

Charlotte nudged Frank with her elbow playfully. "Stop teasing. The less we talk about Mr Hodge the better—or Mr Finch for that matter."

"Mr Finch? Who on earth is that?"

"He is a gentleman who proposed to me before I came to London," she said with a sigh. "My stepmama got quite mad at me when I refused him, and that is why I wrote to Aunt Margaret, asking if I could come and stay with her awhile."

"I take it he did not set your heart afire."

"No, but given my straightened circumstances, I was minded to give his suit a chance until he displayed faults in his personality that I could not accept in a spouse."

Frank regarded her curiously. "What kind of faults?"

"He was cruel to his servants, and added to that, he was stupid."

"And you cannot be marrying someone stupid or cruel."

"Of course not! Frederick understood when I explained it to him, but all my stepmama could see was that I was turning down a gentleman with an income of £3,000 a year. She got so mad at me that she ordered the servants to pack up my things and move them from my bedchamber to a small room in the attic."

Now Frank stopped and stared. "She sent you up to room in the attic, next to the servants?"

"Yes, I had an uncomfortable time there until Frederick came to fetch me. I do believe I heard mice scratching in the ceiling at night."

"If ever I come across this awful stepmama of yours, she better beware for I shall certainly give her a piece of my mind!"

Charlotte laughed merrily, "Just as well then that you are most unlikely to do so."

Frank squeezed her arm and they resumed their walk. "I hope at least that now you are living with the Mortons, you are being well treated. I have known them since forever, and they are good people."

"I cannot complain. They have been kind and generous to one who has been estranged from them all her life."

"I am glad." They walked on in companionable silence for another minute or two, then Frank asked, "If you do not believe you will ever find a love match, then what do you plan for your future? Will you remain unmarried?"

"I do not know. The life of a spinster poor relation is hardly ideal. I still hold a faint hope that someday, some suitor will come my way for whom I can feel the proper tenderness and regard. However, I must be a realist. I know that I am plain looking and poor, so my chances of finding someone other than the likes of Mr Hodge or Mr Finch are low. I am learning to be accepting of my fate. As the great Plato once said, *the greatest wealth is to live content with little,* so I must find my happiness in being content with my lot."

"How utterly depressing!" retorted Frank.

"We cannot all be born with the advantages you enjoy, Frank."

"I am well aware, but you know, my life is not as splendid as you think. You at least, have had the felicity of growing up with loving parents. I did not. My mother, I lost when very young, and my father is a cold, tyrannical being. I am betting you would not swap all my riches for the privilege of having had the parents you did."

"No, you are right. I would not, but in any case, I have you to thank for something."

"Really? What can you thank me for? I have not been kind to you."

Charlotte's lips quirked into a sad little smile. "No, you have not, but you did give me something very precious. In the lonely life of a spinster that stretches out before me, I can at least rejoice that I have had the privilege of being thoroughly kissed."

"I am happy to have obliged," replied Frank with a smirk. "In fact, should you care to replenish your stock of happy memories, I would be more than willing to indulge in a second round of kissing."

Charlotte's heart pounded in her chest as she voiced her next thought, "I was rather hoping that you would give me, not just kisses to look back on fondly, but something more." That last remark was greeted with a stunned silence, so Charlotte hurried on to make her case. "It might be just the thing for the both of us. You have ended your affair with Lady Caroline, so you are free to indulge in another until the time you marry.

139

Why not have a short dalliance with me? In the cold desert of my spinsterhood, I assure you I will not treasure my virtue half as much as the memories of sensual pleasures with you."

Still, Frank did not respond.

"I—I know that I am not much to look at, quite plain really, nothing like the beautiful Lady Caroline, but you said you enjoyed our kiss. I hazard to hope that you would find sufficient pleasure in my body to make this worth your while. Please, would you consider me as your next mistress? I know of course that it would be a short-lived affair and we would have to be very discreet, but nobody cares much about the comings and goings of plain, dowdy Charlotte Harding, so I think it could be done."

Frank remained silent, his face cast in rigidly stern lines. They came to a bend in the road, surrounded by a dense outcropping of trees.

Seeing his lack of response, Charlotte's spirits sank low, and she mumbled, "Let us forget I said anything. Please put this whole conversation out of your head, my lord."

Frank gritted his teeth. "For the love of God, it's Frank, and Charlotte, do be quiet!" Glancing this way and that, in one quick move he pulled her into the thicket of trees and pushed her against the trunk of a wide gnarled oak. A moment later, his lips descended on hers, not gently. His kiss was harsh, practically vicious, and she welcomed it with a soft moan of delight, opening her mouth to his searching, ravaging tongue. Her arms came up to clutch him tight as she kissed him back with innocent yet wanton abandon, her tongue venturing into the velvet heat of his mouth, revelling in the taste and feel of him. He angled his head for more kisses and came against the obstacle of her bonnet. With rough hands, he snatched it off her head and dropped it to the ground before binding his lips to hers again.

His hands roamed feverishly over her body, kneading soft flesh, pressing her to the hardness of his groin. Soon, he was greedy for more, wanting to feel her skin against his ravenous touch. He snatched the skirt of her dress and pulled it up, bunching it at her waist so that his searching hands could explore beneath. His fingers, encountering the thin material of her pantalettes, slid upwards looking for the opening of the garment. While this exploration took place, he kept on with his deep, drugging kisses. Charlotte could not get enough. She wanted more—more kisses, more of his touch, more of everything. She felt his hand slide up her leg, inch by inch. *"He's going to touch me in my special place,"* she realised just a moment before Frank's roving fingers slipped inside the opening of her pantalettes and found her mound.

She gasped into his mouth as she felt him stroke her wisps of hair, then unerringly find that joyous spot below. Why was it that his touch there brought tenfold the pleasure of her own fingers? He seemed to know instinctively how to stroke her, rubbing his fingers in a slow hypnotic motion that had her arching against him.

"Oh!" she moaned. He swallowed her next moan with his kiss. Without her volition, Charlotte ground her hips into his hand, looking for that magical friction that would send her body into ecstasy. Sensing this, his fingers began to stroke a little faster, back and forth. It felt so good! She was nearly there. Just a little more. His lips left her mouth and trailed down her jaw, then nestled into the sensitive skin of her neck. He found the delicate spot he wanted and bit down gently. "Ah!" cried Charlotte and felt a wave of contractions begin at her very core. She pulsed against him, over and over until the pleasurable wave came to an end.

Satiated, she rested her head against the wall of his chest, feeling happier than she had ever felt before in her life. Frank withdrew his hand from inside her pantalettes and brought it up for her to see. It was wet with her sticky fluid. In shock, she watched as he sucked his fingers into his mouth, cleaning them off. He grinned down at her. "Delicious!" he pronounced. Then he became businesslike and purposeful, rearranging her skirts back into place and picking up her bonnet from the ground. Carefully, he placed it on her head and tied the ribbon. Then he stepped back and inspected her. "There," he said, "looking perfectly respectable again. Come now, let us resume our walk."

With her arm in his, they emerged from the thicket of trees and began to walk alongside the road again. No one spoke. Charlotte was too dazed to utter a single word. Her mind was in a muddled frenzy. "*That's it*," she thought. She had crossed the Rubicon, and there was no turning back now. No longer was she a young lady of virtue, but a hussy, albeit disguised in her dowdy outfit. Did this mean that Frank had agreed to her proposition? Would she now become his mistress, for however long he allowed her to be? She hoped that was so. She knew she would treasure every minute she spent with him making memories that would sustain her over the rest of her life.

In another fifteen minutes, they came to the edge of the village, and it was a short walk thereafter to the inn. Frank escorted her inside, requesting a private room and water so that she could wash and refresh herself. "When you are done," he told her, "come down, and we will have something to eat while I arrange for a coach and horses to take us home."

Charlotte gave him a dreamy smile and went up to the room, availing herself of the water closet nearby. Inside the room, she sponged her sticky and still throbbing flesh clean, washed her face and hands, and tidied her clothes as best she could. On her return to the main parlour, she found Frank seated at a table laid out with tea and cake. Without a word, he poured her a cup, knowing just how she took it—milk with one lump of sugar. "Thank you," she murmured, feeling strangely shy.

He smiled, transforming the features of his face from handsome to devastatingly so. "We are in luck. There is an available carriage and horses at the inn, so we may leave whenever you are ready. The innkeeper has also agreed to send out his grooms to retrieve my horses and the wreckage of the curricle. There is a carpenter in the next village that can repair it, and it shall be returned to me, along with the horses, when all the work is done."

"That is lucky indeed." Charlotte sipped on her tea and nibbled on the cake, feeling a little weary. "I hope Helena has fared well at the hands of the physician."

Frank's face lost its smile. "Yes, I hope it is a simple fracture that can easily be mended. Poor thing was in a lot of pain. I must call on the Powells after I drop you at home, to ask after her."

Charlotte knew that was the right and proper thing to do, yet she could not help feeling a little arrow of jealousy pierce her at the thought. She smiled wanly and continued with her light repast.

Frank observed her with concern. "You are worn out! The sooner I can get you home, Charlotte, the better."

"It has been a long day," she concurred.

Once she was finished with her meal, they stood to go. Charlotte thanked the innkeeper and his wife for their hospitality while Frank slipped him a crown for his troubles. Soon, they were settled in the carriage and on their way back to London. Little was said on the journey, each lost in thought. After about twenty minutes, Charlotte felt the rhythmic jolt of the carriage begin to lull her to sleep. She tried to stay awake, but her eyes began to droop. She fell into a light doze, awakening sometime later to find her head comfortably nestled into the crook of Frank's shoulder. It was his gentle shake that had wakened her.

"We are nearly at your home, Charlotte."

She sat up quickly, pink with embarrassment at having availed herself of his shoulder to sleep. His lips quirked. "I had not meant to make you jump like a frightened rabbit. I only wanted a little time to speak to you in private before we arrive." Then, he hesitated. "The arrangement we spoke of... it is not too late to back out if you have changed your mind."

"I haven't," she said quickly.

His smile was relieved. "Still, you ought to take some time to consider such a big step. Charlotte, if I take your virtue, there will be no getting it back. And I can only promise you something temporary until I marry. Are you sure this is what you want to do?"

"I am sure. I will take every drop of happiness you give me and feast on it until I am old and wizened."

"I hope there will be other sources of happiness in your life, Charlotte, not just a few pleasurable hours you spend with me."

"I hope so too, but in any case, I am decided. I want to be your mistress, Frank, if you will have me."

He took her hand and kissed it. "Then that is what you shall be. Give me a few days to make arrangements and wait for my instructions, sweet little hussy."

"You won't change your mind?"

He chuckled, "I won't."

"Good."

The carriage came to a stop in front of 10 Grosvenor Street. Frank alighted and held out his hand for Charlotte to descend. He escorted her to the door and waited until it was opened, then bowed and took his leave.

Chapter 21

It was a few days before Charlotte was to see Viscount Stanton again. She was not to know that he spent that time securing, through his man of business, the rental of a house on Charles Street for the duration of a month. The house was owned by an eccentric gentleman who spent much of his time travelling on the Continent and only occasionally flitted in for brief visits to London. The neighbours were therefore used to the house being empty, and uncurious about its sporadic visitors. It would suit his purposes perfectly. It was located close enough that Charlotte could walk there easily from Grosvenor Street without calling attention to herself. Discretion was of the essence. He was determined for her sake that no one find out about their affair, not even his best friend Rupert.

Charlotte spent these few days in a state of anxious anticipation. With each day that brought no news from the viscount, she began to wonder whether she had dreamed the whole thing—or perhaps if he had had a change of heart.

In the company of Mrs Morton, she called on the Powells several times to enquire after Helena, whose fractured arm had been set and secured in a sling. It was judged that she should stay at home until the injury had healed and not venture out at all. Nevertheless, Miss Powell's popularity was already such that a swarm of visitors came by each day to see the beautiful patient and bring her token gifts. The viscount had not been present on each of their visits so far, though in conversation Charlotte heard that he had been unfailing in his attentions to Miss Powell, coming every day and spending at least an hour in her company.

On the fourth such visit, however, they found the viscount seated close to Miss Powell, reading to her from a book of poetry. He stood as they entered and made his bows to both Mrs Morton and Charlotte, then resumed his position beside Miss Powell. For the half hour of their visit, he spoke not a word to Charlotte, remaining attentive at Miss Powell's side.

Charlotte sat quietly, listening absently to Mrs Morton's and Lady Powell's conversation, her hands knitted together tightly in her lap. It was impossible to believe that the viscount could want her as his mistress. What a fool she had been, throwing herself at him! He could have no interest in her. From him, there was not a word, not a smile nor even a passing look to hint that he acknowledged her presence. It was as if she were invisible to him.

At last, Mrs Morton stood to make her goodbyes, and the Morton carriage was called for. The viscount stood too, and insisted on escorting the ladies out. Mrs Morton smiled at him affectionately as he held out his arm to her. "You are too good, Francis," she said as she took it. Together they stepped out of the Powell house and over to the waiting carriage, Charlotte following silently behind.

The viscount helped Mrs Morton aboard, then held out his hand to Charlotte. As she placed it in his, he exclaimed, "You have dropped your handkerchief Miss Harding!" He bent down as if to pick it up and handed something to her—a note.

"Thank you," she murmured and slipped it into her reticule. He took her hand again and assisted her into the carriage, then bowed briskly and took his leave.

Throughout the journey to Grosvenor Street, Charlotte paid no heed to Mrs Morton's idle chatter, her mind in a whirl, wondering what the contents of the note could be. Once home, she was not to read it straightaway, for Mrs Morton needed settling on her favourite reclining chair, a cup of tea poured and her shawl fetched. It would be another quarter hour before Charlotte could excuse herself and go up to the privacy of Frederick's study. There, she slipped the note out of her reticule and with trembling fingers, broke the seal. The note was brief and to the point.

Go to 4 Charles Street on Wednesday, 3 o'clock. I'll be there.

F.S.

Charlotte's pulse throbbed tumultuously in her temple as she tucked the note away. Full of agitation, she stood and began to pace the length of the room. She took deep breaths to try to calm herself. "*I have a tryst with Viscount Stanton,*" she marvelled. "*He is going to kiss me and do all those wicked things he talked about. Oh dear God!*" She put her hands to her burning face. Could she really do this? Should she back out? No! Her course was set. This was what she wanted.

It would be no trouble to slip out at the allotted time. Aunt Margaret usually took a nap in the afternoons, and Charlotte was known to enjoy lone expeditions to the shops and attractions of London while her aunt slept. It would raise no suspicions. Wednesday was two days hence. How was she to live for those two days? She felt as if her heart would burst from her chest.

———————•———————

The following day crawled by. Mrs Morton and Charlotte paid another visit to the Powells, but the viscount was nowhere in sight. In the evening, Charlotte accompanied her aunt to a card party at Mrs Hurst's, where the average age of the invited guests was at least forty. Charlotte partnered Mr Hurst in a game of whist, though she proved unequal to the task, such was the level of her distraction. Mr Hurst was far too polite to say anything and thanked her cordially for the game.

The evening came to an end and in bed that night, Charlotte tossed and turned, unable to settle to sleep. Tomorrow, she would see Frank. They would be alone in a house. On her return, she would be a virgin no more, her virtue gone.

If she thought Tuesday had been slow, Wednesday morning crawled by at an even more tortuous pace. Charlotte shared a cold luncheon with Mrs Morton, read to her in the drawing room for an hour and finally left her to nap just after two o'clock. Upstairs in her room, Charlotte took great care with her toilette, cleaning her body from top to toe with a wash cloth dipped in a bowl of water infused with a few drops of the orange blossom oil that her Spanish mother had always kept in the house. She brushed her hair and tied it in a loose bun, leaving curled tendrils tumbling at each side. Her toilette over, she pulled on one of her newer gowns, a pale peach muslin affair that Madame Elise had crafted to compliment the rounded contours of her body. Over this, she wore her drab brown pelisse and her oldest bonnet. Nobody looking at her would suspect that she was on her way to a tryst with her lover. Her lover! Who could believe it?

At a quarter to three, she finally stepped out of 10 Grosvenor Street and began to walk to her destination. She had looked it up on the map of London streets which was in Frederick's study. It was not far at all. So close in fact, that she arrived there a good five minutes early. She stood outside number 4 Charles Street and hesitated. Should she walk up to the end of the street and come back for the allotted time, or should she knock on the door now?

The decision was taken out of her hands. The front door of the house opened and a voice whispered sharply, "Come in!" Full of trepidation, she set foot inside. The door shut behind her in the darkened hallway. No light was forthcoming from outside as all the windows were firmly shuttered. "Come along!" A hand grabbed her arm and propelled her forward along the hallway to a set of stairs and up to the first floor which was a little brighter, thanks to a small window at the top of the landing. Frank opened the first door on his left and escorted her into a bedchamber which was lit with several candles casting a welcome orange glow. The room was furnished simply with a large bed, dressing table and chair. In the corner stood an old wooden armoire, and a rich burgundy rug draped the floor in front of the hearth.

Charlotte stood uncertainly in the middle of the room as Frank closed the bedchamber door and leaned against it, his arms crossed over his chest. He watched her hover nervously, a smile playing along the edges of his mouth. Finally, he spoke in a deep, reverberating voice. "Charlotte, are you ready to become my sweet little hussy?"

She looked up at him, her heart in her eyes. "Yes," she breathed.

"Then do as I say, no questions. Are we clear?"

"Yes, my lord."

He scowled. "It's Frank."

"I'm sorry!" she hastened to reply. "Yes, Frank."

"Good. Now take your bonnet off and that dreadful pelisse. Drape them over the chair."

With clumsy fingers, Charlotte executed this task, then stood, waiting for the next instruction.

"That gown is very pretty, Charlotte, but it must come off as well. Do it!"

With a flush staining her cheeks, Charlotte slowly undid the buttons of her dress and pulled it over her head. She placed it carefully on top of her pelisse on the chair, then stood, eyes cast to the floor.

"Now the corset. Do you need help or can you do it yourself?"

She scoffed, "I have been dressing myself without assistance since I was out of the schoolroom."

"Then do it."

With a degree more of confidence, she unlaced her corset and let it fall on to the chair. Now, she stood only in her shift which was tucked into pantalettes, and her stockings. The viscount pointed at the pantalettes. "These off next and the stockings."

With trembling hands, she pulled them down her leg and stepped out of them. Her shift dropped to the top of her thighs, covering her modesty. She went and sat gingerly on the edge of the chair to remove her stockings. The task done, she stood and looked askance at the viscount.

He smiled wickedly, "You know what comes next, sweet girl."

With a deep breath, she took her courage into her hands and pulled off her shift. Now, there was not a stitch of clothing covering her body. For an instant, she was tempted to cross her arms over her chest, but she forced herself not to. Instead, she stood, her arms down by her side, and looked straight at the viscount. His eyes were a molten brown as he took her in from top to toe. "My God, Charlotte!" he declared. "No one seeing you now would ever call you plain. You are magnificent. It should be a crime for you to ever wear clothes."

Charlotte smiled tremulously, "I'm glad, Frank. I want to please you."

"Oh trust me, you do! Turn around, let me have a good look at you."

She pivoted around slowly, letting him admire the creamy line of her back, the soft flare of her hips and the roundness of her buttocks.

He hissed in a breath. "Oh Charlotte, I am undone. You are exquisite." He stepped forwards, stopping a few inches from her. With delicate fingers, he traced a line from her lips, down her throat to one full, rounded breast. He cupped it in his hand, marvelling at how well it fit into his palm. Her pink nipples darkened and puckered at his touch. "So beautiful," he murmured, rubbing the aching tips with his forefingers.

"Oh!" she breathed.

He palmed the other breast and rubbed her nipples, eliciting more moans of pleasure from Charlotte. "So responsive!" he crowed. "You were made for pleasure, my sweet girl."

"It feels so good when you touch me," she murmured. "So much better than when I touch myself."

He laughed, "You touch yourself, do you?"

"Yes, every night. Is that wrong of me?"

"Oh no! Quite the opposite. You are a treasure trove of hidden delights, Charlotte. Come here!"

She stepped into his arms and buried her face into his chest. He pulled her to him, rocking their bodies from side to side as he held her tightly. After a time, he drew back a little and found her lips. They kissed for endless minutes. Each time their mouths pulled apart, they came back together again as if drawn to each other like a magnet, never satisfied, always wanting more — one more tug of the lips, one more lick, one more nibble. "You taste like heaven," he rasped, then sucked her tongue into his mouth.

When their lips parted again, she breathed a response, "So do you. Oh Frank, I don't think I could ever get enough of your kisses."

"Hmph!" he groaned, claiming her lips once more. This went on for some time longer. When Frank finally pulled back, Charlotte's lips were swollen and glistening, her eyes hazy with wanton lust. "Come to bed," he grunted. With strong arms, he lifted her off the ground and carried her over to it, depositing her flat on her back. "I need to taste your cunt, sweet hussy," he growled. "Will you let me?"

"Yes please," she pleaded.

"Then open your legs for me. Let me see you."

In the throes of her need, there was no more shyness. She opened her legs and allowed him to view the most secret place of her body. He knelt on the bed, pressing her thighs apart, and looked his fill. Dark pink folds of flesh peeked up at him, plump and moist, begging to be devoured. And below those folds was the darker coloured, rosebud like entrance to her back passage. He would have that too one day, but not just yet.

151

Soon, it was not enough to simply look. He needed to taste. He bent his head and gave her cunt one long lick from the slit of her opening to the top of her folds. Tremors went through her body at his touch. He needed another taste, so he licked her again. Her flesh was pleasantly musky and sweet. "I just knew it," he groaned. "You taste sweet everywhere."

"Then lick and taste all you wish!" she cried. "My body is yours to do as you please."

Who was he to argue with that? His mouth descended once more to her cunt, and this time, it remained there, licking and savouring her sweet taste. He found her nub of pleasure and fluttered his tongue over it, relishing each moan that came out of her, each entreaty. The sticky substance of her pleasure flowed freely from her cunt, and he lapped at it hungrily. He could feel her swell and throb under his touch. She was close to completion. He licked with more vigour, feeling her come apart beneath him.

"Frank!" she cried, and convulsed under his tongue. He kept on licking and did not stop until she finished riding the crest of the wave. When finally he raised his head, the lower part of his face was wet and dripping. Charlotte stared at him in astonishment. Did this all come from her?

"I have made you wet," she said, disconcerted.

He smirked, "No, my sweet. It is I who have made you wet." He wiped his mouth with the back of his hand and asked, "Have you ever tasted that sweet nectar of yours?"

"Yes, often," she admitted. "I like it."

At her response, he growled, "Oh sweet Lord, you are perfection. Then taste yourself on me!" He leaned over her and put his mouth to hers. She kissed him back with all her might, savouring the essence of herself on his lips. It felt wrong but also so right and so good.

After a long time, Frank ended the kiss and shifted onto his side on the bed to gaze into her eyes. "Charlotte," he said softly. "In the time we have together, I want to know you in every way possible. I want to do dirty, depraved things to you like we just did, and so many things more besides. But I want only truth between us—no lies or any pretence. I have had conversations more honest with you than with anyone else in my life, and it feels so damned good. I love it when you tell me the things you do to yourself in secret. Do not ever hide from me. Sweet hussy, I want to know all your darkest, most shameful imaginings." He dropped kisses all over her face—on her brow, her eyes, her soft cheeks and finally on her lips.

When he drew his mouth away, Charlotte whispered, "I want that too."

He smiled and tucked a stray curl of hair from her face. "Good. If this affair between us is about making wonderful memories, then let us make the very best of them, and not just for your sake but for mine too. Years from now, when you are an elderly spinster and I am a grumpy old man shackled in a loveless marriage, I want us to look back on this time we have together with great fondness. What do you say?"

Charlotte took hold of his face and kissed him solemnly. "I say yes, Frank. Let us have the best love affair there ever was and ever will be."

"Love affair?" he queried with a quirk of his lips.

"Yes, Frank. We are being honest, are we not? Then let us not be afraid to say what we feel. When I look into your eyes, when I touch your lips to mine, when I breathe in your heavenly scent, I feel love. But you need not worry this will ruin things, for in the words of Alfred Tennyson, '*Tis better to have loved and lost than never to have loved at all.*'"

He stroked her face tenderly. "I am not sure if I feel love in the same way you do, but I care very deeply about you, Charlotte."

"That is more than anything any man has ever felt for me, so I am rich and happy beyond measure."

He chuckled and kissed her again.

153

When at last they came up for air, Charlotte said in between panting breaths, "So, if we are to be honest, then I must tell you sir that it is the height of unfairness that I am laid bare to you while you are still dressed."

He drew back to cast an admiring glance at her nude figure. "Yes, it is a trifle unfair from your perspective, but I am willing to even the odds. I will gladly disrobe and allow you to feast your eyes on me. However, I have one condition."

She gazed at him in suspicion. "What would that be?"

His eyes dancing wickedly, he replied, "While I undress, I want to watch you touch yourself the way you do when you are alone each night."

She hesitated, then nodded. "Very well."

He rose then from the bed and began to undo his cravat. She gathered two pillows to prop her head and watched him with fierce concentration until he stopped and raised a brow. "Our deal, madam!"

"Oh yes. Sorry!" She widened her legs and brought two fingers to her special place, then began to rub herself in the way she did every night.

Now it was his turn to stop and stare. She paused. "Our deal, sir!"

"Touché." He began once more to undress, pulling off his cravat. Next, he undid the buttons on his waistcoat and threw it carelessly to the floor. All the while, his eyes remained glued to Charlotte's fingers pleasuring her cunt.

He sat on the edge of the chair and pulled off his boots, then his stockings. Then he stood and took off his shirt. At the sight of his nakedness, Charlotte drew in a sharp breath, instinctively quickening the strokes of her fingers on her cunt. He was broad, with a lean, muscled frame. Crisp dark hair scattered over his chest, thickening as it trailed down towards the fastening of his pantaloons. Taut pink nipples peeked out through the swirls of hair. "*Oh my!*" she thought.

"Talk to me Charlotte," he barked. "What are you thinking?"

Charlotte continued with the rapid strokes on her cunt as she mumbled, "I am thinking you are so beautiful and so male. I want to run my fingers through the hair on your chest and kiss you all over. And also, I very much want to see what lies beneath your pants."

He shuddered at her words, grasping his solid length through the fabric of his pantaloons. "This is what you want to see?" he gritted.

"Yes!"

In one swift move, he pulled his pantaloons and drawers down to the floor, freeing his swollen cock. He kicked them off his feet then stood, legs apart, hands on hips. "Look at me! Tell me what you are thinking." In a repeat of what she had done before, he pivoted around, giving her a perfect view of his smooth back and firm buttocks before turning to face her again.

"I want to sink my teeth into your buttocks!" she blurted.

"Then that is what you shall do. What else?"

He began pumping his cock in one hand. The tip oozed a little liquid, which he picked up with his hand and spread along the length of his shaft. An idea suddenly occurred to her. "I want to touch you the way you are touching yourself."

"Then you will."

"And I—I want to taste you."

He groaned, "Damn it! You are too perfect for words. See what you do to me!" His cock had swelled even more, the tip a dark reddish pink. "Keep touching yourself, sweet girl. I want you to achieve your pleasure before I do."

Charlotte fingers were drenched with her sticky substance as she rubbed herself furiously. She watched Frank approach the bed, his hand stroking his cock up and down with nearly the same fury as hers. "When my cum shoots out," he grated, "I want you to open your mouth and swallow every drop."

"Yes sir!" she breathed.

"But first you must come."

"Come?"

"It means reaching that pinnacle of pleasure."

"I am—so very—nearly there."

"Do it, Charlotte!"

With a loud cry, she came, feeling a wave of contractions in the core of her body.

"Open up!" Frank rasped as he brought his cock to within an inch of her mouth. He gave a strangled cry, "Here it comes!"

And there it was. Pearly white cum shot out from the tip of his male appendage, landing on Charlotte's throat and jaw, before she angled her mouth to receive the rest of it. She swallowed it down, noting the salty but not unpleasant taste. Once he was done, Frank tapped the tip of his cock to her lips. "Clean me up!" he demanded.

Without a thought, Charlotte accepted the wet tip into her mouth and sucked it clean. "Good girl," he purred as he pulled his cock out. A moment later, he was lying on the bed beside her and licking the drops of his own cum that had evaded her lips. He ran his tongue up her throat and along her jaw, then brought his mouth to hers, tasting himself on her in much the same way she had tasted herself on him earlier. It was dirty, wrong, but so good! They kissed long and deeply. Finally, he drew back and rested his head on the pillow beside her.

"That was amazing!" Charlotte whispered wondrously.

He laughed quietly, "That, my sweet sensual girl, was just the beginning."

Chapter 22

Charlotte lay next to Frank on the bed conducting a leisurely exploration of his body, just as she had been promised. She ran her fingers through the hair on his chest and played with his male nipples, then let her mouth follow the path of her fingers. She took her time savouring every inch of his beautiful body, and he indulged her, following her progress with hooded eyes.

Down she went, nuzzling her way along that thickening trail of hair until she found the nest of dark curls at the base of his cock. She kissed him there, burying her nose deep into the tufts to breathe in his dizzying male essence. His cock had already thickened at her touch and now stood proud to attention. She ran a finger along its length, marvelling at the soft satin of his skin. Her small hands wrapped around him, not quite managing to encircle his entire girth. She squeezed him gently, and he let out a long sigh.

"Tell me how that feels," she demanded, mimicking his manner from earlier.

"It feels divine. Do not be scared to squeeze me tight. Yes, like that."

She squeezed again. A drop of liquid emerged from the tip of his shaft. She touched it with the tip of her finger. "That's good," he urged. "Use it to help lubricate your fingers when you stroke me."

She did as he instructed, rubbing him up and down in quick strokes as she had seen him do. He watched her face as she did this, her teeth biting into her bottom lip in concentration. How could he have ever thought her plain?

"Tell me, Frank. Am I doing it right?" she asked.

Her hands were unpractised, yet her touch was bliss. "You are doing it perfectly," he praised. He put his hand to stop hers. "So perfectly in fact, that if you keep going, I shall come again."

"Then why do you stop me?"

He smiled, "Because I do not want to come just yet. I have other designs for you." At her look of enquiry, he explained, "I have not yet deflowered you, my little virgin. If you will allow me, I would like to put my cock into your cunt."

"Yes, I would like that." She thought for a moment. "Will it hurt?"

"Maybe a little. I will stretch you with my fingers first, and you are so wet that your internal passage should be slick and allow me to enter you more easily."

She leaned down and planted a sweet kiss on the tip of his cock. "Then go ahead Frank and take my virtue. It never did bring me much joy."

He pulled her down to him then for a long, satisfying kiss. Their naked limbs twined together as they feasted on each other's mouths. Then it was his turn to trail kisses down her body. He took his time, worshipping her rounded breasts and suckling on their tips till she writhed desperately beneath him. He kissed the soft skin of her belly, dipping his tongue into her bellybutton. Down he went to nuzzle the fragrant wisps of brown hair on her mound, inhaling her essence. "Open up for me," he grunted.

She did as was bid, parting her legs for him. She was still wet and sticky from their earlier exertions. He ran a finger into her folds, coating it in her juices, then rubbed her pleasure spot in the way she had shown him before. She made happy noises, murmuring, "It always feels better when it's you touching me."

"Good. I am glad." Slowly, he slid his finger down to her entrance and pushed it in gently. It was a tight fit. "How does that feel?" he asked.

"A little strange, but it doesn't hurt."

He pushed his finger a little deeper, and she gasped in surprise. He paused, waiting for her to adjust to his presence there, then began to move it inside her in a circular motion. She watched him with trusting eyes. He glanced up at her. "I am going to insert a second finger. Tell me how it feels."

Slowly, he withdrew his finger then pushed in again, this time with two. She inhaled sharply. "That hurt a little," she breathed. Like before, he waited for her to adjust to the intrusion, then began moving gently inside her again. "Hmm," she hummed. "It feels oddly good."

He smiled at her. "It is supposed to." With his fingers still circling inside her, he brought his mouth to her cunt and licked her like she was the finest delicacy. She sighed in delight at his touch. He fluttered his tongue, distracting her so she did not notice when he dipped a third finger into her cunt. He continued in this way until he felt her contract around his fingers as she came. Slowly, he withdrew his hand and looked up at her. "I think you are ready to take my cock," he said in a husky voice.

"Please do it!" she whispered.

He shifted so his body was over hers, leaning on his elbows. Gently, he notched his cock to her entrance and pushed the tip inside. He felt her tense under him. "Hush, my sweet. It will be fine," he soothed. He brought his lips to hers, deepening the kiss as he dipped his tongue into her mouth. At the same time, he pushed his cock further in until he felt the barrier of her virginity. He tangled her tongue with his, sucking gently on her mouth, diverting her attention as he thrust forcefully into her. He felt her gasp but swallowed it down with his hungry mouth. "It is done, sweet girl," he panted between kisses. "Our bodies are joined. Feel me inside you."

She gazed at him with glistening, wondrous eyes. "I do. I feel so full of you."

"Does it hurt still?"

"Only a little. Kiss me more."

So he did, and as they kissed, he began to thrust slowly in and out of her delightfully tight cunt. As she adjusted to his intrusion, he changed the rhythm of his thrusts, quickening his pace then plunging deeper into her slick and snug passage. She gave little moans with each deep thrust, "Oh Frank, that is good!"

After a while, he slipped a hand down her body, unerringly finding her pleasure spot. Her moans became louder as he rubbed her there in tandem with the thrusts of his cock. "Come for me, my sweet girl. You can do it."

Eyes fixed on his smouldering gaze, she let out a cry as she convulsed around his cock. "Good girl," he crooned. "Such a good girl." He began to pound into her, chasing his own pleasure. She felt his cock swell impossibly large, and with a guttural groan he pulled out of her only an instant before he showered her belly with his pearly cum. Breathless, he collapsed against her. She held him tight, not minding his weight on her nor the sticky mess. She clutched him to her heart, feeling pride and exultation and oh so much love. She knew with a certainty that she would never regret giving him the gift of her body.

After a long while, he bestirred himself to go find the basin of water and a cloth. With quick, efficient strokes, he wiped himself clean, feeling a little awed at seeing the blood on his shaft—Charlotte's virgin blood. He dipped the cloth in the water again and wrung it out, then returned to her side. She lay there supine, watching him quietly. He dropped a kiss on her forehead, then began gently to clean her. He returned to the basin several times, the water turning pink as he wiped every trace of blood and cum from her body. When finally she was clean, he lay down beside her. She captured his hand and kissed it. "Thank you," she said simply.

He brought his forehead to hers for a few precious moments before sitting up with a sigh. "It is getting late, Charlotte. Time you should be heading back."

Without a word, they rose from the bed and began to dress. When they were ready, he blew out the candles and took her hand, leading her back down. At the front door, he stopped and took her into his arms. "When can we do this again?" she mumbled into his chest.

"You will need a few days to heal. How about Monday, same time?"

"I'll be here, three o'clock on the dot."

"Good. Sweet Charlotte, I will let you go out first and wait a few minutes here before making my exit. Give me one last kiss before you go."

They exchanged a brief kiss, then Frank opened the door and let Charlotte leave.

Chapter 23

Viscount Stanton assisted Miss Powell into the carriage with all the attention and care that this task required. A week after her accident, her arm was healing nicely, and although it was still held in a sling, it was opined by both her parents that a gentle outing to Hyde Park in the carriage would not do any harm. Accordingly, the viscount had invited her for this promenade.

Having settled her into the seat, he enquired solicitously, "How does your arm, Miss Powell? Are you comfortable?"

She smiled in reassurance, "I am fine, my lord. It was an inspired idea of yours to wedge this cushion under my arm. It feels very comfortable, I assure you."

"I am glad."

Next, Viscount Stanton turned to Charlotte and held out his hand to her. She was on chaperone duty again. This time, Lady Powell had not even bothered with the pretence of an indisposition, merely writing to summon Charlotte for this task.

"Miss Harding?"

Charlotte took his hand and climbed aboard to sit facing Miss Powell. A moment later, he joined them in the carriage, and they were on their way. Immediately, he tilted his body in Miss Powell's direction and began to engage her in flirtatious banter.

"May I compliment you on how well you look today, Miss Powell? The fresh air has put a healthy glow into your fine complexion."

The fair young lady dimpled charmingly back at him. "You flatter me, my lord."

"Never!" he smiled. "Did you perchance read from that book of poems by Robert Browning that I left with you yesterday? What are your thoughts on it?"

While Miss Powell responded to the viscount's enquiry, Charlotte fixed her gaze outside the carriage, wishing she were anywhere but here. It was painful to witness the viscount fussing over Miss Powell and flirting with her. Charlotte knew of course that he intended to make her his bride and that she, Charlotte, had no claim on him. She was only his mistress for the short time until his marriage.

It was Friday, two days after their tryst, and this was her first sight of him since then. Having spent that time in a happy reverie about him and the wonderfully wicked things they had done together, it was quite a jolt to see him act so cool and distant with her. Not by a single look or a word did he betray their intimate connection. No, all his attention was focussed on the beautiful, charming Miss Powell.

Charlotte flicked her gaze to them then hastily brought it back to where it was before. In that brief gaze, she had seen him smile admiringly down at Miss Powell as he teased her about her taste in poetry. No, she would not look at them again if she could help it. Instead, she stared at the changing landscape around her as they left the bustling streets of London and entered the vast fields of Hyde Park. Spring would soon be turning into summer. Back home, the apples would be ripening in the orchards. The strawberries in their kitchen garden would be ready for picking. Robert and Ruth Ellis would be busy in their preparations for their epic journey to America. She missed her friend, now more than ever. There was no one in whom she could confide about her relationship with the viscount. Had she made a dreadful mistake?

No! Her life was barren of joy as it was. She would treasure those blissful moments in the house on 4 Charles Street forever, but they were stolen moments, not part of her real everyday life. She should learn to accept this. She knew where she stood. It would be dangerous and treacherous to her happiness to wish for more.

And so she endured this carriage ride, even began to take enjoyment from it, admiring the verdant fields of Hyde Park, the glint of the Serpentine lake, the bright blue of the late spring sky. There was pleasure to be found in the appreciation of those simple things. She smiled in delight at a family of swans gliding on the smooth waters of the lake.

The viscount, happening to glance up at this moment, caught that serene smile and wondered at it. She had seemed so withdrawn earlier that he had not been able to address a single word in her direction. As ever, she wore that same old dowdy pelisse. However, it no longer elicited the same degree of disgust as it had in him before, for now he knew what deliciousness lay beneath it. Under the tight fabric of his pantaloons, his cock stirred. He should not think about this now. With an effort, he turned back to his fair companion and did not allow his attention to stray again.

———————•———————

"Good day, Miss Powell." The viscount bowed as he took his leave. They were back at the Powell townhouse where he had very attentively escorted the lady inside. Now he turned and bowed to Charlotte, then noticed that she too, was heading out the door.

"Miss Harding, you do not stay here?"

"No, my lord. I shall be walking back to the Mortons' house now."

"I see. In that case, may I escort you there in my carriage?"

She hesitated. "Thank you, my lord, but I would prefer to walk." She did not want prying eyes to see her alone in a carriage with the viscount.

He understood at once. "Of course. Then perhaps I may walk with you the short distance to Grosvenor Street?"

She inclined her head in acceptance, and he instructed his coachman to take the carriage off without him. They began to walk quietly side by side. They were about halfway to the

Mortons' townhouse before the viscount finally spoke. In a low voice, he asked, "How are you feeling? Are you still sore?"

"Much less so than yesterday, thank you for asking, my lord."

"It's Frank," he said in irritation. "That park ride was damned awkward. I wanted to speak to you, Charlotte, but you kept looking away."

"It was better that way. Best when you are courting Miss Powell that I keep well out of the picture."

He huffed, "I did not like it."

"Nor I, but that is the way it is."

He was quiet for a few moments, then blurted, "I am sorry, Charlotte. I know it is not easy for you to watch me with Miss Powell. Would that things could be different."

"Different how?"

"Would that I were free not to marry, or else to marry someone of my choice."

She regarded him curiously. "Why are you not free to do so? I do not quite understand."

He sighed, "My father insists."

"I understand filial duty and your wanting to respect your father's wishes, but if you are truly set against this marriage, then cannot you choose not to be wed?"

"And cause a permanent rupture with my father? You of all people know the consequences of such an action."

"He would disown you?"

"I am not sure, and I am not willing to put it to the test. Of course, he cannot do anything about the title, but the Stanton estate—which is vast—he is free to do with as he pleases. It is not entailed. He could decide to settle it entirely on my younger brother. On the other hand, if I were to fall in line with his wishes and marry Miss Powell, he would as part of the marriage settlement put me in possession of a significant portion of the estate."

165

"And you do not have any other independent means of living? You talked of investing in that American company."

"I have a small legacy from my mother, but it is modest, only a tiny fraction of what is my due as the Stanton heir."

"I see."

"Beside the material things, he is the only family I have, apart from my brother. I cannot think what it would be like to be estranged from him, or cast out as your father was. He may be cold and demanding, but I have a fondness for him—call it love—and there is part of me that still longs for his approval. I cannot go against his will, Charlotte."

She gazed at him sadly. "Say no more about it, Frank. I do understand."

They were coming to the end of their walk, nearly at the Mortons' townhouse. Seeing this, Frank asked hurriedly, "Will you be attending the Grayson ball tomorrow?"

"Yes, we have invitations to go. And you?"

"I had not thought to go, but now I find that I have changed my mind."

"We could not dance. It would cause too much gossip were you to ask me."

"I know, but at least I shall see you, and perhaps find a way to snatch a kiss. You do not know how much I hunger for the taste of your lips, sweet girl."

Charlotte's breath caught. "No more than I," she quivered.

"Then I shall see you tomorrow. Good day, Miss Harding," he said aloud, and bowed, taking his leave.

Chapter 24

Late morning the following day, Viscount Stanton was eyeing a plate of cold beef and eggs with disfavour when a visitor was announced.

"Mr Jasper Stanton, my lord," said Hudson.

Barely had the words been spoken than that gentleman sauntered in and pulled up a chair opposite his brother. Casting an appreciative glance at the breakfast laid out on the table, he began to serve himself, saying with exaggerated cheerfulness, "Morning Frank!"

"Good morning, Jasper," Frank replied, regarding his brother quizzically. "I had not thought your term at Oxford was over."

"It ain't," was the laconic reply.

Frank raised a brow. "Then would you care to explain why you are here?"

Jasper took a bite of beef, chewing on it enthusiastically. "Good slab of beef this. My compliments to the cook." At his brother's look, he confessed, "Little harmless revelry. Only the proctor didn't think so. I've been rusticated till the end of term."

"I see. Does father know?"

Jasper shrugged. "I have not told him, but I am sure that word will reach him soon enough."

"He will not be pleased."

Again Jasper shrugged. "He is so difficult to please that displeasing him has become a habit of mine. I am used to it. We cannot all be good, dutiful sons like you."

Frank looked at him in some surprise. "Is that how you see me?"

"You never put a foot wrong, Frank, at least not to my knowledge. A First at Oxford. A celebrated maiden speech in

167

the House of Lords. Never a hint of scandal, despite your many love affairs. You even managed to turn a profit from that measly little estate mother left you. It is all father talks about, you know."

Frank could not help the leap of his heart at this divulgence. The earl very rarely praised his eldest son to his face; to know that he did so to others was gratifying. In reply to Jasper, he said gently, "I am far from perfect, though I suppose it is true that I have tried, throughout my life, to gain father's approbation. Perhaps as a result, you were spared the weight of his expectations. You should consider yourself lucky."

Jasper grinned, "I do, brother mine. I stand very much in your debt."

Frank smiled back wryly, "So, what do you propose to do now?"

Jasper put his fork down and wiped his lips with a napkin, then said, "I was hoping you would allow me to stay with you until the end of the season—and perhaps let me spend the summer at your estate. That should give father time to cool off on his anger before I have to face him again."

"You are welcome to stay as long as you like, Jasper, though I warn you, the spare room in this apartment is quite small with only a narrow bed."

"It will be more than sufficient for my needs," Jasper said quickly.

Breakfast over, Frank stood, saying to his brother, "A word of advice, Jasper. You are better off coming clean with father and taking whatever consequence he has for you on the chin, than waiting for the whole thing to blow over. Father is not likely to forget or forgive so easily if you avoid him all summer as you propose to do."

Jasper huffed as he got to his feet, "I know you are right, Frank, but I need a little time to prepare myself for the coming confrontation. Let me stay the week, and then I promise I will go see him."

"I have already said you are welcome to stay however long you need," said Frank, clapping him on the shoulder as they headed out of the dining room. "Now come with me."

"Where are we going?" demanded Jasper suspiciously.

"We are paying a call on Sir Horace and Lady Powell, and their beautiful daughter."

Jasper wrinkled his brow. "Never heard of them. Is there a reason why we are making this call?"

"The reason, dear brother, is that Miss Powell is the young lady father desires me to marry before the year is out."

Jasper stopped and stared at his brother before shaking his head and declaring, "God am I glad that I was not the first born."

"You have no desire to be earl and master of Stanton Hall one day?" wondered Frank.

"Not one shred," said Jasper with a shudder.

Frank smiled, "Then it is just as well you are not the first born."

With this, the two gentlemen headed out. Not ten minutes later, they were ushered into the Powells' drawing room. "Viscount Stanton, Mr Jasper Stanton," announced the butler.

The viscount strode in and made his bows to the Powells, then addressed them, "Sir Horace, Lady Powell, Miss Powell, let me make you known to my brother, Jasper Stanton."

Jasper came forward and bowed, greeting the Powells with great civility, the habits of courtesy deeply ingrained. The two gentlemen then turned to the other occupants in the room, and a large smile spread over Jasper's face. "Auntie Margaret," he said, going to embrace Mrs Morton.

That lady gave a pleased chuckle. "Jasper my dear, how good it is to see you. I do believe you have grown another inch since last I saw you."

He grinned, "My tailor would agree with you, for I have had to have my entire wardrobe let out."

169

"Jasper," said the viscount sternly from behind him, "may I make you known to Miss Harding, who is Mrs Norton's niece."

Jasper turned to Charlotte and bowed. "Miss Harding, I am honoured to make your acquaintance. Mrs Morton is almost family to me, so that makes us kinsfolk of a sort, does it not?"

Charlotte laughed, "I think you may be right, Mr Stanton."

With a flourish, Jasper settled himself in the available seat next to her and began an animated conversation while Frank had no option but to make his way to Helena's side, as was expected of him. "Miss Powell, how is your arm today?" he asked her with the utmost civility.

"It is much improved, my lord," she replied. "The physician says I may take off the sling in another week and resume my social activities, though I must continue to have a care of it."

"That is good news indeed!" exclaimed the viscount. "In that case, perhaps we can organise an outing to Vauxhall Gardens, for I know you have long wanted to see it."

Helena beamed, "Oh, that would be marvellous, my lord, as long as mamma agrees."

Lady Powell, overhearing this latest, hastened to give her approval for the outing. During the next half hour, the viscount engaged the Powells in conversation, looking over at Charlotte every now and then as he heard her laughter. "*What could be amusing her so?*" he wondered crossly, but he could not make out what was being said. All he could discern from a distance were grins and chuckles and the occasional loud peal of laughter as Jasper and Charlotte appeared to become fast friends. With an effort, the viscount directed his attention to his intended bride, but that half hour felt interminable.

Finally, he stood and indicated to Jasper that it was time to leave. As they made their farewells, he heard Jasper say laughingly to Charlotte, "You will have to save me a dance or two tonight, Miss Harding. As your kinsman, I insist upon it."

Her responding smile lit up her face. "Then as your kinswoman, I shall hold you to it."

With a barely restrained scowl, the viscount led the way out on to the street, whereupon the two brothers began to walk. "Where to next?" asked Jasper.

"The boxing club," said the viscount in a clipped voice. "I feel the need to spar."

"Yes," said Jasper observing his brother. "You do look like you want to punch someone. What is with you?"

"Nothing at all. It has been at least a week since I last had a boxing session and I simply want to keep in condition."

Jasper eyed Frank shrewdly. "Beautiful girl, that Miss Powell, but what a dull life it will be shackled to her. It is no wonder you are feeling cross at the prospect of it. Is there no way to change father's mind?"

Frank glared at his brother. "What do you think?" he snapped. Just this morning, in fact, a missive had arrived from the earl interrogating Frank's progress in his courtship of Miss Powell and making it known in no uncertain terms what the earl expected. It was no wonder Frank had lost his appetite for his breakfast.

"By gad Frank, you are in a pickle!" said Jasper with some sympathy.

The viscount did not deign to reply. Instead, they walked on in silence. Inside, Frank churned, but his anger was directed at himself more than at his brother. Why was it that Jasper had immediately seen Charlotte's qualities and befriended her, whereas on their first meeting he had dismissed her as a plain, poor relation and had no thought of her until that fateful encounter at the Wilton ball? Was he so blind and full of his own consequence that he had failed to see past the dowdy clothes and unfashionable looks?

Not that it mattered in the grand scheme of things. She was his mistress now, and the clock ticked on the time they had together. Once he was engaged, he would have to end his association with her. Surely by then, he would have grown tired of their dalliance, as he always did with his mistresses. Somehow though, he wasn't so sure he would this time.

His blood stirred as he recalled how she had looked, lying naked on the bed, stroking herself to pleasure. He wanted nothing more in that moment than to drag her back to the house on Charles Street, rip off her clothes and spank her for having had the temerity to charm his brother. Then he wanted to drive himself into her tight body until she screamed his name and begged for more. He let out a long, frustrated breath and tried to calm himself. By gad, he did feel the need to punch someone.

Chapter 25

The Stanton men arrived at the Grayson ball more than a little fashionably late. It was all Jasper's fault. He had kept his brother waiting while he got Hudson to tie his cravat in an intricate new knot that was all the rage, and then he had needed his hair coiffured just so. While this was done, Frank had kicked his heels in the drawing room, fists clenching and unclenching in his irritation and desire to be on his way. It was not a minute too soon that they finally set out and arrived at Lord and Lady Grayson's stately house on Grosvenor Square.

They greeted their hosts and entered the spacious ballroom that was already alive with the hum of voices and the jaunty sounds of a country dance. Frank's gaze immediately tracked the room, searching until he found what he was looking for. In the heart of the dancefloor stood Charlotte, moving to the steps of the dance with a merry smile and a nimble foot. She wore the same gown of pale blue silk that he had seen on her at the Wilton ball. It showed off to perfection the delicate line of her neck and shoulders, and clung enticingly to the bountiful breasts beneath. She looked radiant and lightly flushed from her exertions. Once his eyes found her, he could not look away. He wondered yet again how he could ever have thought her plain.

A light jostle of his arm brought him back to his immediate surroundings. It was Jasper that had nudged him, for they had been joined by Sir John and Lady Pemberton, with their daughter in tow. Greetings, bows and curtsies were quickly made, then mindful of his social duties, the viscount requested a dance from Miss Pemberton. This request was seconded by one from Jasper, after which the little group stood for a few minutes, exchanging polite conversation. Frank noted with cynical amusement the enthusiasm with which the Pembertons vied for his attention, all too clearly trying to take advantage of Miss Powell's absence to fix his affections on Miss Pemberton. If only they knew where his interest really lay.

As the country dance came to an end, the viscount excused himself and began to make a circuit towards Mrs Morton, who sat with another matron, a Mrs Hurst, in one corner of the ballroom. Jasper ambled amiably at his side. They stopped a few times along the way to greet other acquaintances and request more dances. It seemed an age before they finally made it to their destination, by which time a rosy-cheeked Charlotte had been returned to Mrs Morton's side by her dance partner.

"Evening, Aunt Margaret," Jasper boomed. "Evening Miss Harding. You are looking mighty fine tonight. I had best claim my dances with you before it is too late. Are you free for the next quadrille? And how about the waltz?"

Charlotte curtsied prettily and replied with a smile, "I kept the quadrille free for you, Mr Stanton, though I had begun to worry that you would not show up tonight."

Jasper grinned, "It is called being fashionably late."

At which the viscount snorted, "It is called spending an obscene amount of time fashioning that abominable cravat."

"Abominable! I will have you know *this* is the height of fashion," riposted Jasper.

"It certainly is an impressive looking cravat," soothed Mrs Morton. "Jasper, I do not believe you have met my dear friend Mrs Hurst. Let me make you known to her. Mrs Hurst, this is Jasper Stanton, the Earl of Stanton's younger son."

Jasper bowed correctly. "At your service, madam."

Mrs Hurst smiled warmly at him, "Good evening Mr Stanton. Even had you not been introduced, I would have guessed your kinship with the viscount, for the resemblance between the two of you is remarkable."

"Except I'm the handsomer one," quipped Jasper.

"As to that, I couldn't say!" laughed Mrs Hurst.

During this exchange, Charlotte and Frank cast lingering glances at each other, drinking in the sight of the other. Now, the opening notes of the quadrille could be heard, and Jasper put out his arm to Charlotte. "I believe this is my dance, Miss Harding." She put her hand through his arm and allowed him to escort her to the dancefloor. The viscount, reminded of his duties, perforce made his way to Miss Fortescue, whom he was to partner.

Throughout the dance and the ones following, as they executed the intricate steps, hopping and skipping to the lively music, the viscount was acutely aware of Charlotte's presence, wherever she was on the ballroom floor. It was as if an invisible cord were tied between them. He might be smiling down at his partner, or exchanging little words here and there with her, but his entire focus was on what Charlotte was doing. He caught her delighted peal of laughter at something Jasper whispered to her. He saw her teasing smile as she twirled with Mr Hurst. He felt an illogical resentment at each laugh and smile she bestowed on someone else. Those smiles should be for him and him alone. With each minute, his irritation increased and the fire of his desire got stoked. He needed to feel her in his arms again and inhale the delicate floral scent of her skin. He needed to stop these other men fawning over her. Blast it, what was wrong with him?

Things got even worse when the music struck up a waltz. He was promised to Miss Pemberton for this dance, but she might as well have been invisible, such was his frustration at seeing Jasper clasp Charlotte close in his arms and smile mischievously down at her. *Damnation!*

That was it! He could not take another moment of this agony. As soon as the dance ended and he had jettisoned Miss Pemberton with as much civility as he could muster in his state, he marched towards Mrs Morton just as Jasper returned with Charlotte on his arm.

"Miss Harding," he said curtly. "I believe the heat of the ballroom has affected you, for you are looking alarmingly flushed."

Mrs Morton glanced at Charlotte worriedly. "He is right Charlotte. Are you feeling quite well? Perhaps you should go out into the garden for some fresh air."

"A capital idea!" exclaimed Jasper. "Auntie Margaret, will you allow me to escort Charlotte out for a few minutes? We are practically kin, you know, and you can rest assured she will be in good hands."

"Of course, dear boy. Please do so. I would not like to see you faint in this ballroom, Charlotte," said Mrs Morton with great concern.

Charlotte had barely a chance to speak for herself before she was whisked away by an eager Jasper, much to the viscount's dismay. He watched them walk away, astonishment warring with annoyance. How dare his brother steal a march on him? An instant later, he recovered enough to make his excuses to Mrs Morton and follow in their footsteps towards the garden.

He was very nearly at the edge of the ballroom when something else happened to vex him, or rather someone else. Lady Caroline Drake stepped into his path with a winning smile, exclaiming, "Viscount Stanton! What a surprise! We have not seen you out and about in ages, not since Miss Powell's unfortunate accident. We were beginning to wonder what had become of you."

"Lady Caroline, as you can see, I am hale and hearty. Perhaps you will excuse me—"

"Oh but do stay a moment, viscount. Tell me how dear darling Miss Powell is doing."

"She is much improved, though if you have such concern about her wellbeing, then perhaps you should be calling on the Powells to enquire after her."

Lady Caroline rapped his arm with her fan. "How droll you are, sir! I was merely enquiring of you as it is all but common knowledge that she is soon to become your bride."

The viscount eyed her with growing irritation. "Caroline," he muttered under his breath. "I have told you before that this is none of your concern. Now, if you will excuse me, I must find my brother." And with that, he strode away, unaware of the possessive and angry gleam in Lady Caroline's eyes as she watched him go.

Leaving the ballroom, the viscount found his way towards the back of the house where a large door opened into the garden, lit softly by several glowing lamps. He walked past some acquaintances, nodding to them absently, and looked around for a sighting of Charlotte's pale blue gown. A moment later, he spied her and Jasper sitting on a wooden bench next to a water fountain. He made his hasty way over to them.

Charlotte looked up in surprise at the sound of his footsteps, but it was Jasper who spoke first. "Frank," he said, amusement lacing his voice, "don't tell me you too are in need of some invigorating fresh air!"

"Jasper," Frank said between gritted teeth. "It would oblige me if you could make yourself scarce and leave me alone with Miss Harding."

"Easy Frank. No need to get into a tizzy," Jasper spoke as if gentling an agitated horse. "If you will but consider this rationally, I did you a favour by bringing Charlotte out here. My escorting her did not occasion any gossip, but had you led her out of the ballroom, all eyes would have followed you."

Frank had to acknowledge the truth of these words. "I am duly grateful, Jasper. Now for the love of God won't you please go?"

"Not so quick," said his brother smoothly. "I cannot return to the ballroom without Charlotte, as everyone saw me taking her out for some reviving fresh air. There is a clump of trees over there which is far enough from here that I will not overhear you. Take Charlotte and be back in no less than five minutes, or else I shall come looking."

The anger drained from Frank. He gave his brother's shoulder a squeeze of thanks, then held out his hand to Charlotte. "Sweet girl, come with me," he said in that commanding tone she was growing to love. She stood and put her hand in his, walking with him towards the privacy afforded by the trees. No sooner were they out of sight than he spun her around to face him and brought his lips to hers in a punishing kiss.

Oh the sweet relief of holding her in his arms! Like a parched traveller in the desert, he drunk her in, holding her tight to his chest as he ravaged her mouth. She clutched at him, kissing him back with equal ardour. "Frank," she murmured in between kisses. "Oh Frank."

He responded by sucking her tongue into his mouth then biting her lower lip, only to lick the stinging flesh. "Sweet girl," he groaned. "I cannot wait until Monday. I am burning for you. Let me have a taste of your nectar." And with that, he dropped to his knees on the mossy ground and burrowed under the skirt of her gown, finding the slit of her pantalettes and parting the fabric. Like a starved man, his mouth clamped on her mound, finding her pleasure spot with uncanny precision.

Charlotte gave a stifled gasp, drowning in the feel of his mouth as he licked and sucked on her as if his life depended on it. So intense was the feeling that it did not take long at all for her to reach that precipice of pleasure. In moments, her body erupted in wave after wave of blissful contractions. She clamped her teeth over her gloved arms to stop herself from crying out, then gave a long sigh of relief as Frank emerged from the tent of her gown, his mouth glistening with her sticky juices.

His eyes burned with passion as, with unsteady fingers, he unfastened the front of his breeches and took out his swollen cock. "See what you do to me!" he grunted as he jerked a hand frantically along his length. In an instant, he too was reaching his climax, spurting his pearly emissions all over the ground before him. He gave his cock one last tug, then rasped his order, "Put your mouth here and clean me up."

Without hesitation, Charlotte knelt down and licked his cock clean, revelling in the musky, salty flavour of him. "Good girl," he whispered, stroking her hair gently. "My sweet wanton girl." With great care, he helped her back to her feet. Using his handkerchief, he wiped his face, then rearranged his clothes. He looked at her ruefully. "You have driven me to madness, Charlotte."

"The feeling is mutual, Frank. Sometimes, it feels as if I shall combust if I do not feel your lips on mine."

He drew her to him, dropping a light kiss on the top of her head. "Our five minutes are up," he said softly. "Before I let you go, please say you will meet me at Charles Street tomorrow. I do not think I can wait until Monday."

She thought quickly. "I'll be there," she promised.

Without another word, he led her back to the fountain where Jasper waited patiently. His brother stood on seeing them and scrutinised their persons with a frown. "I do hope the two of you know what you are about," he said. Taking out his handkerchief, he bent and wiped some dirt from the bottom of Charlotte's gown. "Come on Charlotte," he added. "It is high time we returned to the ballroom. As for you," he told his older brother, "best you wait a while before following us back inside."

Frank nodded briskly in acquiescence.

•————————————•

Much later, the Stanton gentlemen left the Grayson house together, electing to walk home instead of going by carriage. Both were silent as they walked, deep in thought. Finally, Jasper could stand it no more. "For the love of God, Frank, why are you conducting an illicit affair with Charlotte? She is an innocent, not your usual type at all. Have you any idea what this could do to her reputation if word got out?"

"Would you believe me if I said it was Charlotte's idea, not mine?" retorted Frank.

Jasper huffed in annoyance, "You cannot have put many objections in the way of that idea then."

"No," admitted Frank. "My heart leapt at the chance. I do not think I have ever wanted anyone the way I want Charlotte."

"If your feelings are so strong, why do you not marry the girl instead of tarnishing her with a tawdry affair?"

Frank's lips thinned. "Do you see father ever accepting a match with her?"

Jasper considered the question. "Granted, she has no fortune, but the Stantons are rich enough that it should not matter. She is genteel and well born, and I know for a fact that father holds Auntie Margaret in high esteem. The friendship between our families goes back a long way. If you were to insist, he would come round."

"I do not believe he would," sighed Frank in frustration. "In some people's eyes, Charlotte is not well born. Her mother was a tradesman's daughter from Spain. Hugh Harding was disowned by his family when he married her."

"Ah, that complicates things." Jasper brooded on the matter, then shook his head sadly. "I feel for you Frank, but still I think you are doing wrong and putting her at grave risk. She is dependent on the bounty of her aunt and cousin. What would they do to her if this came out? What if she were to become with child?"

"I am taking precautions, so that is unlikely. And if it did happen, then I would make sure she and the child were well provided for."

"I hope you know what you are about, Frank. I like Charlotte a great deal and would hate to see her brought down by this."

"We are being very careful and discreet—" began Frank.

"So discreet that you planned to take her out into the garden for a frolic. I do not know what would have happened had I not caught on to what you were about and pre-empted you." Jasper snorted and added, "I feel like an older brother right now, you know, not the other way around."

Feeling chastened, Frank muttered, "It won't happen again." Then, in a plaintive voice he added, "It did not help to see you waltzing with her. Nobody's arms but mine should hold her so close!"

Jasper threw him a pitying look. "My but you have it bad. Would you have preferred someone other than your brother, whom you trust, had waltzed with her?"

Frank sighed deeply, "I suppose not."

"Then do not let that green-eyed monster of jealousy take over whenever I am with Charlotte. I have no designs on her at all, and in any case, I can see just how smitten she is with you. She should have a care that no one else sees it too."

With that, they completed the rest of their walk in silence. As they approached their lodgings on Wimpole Street, Frank stayed his brother with a hand on his arm. At Jasper's questioning look, he said simply, "Thank you. I am glad you have come to stay."

Jasper winked. "Had to earn my bed and board somehow."

Frank chuckled. "It's good to have you here," he said softly.

Chapter 26

Charlotte and Frank met in Charles Street the following afternoon, and every day thereafter, with the occasional exceptions when his social obligations got in the way. Their appetite for each other was insatiable, but there was to be no repeat of the dangerous public frolics such as had occurred at the Grayson ball. Their liaison was kept to within the confines of the house where they had their trysts.

Frank ravished Charlotte in every room of that house, and even had his wicked way with her on the staircase one day. Like the most apt of students, Frank learned everything there was to learn about Charlotte's body and her desires. She too, studied every facet of Frank—the wild look in his eyes when he came, the great pleasure he got from having the lobes of his ears nibbled, the way his face and neck flushed when desire raged within him.

It was as if they lived two very distinct lives. Outwardly, he was Viscount Stanton, correct in every way, paying court to his intended. The minute he crossed the threshold of Charles Street, however, he became Frank, enslaved to his passion for Charlotte.

Once their passion was sated, they would lie together in bed and talk softly, sharing parts of themselves to the other. One such afternoon, Charlotte lay on her back while Frank's hands roamed idly over her breasts. Out of the blue, she asked, "Did I ever tell you about my good friend Ruth?"

"Is this the one going to America? Yes, you did."

"Oh yes, now I remember. I was thoroughly lectured on the perils of disclosing my friendship with her."

"I'm sorry," murmured Frank. "That was incredibly pompous of me."

"No, it wasn't. You meant well. I am sure the fine people of the ton would not understand a gentlewoman befriending a farmer's daughter." With a sigh, she added, "Ruth sails on the Hibernia to New York on the seventh of next month. After which, I do not know when or if I shall ever hear from her again."

Frank dropped a kiss on Charlotte's collar bone, then her neck. "I am sorry," he said. "It is hard to say goodbye to someone who is more family to you than a friend."

"Yes, she is that. You know, in a way, I do envy Ruth. She and her brother Robert are taking their fate into their own hands and deciding to forge ahead towards their objective. I on the other hand, am stuck, with very little power to do much to change my fate beyond accepting or rejecting a marriage proposal. I wish sometimes I could be more like Ruth, and bravely go forth towards my destiny."

Frank let out a long breath. "I wish that too, sometimes. My life has been shaped by what father wants for me or what society expects from me as the Earl of Stanton's heir. I dream at times of what it would be like to be an ordinary Mr Stanton, with no title or great fortune, free to decide my fate."

Charlotte stared. "Frank, I do believe we are not too dissimilar, you and I. We are both trapped. Myself in poverty and dependence on my relatives, and you in your father's great wealth and power. Neither of us are free, are we?"

"I suppose not," he agreed reluctantly. "But let us not become morbid. We are here for happy memories, are we not? Then I think, I would much rather do this." And he started kissing his way down her lush, smooth body.

The days flew by until two weeks had passed since that first time they made love. There was no sign that Frank's hunger for Charlotte was waning—quite the opposite. He occasionally wondered how he was going to wean himself from his craving for her. Then he would push the thought aside. When the time came, he would deal with it. In any case, the longer this went on, the more likely it was that his naturally fickle nature would bring things to a close.

On a bright morning in late May, two missives sat on the breakfast salver, the franking on both indicating they had come from Stanton Hall. Frank opened the first. It was from Jasper, who as promised, had made a penitent return to the family home. In the letter, he wrote that after abasing himself in confession and promising to mend his ways, he had earned his father's forgiveness. For his part, the earl had contented himself with a few acerbic words and a threat to halve Jasper's allowance if this occurrence were to be repeated. Frank snorted. On balance, he thought his brother had gotten off lightly.

Frank read on, frowning as he came to the following passage.

I should warn you, Frank, that father has talked incessantly of your forthcoming nuptials. He has taken it into his head to go to London this week, despite his repugnance for the city's putrid air, in order to nudge things along. Expect his arrival, and mine, by mid-week. And if I were a betting man, which I am by the way, then I would bet that the announcement of your engagement to Miss Powell would ensue shortly afterwards.

Gird yourself dear brother and send my best wishes to Charlotte. You know, don't you, that it is not too late to change your mind and choose her over Miss Powell as your bride. That's what I would do, but there again, I have never had a massive fortune and dad's approbation dangled over my head. Whatever you decide, you have my lasting support and love.

Yours,

Jasper Stanton

With hands that were not quite steady, Frank opened the second missive. In it, the earl stated his intention to decamp to London by the middle of the week and his wish to hold a dinner party on Thursday 1st June, inviting the Powells and the Mortons. He instructed Frank to have the invitations sent out and to arrange with the cook and housekeeping staff a suitably impressive meal with a good set of wines. The subtext of the letter made it clear that the earl expected an engagement to be announced shortly thereafter.

Frank put the letter down, his chest suddenly feeling constricted. It had to happen eventually, he told himself. This was no surprise, yet it felt like a wrench. There was less than a week to go before he had to end his relationship with Charlotte. Good God, how was he to do it?

He recalled Jasper's words. It was not too late to change his mind and ask Charlotte to marry him. Could he do it? He closed his eyes and imagined how that would play out. Every time he envisioned telling his father he would not be marrying Miss Powell but would be proposing to Charlotte Harding instead, he balked. It was an impossibility. This could send his father into an apoplexy—perhaps even be the death of him. There was no earthly way the earl would accept Charlotte as his daughter-in-law. Frank would become estranged from his own father and perhaps be dispossessed.

Would such an upheaval of his life be worth the trouble? He was still in the throes of his desire for Charlotte, but he was not known for his constancy. A few months or a year down the line, when the passion had finally run its course, he could rue the day he gave up everything for her.

Scrubbing a hand over his eyes, he stood and took a deep breath, his breakfast uneaten. There was nothing for it but to end things with Charlotte as amicably as possible and then to do his duty. He would settle down to a life of domestication with Helena Powell. Once married and in possession of a large chunk of his fortune, he would be free to live life on his own terms, for there would be little more the earl could do to exert his power over his son. This marriage would emancipate him. That is what he told himself anyway. He ignored the persistent little voice that said that far from being free, he would be entering a gilded cage.

The day passed with interminable slowness. He made a social call to the Powells, visited the Stanton town house to begin the arrangements for the earl's arrival, called on his man of business and even managed a bout at his boxing club. All the while, he counted the minutes until three o'clock.

Inside the house on Charles Street, he waited by the door for the four knocks that would signal Charlotte's arrival. When they finally came, he whipped the door open and pulled her inside. A moment later, he was upon her, ripping the bonnet from her head and pushing her against the back of the door.

"Frank!" she cried, startled at the vehemence of his welcome.

He didn't reply. Instead, he dug his fingers into her hair, uncaring of the pins that fell to the floor, and brought his mouth to hers in a bruising kiss. As he did so, he pressed the hardness in his groin to her, making her feel his intense, raging need. "If you don't undress right this minute," he snarled, "so help me God I will rip the clothes off you!"

With that, he released her and began to tear off his own clothing with wild, disjointed hands. After a moment's hesitation, she followed suit. With trembling fingers, she undid the fastenings of her dress and threw it over her head. Her shoes, corset, chemise and pantalettes came off next. As she bent to pull down her stockings, he stopped her. "That's good enough," he grunted, and took her back into his arms. Without the barrier of clothes this time, he ground his hard cock into the softness of her belly as he took her mouth in another punishing kiss.

Other females might have taken exception to such brutish treatment. Not her. She revelled in his need, which only matched her own. With two firm hands, she drew his head to hers, raking through his dishevelled hair, and plundered his mouth. "Frank," she sighed as he trailed a path of kisses down her neck, "I have such need of you."

He sucked in the hardened nipple of one breast, letting it out with a squelching sound. "Then hold tight, for I mean to have you against this door."

With the strength honed from hours upon hours of sparring at his boxing club, he put two hands to her buttocks and lifted her against the door so his cock was at the right height to enter her slick, tight cunt. "Spread your legs, Charlotte, and let me in!" he hissed. She did as asked, and with one forceful thrust, he plunged inside her to the hilt.

"Ah!" they both cried in unison.

He pulled out and plunged again even more forcefully, his teeth gritted and his face set in a grimace. "This cunt," he cried in between thrusts, "is mine!" And he set to a punishing rhythm, driving in and out while she held on to him for dear life.

She gasped with every thrust. "All yours," she breathed.

"Damn right!"

He nailed her to the door, hammering his need of her. He was not gentle. Nor did she want him to be. And when the time came, they both reached their climax as one. With loud cries, they pulsed their pleasure, her cunt tightening around his cock in sweet agony while he released his seed deep inside her. In that moment, no force could have wrenched him from her. He held her tight to him, burying his face in the crook of her neck.

Eventually, he regained his senses enough to lower her gently to her feet. The action caused his cock to withdraw from her cunt, and a gush of cum spilled down her thighs. He watched it in savage satisfaction. In the recesses of his mind, he knew he had done wrong and taken an unacceptable risk, but he could not find it in himself to regret what had just happened between them. He dropped a kiss to her mouth. "Stay here, sweet girl, and I will get a cloth to clean you."

He flew up the stairs to their bedchamber and came out a moment later bearing a dampened cloth. Back at her side, he knelt and wiped her clean. "There you go," he smiled. "As good

187

as new." He stood and held out his hand. "Come, let us go to our bed for a while."

He led her upstairs to their room and pulled down the bed covers. Pausing only to throw the cloth on to the table, he went to lie beside her. She turned to face him. "Frank, do not get me wrong, for I enjoyed that immensely, but what on earth is the matter?"

"I am sorry if I was rough with you, and for not pulling out when I should have. If a child results of this, I promise you will be well cared for."

She gave an impatient huff. "You have not answered me. I know something is the matter. What is it?"

He took her hand and kissed it, then brought it back down with a sigh. "I have had word from father. He intends to come to London mid-week and to hold a dinner party for the Powells—by the by, the Mortons are invited; that means you too. He expects me to propose and to have the engagement announced before his return to the country." Frank traced a gentle finger along Charlotte's cheek to her lips. "You know what this will mean. Very soon, we shall have to end this affair between us."

Charlotte did not reply, making her own explorations of his face with her fingers. At last, she said in almost a whisper, "We expected this."

"Yes."

She gave a sad little laugh. "We have achieved what we wanted from this affair of ours, have we not? I for one have memories galore to take with me."

"I would have liked to make more."

"Life is not always about what we would like."

He grimaced. "That much is true."

"So, was this our last time?"

He drew her to him, running a hand down the velvet softness of her back. "Call me selfish Charlotte, but I am not ready to let you go just yet. We have until Thursday. I wish to see you every day until then."

"Then we shall make it so."

Chapter 27

On her return to the Mortons' townhouse, Charlotte was surprised to learn that Frederick was back in residence. After a hasty toilette in her room, she came down to find him comfortably ensconced in the drawing room by his mother's side, regaling her with stories of Edwin. He stood when Charlotte entered the room and greeted her warmly, "Charlotte, it is good to see you."

"And you, Frederick," she smiled.

"You are looking well. London life agrees with you it seems." Then he frowned as he noticed something on her face. "What has happened to your lip? There is a cut on it."

Charlotte touched her finger to it, remembering the rough bite of Frank's teeth as he had pushed her against the door. Thinking quickly, she replied, "It is nothing, just a moment of carelessness on my part which resulted in a book falling over my head."

"You must take greater care, Charlotte," he said sternly.

"I will. Do you remain with us long?"

"I'm afraid not. I have a meeting with my man of business tomorrow and must pay a visit to the bank, then I promised Harriet to come straight back. After our recent worries, she does not like to be left long alone."

"The poor dear," said Mrs Morton. "She is understandably still shook from Edwin's illness. I believe, Frederick, that I will cut short my stay in London and return to Stanbourne in a week or two. I wait only until the announcement of dear Helena's engagement to Frank."

"Has he proposed?" asked Frederick curiously.

"Not yet, but from what I hear, it is imminent. Perhaps you do not know that Earl Stanton will be arriving in town this week and holding a dinner party in Helena's honour. I expect to hear of an engagement soon after."

"Nice girl. He could do a lot worse," remarked Frederick.

"She is a delightful girl—beautiful, accomplished and of excellent parentage. I think it will be a splendid match."

Charlotte sat quietly, listening to this painful conversation until Frederick drew her in. "What think you of it, Charlotte?"

"I—I do not know. They appear well matched in looks, wealth and breeding."

Frederick chuckled, "And of course that is all that matters in the affairs of such grand people. I count myself lucky that I was able to marry my Harriet for other, better reasons, for you know, she is a parson's daughter with little cachet in society."

"Are you not rich too, Frederick?" wondered Charlotte.

"I am comfortable enough, but nothing on the same scale as the Stantons, and I am a mere commoner with no title. I do believe that the huge Stanton patrimony is a yoke around Frank's neck. Much rather him than me."

"Nonsense," rebuked his mother. "He should count himself lucky to be so well endowed and win the hand of so lovely a girl as Helena."

"I'm sure he shall," smiled Frederick, soothing Mrs Morton's ruffled feathers.

The conversation drifted to other matters then, as Frederick and Mrs Morton talked of Edwin and his fortunate recovery. Charlotte only half listened. A residual pain remained in her heart at the thought of Frank's impending marriage, but she told herself to be strong and to bear it. As always, she would endure.

The week flew by. Each day, Charlotte and Frank stole precious moments together to make love with ferocious, ardent passion. All too soon, however, it was Thursday. Charlotte arrived one last time at the house on Charles Street. This would be a brief assignation, for the earl had informed Frank that he

191

should get to the Stanton townhouse no later than five o'clock. Matters were to be discussed prior to the dinner party guests making their appearance. So, for this last tryst, they would only have one hour.

Charlotte knocked four times, and an instant later, the door opened. Unlike before, Frank did not pull her roughly to him. Instead, he held out his hand and walked her silently up to the room. Inside, they undressed with care until they were both totally bare. They stood facing one another, taking an inventory of each other's body. Frank's eyes caressed the delicate line of Charlotte's shoulders, the roundness of her breasts, the soft skin of her belly and brown wisps of hair on her mound. Charlotte's eyes embraced the broadness of his chest, the fine black hair that adorned it and the majesty of his cock nestling proudly in the dark curls of his groin. She made a concerted effort to imprint this sight on her memory.

Finally, Frank said, "Come to bed."

They climbed on to the bed and came together, legs entwining, arms holding the other close. Charlotte raised her lips to his and they kissed, long and leisurely. "After today," she murmured, "I will be Miss Harding to you, Charlotte no longer."

He chuckled, "You will always be sweet wanton Charlotte in my mind."

"We will still see each other every now and then. Your family is close to the Mortons, so we cannot avoid being in each other's presence—although you will be with your wife. I shall have to learn to think of you as Viscount Stanton, not as Frank who ravished me in this bed."

"Ah," Frank kissed her nose lightly, "but wasn't the purpose of this affair to amass sweet memories?"

"I will unwrap those memories when I am alone in my bed at night. Other times, they shall remain firmly locked away."

He nuzzled the soft skin of her neck. "I do not know how easy it will be to do it, but I think you are right. I cannot be envisioning your naked beauty each time I look across the dining table at you. I hope in time, it will become easier."

Charlotte placed a hand above his heart. "Frank, I want to say this to you one last time, and then we can put it out of our minds. Thank you for these happy weeks we have had together. I have loved you fiercely. I do love you. And because I do, I wish you only happiness, even if it is with Miss Powell and not with me."

He trapped her hand, letting her feel the hammering of his own heart. "Charlotte, my darling. I know not of love. I have not been known for my constancy and I cannot say truly if what I feel for you is love, but I have never cared for another woman the way I care for you. I will always be grateful that you gave yourself to me these short few weeks. And I also wish you only happiness. I want you to come to me if ever you are in need, for I shall always be your friend."

"Make love to me, Frank."

Gently, he brought his body over hers, bracketing her head with his elbows. His face swooped down to capture her lips just as he pushed his cock into her welcome heat. For this last time, they made love slowly, purposefully. In between kisses, they stared into each other's eyes as their bodies were joined. Frank felt the contractions of Charlotte's cunt as she reached the culmination of her pleasure.

With a wrench of regret, he pulled out and spilled his cum over her belly. Then with a sigh, he went to get a cloth and cleaned her. Just before he stood again to dress, he dropped his head between her legs and kissed her deeply in that most intimate part, tasting the residue of his cum and hers. Then without a word, he got up and dressed. She too stood and dressed in silence. When they were done, they walked downstairs slowly, hand in hand. At the door, he kissed her one last time, still silent, for there was nothing more to say. With a final stroke of her cheek, he opened the door and let her leave.

Chapter 28

The earl gazed with satisfaction and pride at his eldest son who sat across from him in his study. They had just spent a half hour discussing settlements, proposed wedding dates and honeymoon destinations. The earl was prepared to be generous. The papers had already been drawn up with his man of business. As part of the wedding settlement, Francis would receive a good half of the Stanton land, including a large country house—Netherwick Hall—which stood in its own extensive acreage, not ten miles from Stanton Hall.

It would be a fitting place in which to establish himself and his new wife. Altogether, these lands would give Francis an income exceeding £15,000 a year in addition to that paltry estate he had inherited from his mother.

"You have done me proud, Francis. All that I have asked of you, you have accomplished, and you have shown yourself worthy of the title that will be yours one day."

"Thank you sir," replied the viscount. "I have always strived to merit your approval, though at times, it felt sadly elusive."

"It was to build up your character, Francis, and look how well it worked."

The viscount nodded. "I see that now."

"Miss Powell will make an excellent wife for you. I have made extensive checks as to the Powells, their character, their breeding and their connections, as well as made several enquiries as to how well Miss Powell is regarded in their locality. I have looked into her childhood friends, her education, her charitable works. Believe me when I say I have left no stone unturned to ensure you achieve the right marriage. This will be the making of you, Francis, not just in your private endeavours but also in your public life. As a married man, with a wife such as Miss Powell at your side, you will be well placed to seek advancement in government or in the civil service. I have several ideas for you, which we can discuss further when you are back from your honeymoon."

The earl failed to notice how his son's face paled at these words and how one hand tightened into a fist. He continued blithely, "I will let you go now to get yourself ready for dinner. Our guests arrive in an hour. Know that I plan to invite Sir Horace up to my study after the meal, where the three of us may discuss this proposed marriage."

The viscount nodded again. "Yes sir," then stood and took his leave.

•———————————•

Charlotte and Mrs Morton arrived on the stroke of seven at the Stanton townhouse. They stood in the magnificent entrance hall, waiting to be announced, gazing up at the sparkling crystal chandeliers, the decorative mouldings and a life sized portrait of the previous earl. This was opulence on a scale Charlotte had rarely seen before. She had known, of course, that the Stantons were very rich, but this fact had not been brought home to her in quite such a manner as now.

"Mrs Morton, Miss Harding," announced the butler, opening the double doors to usher them in.

With a pounding heart, Charlotte walked in behind Mrs Morton, her eyes searching the vast room. In the centre, she saw a tall grey-haired gentleman who bore a striking resemblance to Frank—his father no doubt. Beside him stood Sir Horace and his lady. To the right of them was Frank, and beside him, looking remarkably beautiful, was Miss Powell. Further along to the left of the earl, a little apart from everyone, stood Jasper Stanton.

It was he that came forward first, a sunny smile on his face. "Aunt Margaret," he said, embracing Mrs Morton. Turning to Charlotte, he bowed. "Miss Harding, I am delighted to see you

195

looking so well. Let me introduce you to my father." In a whisper, he added, "Just remember, his bark is worse than his bite."

Mrs Morton was first to curtsy to the earl and the others present, after which it was Charlotte's turn. "Father," said Jasper. "This is Miss Harding, who is currently staying with her aunt, Mrs Morton."

Charlotte curtsied and murmured, "An honour to make your acquaintance, my lord."

The earl bowed formally and inspected her from head to toe with a frown. "Are you perchance Hugh Harding's daughter?" he demanded.

"Yes, my lord."

"And that Spanish woman he had the misfortune to marry?"

"I would not call it a misfortune, my lord, but yes, my mother hailed from Spain."

"Hmph. You look nothing like her."

Charlotte's eyes flew to his in surprise. "You knew my mother?"

"I was a colonel in the army before I acceded to the title upon my older brother's passing—in the same regiment as Hugh. In fact I was there when he first met the beautiful Juana. All the officers were vying for her attention. I think that snake of a father of hers brought her along with him purposely to be a distraction while he swindled us with his overpriced grain. Though I must say, I was surprised when it was Hugh that won her favour, for he was never one for the ladies—his head always buried in a book. But she set her cap at him, and he fell for it, more fool him."

At these words, Charlotte stiffened. "I will have you know, my lord, that you are speaking ill of my mother, for whom I have a high regard."

"I tell it the way it is, Miss Harding," responded the earl coldly. He sat back in his chair, clearly dismissing her.

"Come sit beside me," urged Jasper, and he led her to his side of the room, out of earshot from the rest. She cast one last glance at Frank, whose eyes were fixed on hers, and followed Jasper. "Don't mind my father," he said quietly as they settled on a yellow brocade settee.

"I had not realised he knew my parents."

"Nor had I. Your mother was quite unforgettable, by the sounds of it."

"She was, and I do not like her character to be impugned, for I have never known a better Christian than she."

"I do not doubt it, Charlotte. Now, on to other matters. How goes it with you and my brother? I have not had a chance to talk with him since arriving."

Charlotte looked down at her hands, held tightly in her lap. "It is all over with us. We said our goodbyes, and he is set now to propose to Miss Powell."

Jasper snorted, "More fool him!"

Charlotte gazed at him in surprise. "You do not approve of the match?"

"I have learned, Charlotte, that there is little happiness to be found in following my father's wishes—but Frank was always the obedient one."

"Well I hope for his sake he does find happiness," murmured Charlotte.

"I hope so too. Now, I am going to make it my business to distract you from that spectacle over there. We need some light-hearted fun."

"I am all for being distracted. What do you have in mind?"

"Fancy accompanying me tomorrow to the races? It's the Epsom Derby."

Charlotte's face lit up. "I would love to!"

"Then that's what we shall do. I will speak to Aunt Margaret about it this evening, but I'm sure she will raise no objections. I'll come pick you up in Frank's curricle, which has been returned, good as new. And I promise to avoid any mishap on the road."

"I do not need any convincing," replied Charlotte with a smile.

From across the room, Frank watched jealously as Charlotte and Jasper engaged in a lively conversation. He trusted his brother and knew he was not flirting with her, but nevertheless he envied their blithe conviviality. With an effort, he brought his gaze back to Miss Powell, who looked exceptionally fine tonight. He should be content. This lovely young lady would soon be his if all went as planned. He had finally won his father's approval. Soon, he would be in possession of a large fortune. Most others would envy him. He was the most fortunate of men.

The evening dragged on. They sat through an elaborate meal of ten courses, then the men lingered over their port. That was when the earl suggested Sir Horace join him upstairs in the library. Frank followed them, taking a seat beside Sir Horace. The earl did not beat about the bush. In a forthright tone, he spoke, "Sir Horace, I am sure you have an inkling as to why I wished a private audience with you. I am hoping for a match between Francis here and your lovely daughter. They have had some time to get to know each other, and to decide whether or not they would suit. I know you too have had an opportunity to get to know my son, so I ask you. Do you have any objections to Francis paying his addresses to Miss Powell?"

Sir Horace regarded Frank thoughtfully before answering the earl, "My lord, I have had an opportunity to get well acquainted with Viscount Stanton and to observe his manner with my daughter. After her unfortunate injury, he was everything that one could ask for in solicitousness. I can have no objection to a match between him and my daughter, though of course I cannot vouch for her answer were he to propose."

"Sir Horace," began Frank, "I thank you for your kind words. It would be a great honour to have Miss Powell as my wife, and I would like to call on you tomorrow morning, if I may, and put my suit to your daughter."

Sir Horace smiled kindly, "I have no objection to that, viscount. Do your best, but know that Helena has a mind of her own. I cannot say whether or not she will welcome your suit with any degree of certainty."

Frank nodded. "That is how it should be. I look forward to paying my addresses and discovering the truth of her feelings for me."

"Then it is decided," said the earl. "Tomorrow, Francis will propose and should Miss Powell accept, we shall meet again to discuss settlements. I will have you know, Sir Horace, that I am prepared to be extremely generous in the lands I settle on my son in the event of his marriage."

"While that is of course good to know," replied Sir Horace, "my object is to see Helena settled happily with a spouse that will show her care and affection, as well as provide well for her."

"I assure you that she will want for nothing should she do me the honour of becoming my wife," said the viscount, and he meant those words. On his marriage, he would endeavour to be as good a husband to Helena as he could, giving her his fidelity, his care and his affection. Perhaps in time love too would grow. An image of Charlotte came into his mind, but he resolutely pushed it away. His course was set. He would not deviate from it.

Chapter 29

The following morning, Jasper arrived as promised to take Charlotte to the races. He helped her up into the curricle, and soon they were on their way. The day was warm and partly sunny, with a light breeze to keep them from overheating. Throughout the journey, they conversed like old friends. It was strange how easy she found Jasper's company. It was as if they were indeed the kin he claimed them to be.

They stopped along the way for a light repast, then continued on their journey, arriving at Epsom race course a little before noon. The place was heaving with a crush of carriages, curricles and phaetons. Jasper helped Charlotte down and found a young groom to care for his horses, handing him a shilling for his troubles. With Charlotte on his arm, he made his way through the jostling crowd, purchasing a ticket for the two of them in the stands—for neither of them had any notion of joining the uppity folk sitting above.

"Let us go place a bet," suggested Jasper. They went to find the betting clerk, looking at the list of horses and the odds against them. "I think I shall place a shilling on Bay Middleton," decided Jasper. "How about you Charlotte? Here is a shilling for you to bet with."

Charlotte frowned in concentration, then made her decision. "I will bet on Mundig," she said.

The bets were made and receipts written out. Jasper pocketed them then went to look for some refreshments, returning laden with a bottle of lemonade, two glasses and spiced buns for each of them. "Come along, Charlotte," he said. "Let us find ourselves a good spot from which to watch the races." With some deft manoeuvring, he steered her to a good vantage point a little way along at the front of the stands.

They stood happily watching the first heats of the race, munching on their buns and sipping their lemonade. Charlotte felt carefree, almost forgetting the pain of her loss. With Jasper's close resemblance to his brother, it was as if she remained connected to Frank somehow, even though he was now well out of her reach.

It was a few races in that they found themselves being hailed by a gentleman standing a little way from them. "Well if isn't Jasper Stanton," he called.

Jasper turned, and on recognising the gentleman, grinned in delight. "Oliver Stanley as I live and breathe!" he cried.

The gentleman in question made his way over to them, clapping Jasper on the shoulder. "I had not expected to see you here, Jasper. Were you not at Oxford?"

Jasper made a face. "I have been rusticated, Ollie, but let us not talk of it." Turning to Charlotte, he said, "This is Oliver Stanley, a very good friend from Eton. Ollie, let me introduce you to Miss Harding, a kinswoman of mine."

Oliver bowed with a flourish. "At your service, ma'am." He was lean and dark, with slightly crooked features that gave him a charming, rakish air. Over the next hour, he regaled Charlotte with entertaining tales of their antics at Eton. His manner was so easy and friendly, that Charlotte soon lost her reserve. As she became comfortable in his company, her natural ebullience and good humour emerged. She laughed and joked, sharing her own tales of childhood pranks—for there had been a good many with Robbie and Ruth as conspirators—and was such an entertaining companion that Oliver was soon charmed by her.

A hush came over the crowd as the final race of the day was announced. Charlotte, Jasper and Ollie watched eagerly from the front of the stands, cheering on the different horses they had placed their bets on. All of a sudden, from the back of the race, a single horse and rider began to work their way to the front. "It's Mundig!" cried Charlotte beside herself with excitement. She watched them with baited breath as they edged closer and closer to the front, urging them on. It was a close call, but at the very last moment, Mundig nosed ahead into first place. Charlotte jumped in elation. "My horse won!" she exclaimed.

Jasper watched her in amusement. "So it did. Let us go collect your winnings."

It took some effort to weave through the crowd and find the betting clerk, but eventually, Charlotte was the proud recipient of two shillings, one of which she immediately gave to Jasper as a payback for the initial loan. He refused to take it, however. "It's all yours Charlotte. Do with it what you will, but we should be heading back to town now, before it gets late."

They said their goodbyes to Ollie, Charlotte promising him a dance at the following day's ball being held at Lord and Lady Beaumont's house. It would be Charlotte's last ball of the season before she returned to Stanbourne with Mrs Morton. Then, spirits flying high, they got into the curricle and began their journey back to London. They talked animatedly about the day's events, then fell into companiable silence until their arrival at the Mortons' townhouse. Jasper helped Charlotte to dismount and walked her to the door. She turned to him. "Thank you, Jasper. That was the best day out, so good in fact that it almost made me forget my woes."

He beamed, "That was the objective. Though it should be me thanking you, for you are capital company. I had great fun! Good evening, Charlotte. I hope to see you at the ball tomorrow."

"Good evening."

———•———————•———

Frank's day had been decidedly different. In the morning, as promised, he paid a call on the Powells and was given a private audience with Helena. He bowed over her hand then took a seat at her side. "Miss Powell," he said, "it cannot come as a great surprise to know why I am here this morning. I have come to ask if you would do me the very great honour to be my wife. Should you say yes, you would make me the happiest of men."

Miss Powell flushed rosily but surprised him with her response, "Viscount Stanton, may I ask you one thing?"

"Of course."

"Are you in love with me?"

He looked down at his polished boots, then raised his eyes to hers. "I care very much for you," he said gently, "and I hope in time my great affection will grow into love. I do promise that I will do everything in my power to be a good husband to you and ensure your happiness."

"I see," she said. There was a pause as the viscount waited for her to continue. Finally, she spoke, "I too feel great affection for you, viscount, but I am not in love. I believe that we stand as much chance at felicity as others who do profess their love, and as long as I have your promise to always to be truthful with me, then my answer is yes, I will marry you."

The viscount took her hand and kissed it. "I give you my word, Helena."

"Then tell me this, Frank. Is Lady Caroline Drake your mistress?"

"This is a delicate matter, Helena, and not something that should concern you."

"But if I am to be your wife, then it does concern me, and you have promised to be truthful. So, tell me."

He sighed, "She was my mistress for a brief time, but no longer. It has been several weeks now since we parted ways."

"And have you had another mistress since?"

He hesitated, then honoured her with the truth. "Yes, Helena, but that too is over."

"I have not heard rumours about this other person. Who might she be?"

"I cannot betray her trust by telling you, Helena, but believe me when I say that it is over, and that I plan to be faithful to you from this day forward."

Helena scrutinised his face for several moments in silence. "I see. I think we shall deal well with each other."

He stood and so did she. Gently, he drew her to him and kissed her lips. It was a chaste kiss, nothing like the ravenous hunger of Charlotte's kisses. *Damnation!* Why was he thinking of her now? He tried to dismiss these thoughts and keep all his attention on the lovely lady in his arms. Her skin was soft and fragrant, but it felt foreign to him. Instead, he craved that familiar scent of orange blossoms and feminine musk that was uniquely Charlotte's. Cursing himself inwardly, he stepped back and smiled, "Well then, let us break the good news to your family."

Chapter 30

Next evening, Mrs Morton and Charlotte made their entrance at the Beaumont ball among a thrum of other guests. They greeted their hosts then wandered over to the large ballroom where the strains of a quadrille could be heard playing. Charlotte was dressed in the white satin gown she had last worn at Almack's, her hair piled above her head in artfully designed curls. She was glad to look her best on this, her last ball of the season.

"Let us see if we can locate the Powells," said Mrs Morton, and Charlotte dutifully cast her eyes around the ballroom for them, knowing full well that Viscount Stanton would be in attendance with them now that he was affianced to Helena. She caught sight of him at the same moment that he saw her. They stared at each other across the room, the viscount's mouth pressed into a thin line.

"There they are," said Charlotte, and she guided Mrs Morton towards that part of the ballroom where they stood. A few moments later, they had reached the Powells and made their hellos.

The viscount bowed curtly as Charlotte dipped a small curtsy, but that was all the attention he gave her. Quickly, he turned to his intended bride and said, "Helena my dear, will you do me the honour of this dance?"

"Of course, my lord," she dimpled at him.

Without further ado, he swept her off to take their positions for the quadrille. Charlotte followed them with her eyes, unable to stop the lancing pain in her chest. "*I must get used to this,*" she told herself sternly. She would be encountering the viscount and his bride often enough in days and months to come. Seeing the man she loved with another should become so common an occurrence that over time, the pain would be blunted.

She stood with her older companions, paying desultory attention to their conversation. Lady Powell was in her element, having achieved the match of the season for her daughter. Although the announcement had not yet been made in The Times, it was common enough knowledge among the ton that Helena Powell had nabbed its most eligible bachelor.

Charlotte was jolted out of her reverie by Lady Powell addressing her, "Such a pity, Charlotte, that Mr Hodge's interest in you seemed to wane all of a sudden. I do wonder what caused it, as I had high hopes we could have been celebrating two sets of nuptials this season."

Something made Charlotte retort, "Lady Powell, the explanation is simple. I told Mr Hodge that I did not welcome his suit, and he very kindly obliged me by ceasing his visits."

Lady Powell stared at her in shock. "Whyever would you do that?"

"I may be poor and plain, Lady Powell, but even I am sensible to feelings. I did not want to spend the rest of my days with a man that evinced in me a sense of disgust."

"Do you prefer then to end your days a spinster, your future unsure?"

"As you so kindly point out, both sets of choices are stark, but on balance I would prefer not to be bound to someone for whom I could never feel the least shred of affection."

Lady Powell glared at her in disapproval. "Do you hear that, Margaret? I do believe the poor girl has lost her senses."

"Let her be, Julia," said Mrs Morton, surprising Charlotte. "She is young still, and there may be other suitors that come her way. In the meantime, I am happy to have my lovely niece's company. She has been such a comfort to me, especially during that difficult time when Edwin was sick."

"I only have her best interests at heart, Margaret," huffed Lady Powell, still much put out.

"As do I," smiled Mrs Morton. "Come now, Charlotte, and get yourself a dance card. This is your last ball of the season, and I mean you to dance."

With this, Mrs Morton marched her towards the master of ceremonies and obtained a dance card for her. "Now as to a dance partner," she said, looking around the ballroom. Suddenly, she spied Rupert Weston a few feet away. "Just the person!" she cried and waved him over.

A moment later, Rupert was bowing to both ladies. "Mrs Morton, Miss Harding, a pleasure as always."

"Mr Weston," said Mrs Morton firmly. "This is Miss Harding's last ball of the season as we shall be returning to the country within the week. I am determined she must have as many dances as possible. Would you be a dear and help fill out her dance card?"

Rupert smiled, "Of course. Miss Harding, will you reserve the next country dance for me?"

"I will," replied Charlotte, touched and ashamed all at once. She appreciated her aunt's efforts but did not wish to feel like a charity case. Nevertheless, she took out her dance card and jotted down his name.

"Excellent," said Mrs Morton in satisfaction. "Mr Weston, if you will excuse us, we must mingle a little more and add dance partners on Charlotte's card."

He bowed. "I shall return to claim my dance in due course, Miss Harding."

"Thank you. I look forward to it."

Mrs Morton was as good as her word. They mingled, and soon Mr Hurst had added his name to the list of dance partners. It was then that they were joined by Jasper Stanton, in the company of Oliver Stanley. Introductions were made and dances eagerly booked. Jasper claimed the cotillion and the next quadrille, while Oliver put dibs on both the gavotte and the waltz. With surprise, Charlotte glanced at her dance card to see it had been completely filled. Not one dance would she sit out on her last ball. Before long, Mr Weston was back to take Charlotte to the ballroom floor.

"It has been a while since I last conversed with you, Miss Harding," he said as they took their positions for the country dance. "Tell me, how have you been enjoying your stay in London? Has the great metropolis lost its shine at all or are you still impressed with it?"

She laughed, "I adore it still, though I own I will be glad to return to the peaceful quiet of the country."

"That I do understand," he replied and moved along in the dance line. They talked again at sporadic intervals, and Charlotte began to enjoy herself in the simple pleasure of dancing, which was after all one of her favourite pastimes.

The evening flew by as she flitted from partner to partner. She laughed merrily with Jasper and enjoyed a light flirtation with Oliver Stanley. She knew instinctively that it was harmless flirting and that he meant nothing by it, but it was a balm to her soul nevertheless. She caught brief glimpses of the viscount here and there, and each affectionate smile she saw him give to Miss Powell pierced her heart. After a few such glimpses, she decided it was best to look away and try to avoid sightings of him as much as possible. That chapter in her life was over.

Soon, it was time for the waltz. As she went to take her position with Ollie for the dance, she could not help but catch sight of the viscount placing his arm around Miss Powell's waist. He looked across at her in that moment, and at her dance partner, his eyes blazing. She looked away. She was not going to put herself through any additional heartache if she could help it. What was done was done, and she and the viscount were over. She had to be strong and firm in her resolve. After all, she had gotten what she wanted out of the affair—three glorious weeks that would live in her memories forever. She should not be greedy and hanker for more.

Instead, she smiled up at Ollie as he took her hand in his and the opening strains of the waltz began. How flattering, on her last ball of the season, to waltz in the arms of such a good looking gentleman. Putting a hand to her waist, he said, "I hope you will keep up, Miss Harding, for I mean us to fly across this ballroom floor."

She laughed, "I will but try, though I warn you that this is only the third waltz I have ever danced."

"Ouch!" he cried. "Never mind, just follow my lead." And with that, they were off. Ollie was not jesting when he claimed they would fly across the ballroom floor. With high exuberance, he twirled Charlotte around, nearly to the point of dizziness. At first, she stumbled and struggled to keep up with his energetic steps, but eventually she picked up his rhythm, laughing breathlessly as he swung her around in his arms.

Spinning around more sedately were the viscount and Helena Powell. His face became set in forbidding lines as he observed Charlotte and her eager suitor enjoying themselves on the dancefloor. His eyes settled harshly on the hand around Charlotte's waist, noting the way that arrogant pup was holding her so closely. He ground his teeth in frustration while Helena looked up at him, her face creased in a puzzled frown. "Is all well with you, my lord?" she asked in concern.

He schooled his features with an effort and smiled, "Yes, my dear. I was only trying to remember the name of that gentleman dancing so energetically over there."

As they turned, she cast a quick glance their way and replied, "That is Oliver Stanley, Lord Stanley's younger brother."

Now he remembered. The young pup had been at Eton with Jasper, helping him get into all kinds of scrapes. His damned brother must have made the introductions. What on earth could Jasper have been thinking to make such a flirt known to Charlotte? He would have words with his irritating brother at the soonest opportunity. This Oliver Stanley might lead Charlotte astray, perhaps even proposition her. Newly acquainted with the joys of lovemaking, she would be ripe for the taking and innocently agree to another liaison. At this thought, the viscount's countenance turned thunderous.

Seeing it, Helena ventured to ask, "You do not approve of the gentleman?"

His nostrils flared. "I do not understand why Mrs Morton has allowed him to dance with Miss Harding. He had a reputation for wild behaviour when he was at Eton with my brother."

She glanced at them again, then said reassuringly, "I do not believe he means anything other than a light-hearted enjoyment of the dance, Frank. He can surely have no designs on Miss Harding." That latter was said with obvious disbelief that any young gentleman could harbour a desire for plain Charlotte Harding.

Frank's lips tightened. Now that his eyes were open to Charlotte's charms, he could see no reason why other males might not notice them too, and prey on her. His heart beat in a furiously anxious rhythm. Had he made a colossal mistake, ending his relationship with Charlotte? Cast adrift after their tumultuous affair, she was vulnerable, and he was unable to protect her. Perhaps he should have agreed to set her up as his mistress in her own home, lavishing her with an income so she was not reliant on her relatives—even if that would guarantee her fall from society's graces. He would have money aplenty to ensure her future, wouldn't he? Instead of being hellbent on fidelity, he could have come to an arrangement with Helena, keeping a mistress alongside his wife, as others did in the ton. Why had he not done so? What a fool he was!

Maybe it was not too late to change the terms of his relationship with Helena. She did not seem the overly sentimental type. All she asked for was honesty. He could make his confession and ask her to allow him a mistress, promising his discretion and continuing affection in the marriage. Yes, that was what he needed to do.

With Charlotte set up as his mistress, he could ensure that no other man dared make advances on her. He could keep her safe. Then, he could continue to enjoy making love to her anytime he wished, without having to make secretive trysts. He would purchase a house in a quiet London neighbourhood and establish Charlotte there. Would that not be better for her than to live an unfulfilled and uncertain life as a poor spinster reliant on the charity of her relatives? When not in London for the Season, he could have her live at Hartley Court, the small estate his mother had bequeathed him in Wiltshire. It was a two-hour ride at most from Netherwick Hall. He could go visit her there regularly.

The plan was forming in his mind. At the earliest opportunity, he would have a talk with Helena about changing the terms of their arrangement and keeping a mistress after their marriage. Once in possession of his fortune, he would be free to put it all into action. But first, he needed to get Charlotte well away from Oliver Stanley.

The waltz came to an end as these thoughts battled frantically in Frank's mind. He bowed to Helena and escorted her back to Sir Horace and Lady Powell's side. Then, with another bow, he excused himself. Darting his eyes across the ballroom, he looked for Charlotte and found her laughing gaily with Jasper and that rake, Oliver Stanley, as they partook of refreshments. With fire in his brown-eyed gaze, he began to make his way towards them, failing to notice Lady Caroline Drake's eyes following his trajectory with interest.

"Jasper," Frank hailed his brother upon reaching them. "How goes it with you?"

"I am well thank you. What brings you here Frank, when you should be at your future bride's side?" asked Jasper with an amused quirk to his lips.

"I shall return there shortly, never fear." Frank turned to greet Charlotte. "Miss Harding," he said, with an inclination of his head. Then, "Stanley," his expression going frosty.

Ollie grinned back irrepressibly, "Viscount Stanton, a pleasure to meet you again."

"That was quite a lively waltz you danced just now," remarked the viscount. "I do believe you have overexerted Miss Harding, for she is looking quite flushed."

She was, in fact, pink-cheeked, though this was only partly due to the exertions of the dance. "It is very warm in here," continued the viscount, "and we would not want you to faint, Miss Harding. Perhaps Jasper should take you out to the gardens for some fresh air."

"I would be happy to—" began Ollie, but then Jasper, with a quizzical expression, interrupted him.

"That's alright, Ollie. You are promised to Miss Cartwright for the next dance, are you not? Do not fret, I shall take Miss Harding out for a short breath of air outside." With a pointed glance at his brother, Jasper swept Charlotte away on his arm.

As they weaved their way through the crowded ballroom towards the back of the house where balcony doors opened onto the garden, Charlotte breathed, "Oh my. It is like the last time. I am sorry to have you forced into taking me out again, Jasper."

He patted her hand. "Not to worry, though I do wonder what Frank has in mind. I thought you said the two of you had ended this thing between you."

"We have," avowed Charlotte.

"Then why is he setting up this private encounter with you?"

"I do not know," responded Charlotte as they stepped out into the breezy moonlight.

They stood on the balcony, from which a set of steps went down to the garden. Other guests thronged the space, also taking in the fresh air on this warm summer evening. With aplomb, Jasper led Charlotte down the steps, saying loudly, "A good turn around the gardens will help you recover, Miss Harding, for you look mightily flushed."

Once at the bottom of the steps, he began to walk her away from the house, down a winding path surrounded on both sides by tall rose bushes, obscuring them from view. "I wonder how long it will take Frank to shake Ollie off and come looking for you," he wondered idly.

He was not to wonder for too long, for in less than a minute or two, a brisk stride heralded Frank's appearance. He came upon them, a sober expression in his eyes. "Charlotte, I need have words with you," he spoke firmly.

With an ironic lift of his brow, Jasper replied, "I shall leave you two lovebirds and go wait at the end of the path for Charlotte's return. Do not tarry Frank, or questions shall be asked."

Frank nodded, impatient for his brother to leave. A moment later, they were alone.

"Frank," murmured Charlotte. "What is it? I thought we had said all that needed saying."

He took her hands in his, drawing her close to his body. "No, there is more that needs to be said. Charlotte, I have been a fool. A stupid, blind fool. I should never have let you go."

At this, Charlotte's hopes, hidden deep within her soul, set themselves loose and flew to the surface. She gazed at him, her heart in her eyes. Was he finally going to declare himself? Ask her to be his wife, no matter the consequences? Her body trembled in his grasp.

"Charlotte, I want you to be my mistress permanently," he said quickly, dashing all her hopes.

"Oh," she replied, unable to say more.

He shook her gently. "Listen to me. Once I am married and in possession of my fortune, I can set you up in luxury. You will want for nothing, my sweet wanton girl. All the comforts you will have, and your future will be assured. I will be generous—you have my word on this. I shall give you the means to live in comfort for the rest of your days. What do you say?"

"I—I," she stuttered.

He smiled, stroking her cheek and running a finger along her quivering lips. "Say yes," he chided, but the opposite word came out of her mouth.

"No."

"No?" he questioned, his voice rising.

"I cannot do what you ask, Frank, even though, believe me I am so tempted. Consider how this would affect my aunt and my cousin. I could not repay their kindness by shaming the family. You know that by becoming your mistress openly as you describe, I would fall from grace and be a pariah in society. I could not do this, my love, not even for you."

He growled in irritation, "You would prefer to live a barren life as a spinster, your future uncertain, always reliant on the charity of others?"

"At least I would hold my head high. I could not tolerate the whispers and sneers of others, Frank, nor could I bear to hurt Aunt Margaret."

"She would get over it, and the whispers would only last a short time until the next scandal hit the news. Charlotte, my sweet, do you not long to tangle with me between the sheets and have my cock fill you? I could even plant my seed in your womb. Think of it! You and our children would be cared for. Every material need you would have, your future assured. I promise you." He pulled her to him then and brought his lips to hers in a hungry kiss.

Her mind held out against his offer, but her body could not resist him. She kissed him back. The feel and taste of him brought out a hunger in her such as she had never experienced before. Oh how she wanted him, craved him! It seemed he felt it too, for he consumed her with his mouth, his tongue brushing roughly against hers then sucking her essence frantically. His hands grasped her close, pinning her to his searching mouth. They were so in thrall to each other that they did not hear the soft footsteps approaching nor the low murmur of female voices.

Chapter 31

Jasper had been loitering by the first bend of the rose-lined path, wondering what his brother was up to. He hoped it was not anything that would embroil Charlotte in any trouble, for he had grown rather fond of her. His pulse quickened as he heard the sound of voices approaching. A moment later, the ladies were upon him—Lady Caroline Drake and with her, an older matron named Mrs Grantley.

"Mr Stanton," exclaimed Lady Caroline. "What are you doing standing here alone? Was not Miss Harding out with you for some fresh air?"

"Er—" His mind searched rapidly for an appropriate response. In the end, he said, "Yes, she is."

Lady Caroline looked left and right. "Where is she?"

"Umm, it is a delicate matter, Lady Caroline."

Mrs Grantley raised her brows at this. "Whatever can you mean, Mr Stanton?"

"Miss Harding was feeling unwell and, erm, she felt the need to run ahead behind the bushes to discharge what had been ailing her. I of course stayed behind to allow her a modicum of privacy. She will return shortly, and I will be sure to procure some lemonade to refresh her."

"Oh, the poor dear!" cried Mrs Grantley. "I had best go look for her."

"Oh no!" said Jasper quickly. "I do not think she would like having company in this moment of weakness."

"Nonsense," retorted Mrs Grantley. "If as you say she has been unwell, then I may help revive her with some *sal volatile.*" And with that, she marched ahead before Jasper could stop her, followed closely by a smirking Lady Caroline. Jasper had no choice but to follow at their heels, earnestly hoping that the sounds of their voices had warned Frank and Charlotte of their impending presence.

That hope was dashed when he heard Mrs Grantley exclaim, "What is the meaning of this?" A moment later, he saw what they had seen—Charlotte and Frank wrapped in a passionate embrace, only now pulling apart as they realised they were not alone. Charlotte's eyes filled with horror while Frank shot a fuming look at Lady Caroline. This was all her doing.

"Why you hussy!" cried Mrs Grantley in outrage. "The apple does not fall far from the tree it seems. A jezebel, just like your Spaniard mother!"

Lady Caroline clutched her hands dramatically. "Well I never!" she exclaimed.

All this was too much for poor Charlotte. With a mumbled, "Excuse me," she ran back towards the house before either Frank or Jasper could stop her.

"And you!" Mrs Grantley continued in tones of deep disgust. "Newly betrothed to that lovely Miss Powell. I am shocked at this depraved behaviour, viscount."

"This is none of your concern, madam," snarled the viscount.

He made to follow after Charlotte, but Jasper laid a hand on his arm. "I will go find her. You had best return to Miss Powell's side."

With that, Jasper walked rapidly back to the ballroom, casting his eyes for Charlotte. He found her, heading towards Mrs Morton, who was sitting with Lady Powell in a bank of seats to his right. He hurried after her, arriving just as she made it to the older ladies.

"Aunt Margaret," she breathed in shallow pants. "I—I am unwell and need to return home urgently."

"Oh my dear!" exclaimed Mrs Morton in concern.

Jasper spoke from behind her, "If you will allow me, Auntie Margaret, I will escort her back home."

217

"Give me a few minutes to go find our hosts and make our goodbyes, and I shall come with you," said Mrs Morton, but Jasper cut in.

"I do not think she can manage a minute longer. I must take her home now."

"Oh," flapped Mrs Morton. "Very well. I shall follow shortly in my carriage. Take care, my dear."

Charlotte nodded wanly and hurried along beside Jasper as they left the ballroom. After she had collected her wrap from the powder room, he took her out the front door and hailed a passing hackney-carriage. He assisted her inside, calling out the address to the coachman, then joined her.

Charlotte was shivering, despite the warmth of the summer evening. He took her hands in his and began to rub them.

"What is going to happen?" she asked worriedly.

He sighed, "You are going to have to brace yourself, Charlotte, for some unpleasant days ahead. Mrs Grantley is a known gossip, and I would not be surprised if news of your affair with Frank were being spread all around the ballroom as we speak. Auntie Margaret will be sure to have heard of it by the time she returns home."

Charlotte took a sharp breath in. "Oh Lord! What will she say?"

"I imagine she will be very shocked and disappointed."

"W—will she boot me out of her house and make me homeless?" stuttered Charlotte, becoming aware of the grimness of her situation.

"I do not believe so, but she may wish to hasten her departure from London to spare you and herself any further gossip."

"I don't know how I am going to face her," bemoaned Charlotte.

Jasper injected a briskness to his voice. "You will have to, and you will get through this, trust me."

She nodded, trying to brace herself for what was ahead. A minute later, the carriage came to a stop in front of 10 Grosvenor Street. Jasper jumped down and assisted Charlotte out, walking her to the front door. He rang the bell a few times, then turned to her, saying cheerfully, "Courage! This will blow over eventually. Remember you have a friend in me."

The door was opened by a sleepy footman.

"Goodnight, Miss Harding," Jasper said.

"Goodnight, Mr Stanton."

Charlotte disappeared inside, and with another long sigh, Jasper returned to the carriage and instructed the coachman to take him to Wimpole Street.

Chapter 32

Frank returned to the ballroom in a foul mood. Caroline would pay for this! He was as certain as it was possible to be that it was her that had engineered this situation, following them to the garden with the biggest gossip in town. Taking deep breaths to calm himself, he scoured the ballroom, looking for Helena. He had to reach her before the gossiping matrons spread their tales, as they inevitably would. At the same time, his mind was preoccupied by Charlotte. How would she deal with the consequences of their discovery? He ached to be with her and reassure her that all would be well. He would make sure of it.

He spotted Helena at the opposite end of the ballroom, and began to make his purposeful way towards her. She was dancing a quadrille with Sir George Draven, a wealthy gentleman who could be counted amongst her most ardent admirers. That did not worry Frank too much. Draven's fortune was modest in comparison with the magnificent Stanton patrimony, and moreover, Helena had already accepted his proposal. Her manner towards him was all that it should be— cordial but formal and correct. The poor man did not stand a chance.

Frank waited until the dance came to an end, then approached Helena as she curtsied to her partner. "Miss Powell," he said emphatically. "Will you honour me with your company awhile? I feel sure you are in need of some refreshment after this vigorous dance."

"Of course, my lord," she replied. With a final nod of dismissal towards Draven, she allowed him to escort her to the refreshments table, where he quickly procured her with some lemonade. He led her then to the semi-privacy of a quiet nook located behind a thick Grecian column.

She raised her brows at this. "My lord?"

"I need to speak with you, Helena. You asked me to always be truthful with you, so I will speak frankly. Yesterday, I told you of my having had a mistress recently, a relationship which I ended upon my proposal of marriage to you. I—I have come to regret that decision, Helena. I must admit to you that while we were waltzing earlier, I saw that lady in the arms of another and felt an intense jealousy."

Helena studied him in curious fascination. "You are talking of Miss Harding, are you not?"

"Yes."

"All this time she was acting as my chaperone, you were conducting an illicit relationship with her?"

A little uncomfortable, he replied, "Yes, more or less. It began on the day of your accident, when I walked her back to the inn."

"I see."

"There is more I must confess, and it must be done now before gossip reaches your ears."

She looked at him warily. "What is it?"

"I resolved during that dance to talk with you and ask if you would agree to different terms for our marriage. I know you are not in love with me, Helena, and neither I with you, although I care a great deal for you. I plan to be a considerate and affectionate husband to you, and to make your comfort and wellbeing a priority. However, I would also like to keep Miss Harding as my mistress, very discreetly of course."

She took in a deep breath. "I see."

"Speak to me Helena, before I tell you the rest. Is this something that you could live with?"

"Do I have much choice," she asked dryly.

"You do. You could break off our engagement, should you so wish. Or you could agree to the terms I have just set out. In truth, I cannot see myself resisting Miss Harding's charms in perpetuity."

She regarded him thoughtfully. "I must confess to some surprise, Frank. Those charms you speak of are not immediately obvious to me."

He laughed without amusement. "Neither to me at first, but once my eyes were opened, Helena, I could not unsee."

"Do you love her?"

Frank experienced a tight feeling in his chest. "I do not know. I have never been in love before. All I know is that I care greatly for her and I ache to be with her."

"Yet you propose marriage to me."

"You must know that father would never accept Charlotte as his daughter-in-law due to her parentage."

She nodded. "I can see your dilemma, Frank."

He braced himself for her response. "So I ask you again, Helena. Could you live with such an arrangement as I propose?"

She was silent a long moment, then eventually murmured, "I could. However, I must ask you to keep your promise of always being honest with me. I do not mind a mistress as much as the lies that come with having one."

"I will never lie to you, Helena. I promise."

"Tell me the rest then and be quick."

Frank took a deep breath and launched into his story. "Just now, I met with Charlotte in the garden. I wanted to convince her to take me back. Unfortunately, we were discovered in a compromising position by none other than Caroline Drake and Mrs Grantley."

Helena flinched. "Then I take it the story has now spread throughout this ballroom."

"I'm afraid so."

She nodded mutely, then her face took on a resolute expression. "We must make a show of unity, Frank. If people

222

see us laughing gaily with not a care in the world, they may question the truth of these rumours. At the very least, they shall see that we are unconcerned about them and still intent on following through with our marriage."

Frank smiled in relief, "Has anyone ever told you what a formidable person you are, Helena?"

"Many, and on several occasions," she retorted.

He chuckled, "Then, shall we dance?" He held out his arm, and she took it. Without another word, they stepped away from the column that had been sheltering them and made their way to the centre of the ballroom floor to take their position for the next country dance. Eyes turned to them from all directions. As the first few notes of the dance were heard, Frank whispered to her teasingly, "What a magnificent goddess stands before me."

She gurgled with laughter. "Oh sir, what a flatterer you are."

He bowed with a flourish as they began the dance. "I tell none other than the truth," he stated with a devilish grin.

To all the avid onlookers, Frank and Helena appeared the epitome of a happy, newly engaged couple. For the rest of the evening, they played their part well, never faltering, even under Lady Powell's indignant stare.

After saying his farewells and leaving the ball, Frank took himself walking to a certain address a few streets away. There, he awaited Lady Caroline's carriage to deposit her home. It arrived not a few minutes later. As she climbed the steps towards her front door, he followed her, stepping inside the house before she had a chance to refuse him entry. "Frank!" she cried out in alarm. "What are you doing here?"

"Upstairs, madam, or would you like to have this conversation out here in front of the servants?"

She shook her head suspiciously.

Frank pointed to the stairs. "After you."

She paused, undecided, then shrugged and made her way up the stairs towards her bedchamber, Frank at her heels. Once inside the room, she dismissed her maid with a flick of the wrist and turned to Frank with a sneer. "I didn't know that you were into plain, busty girls, Frank. I'm afraid I cannot congratulate you on your newfound taste in women."

"Leave Miss Harding out of this!" rasped the viscount.

She snorted, "Then tell me why you are here!"

"I am here, Caroline, to tell you that I know your coming upon us in the garden was no mere accident but premeditated. What did you hope to achieve by exposing our affair? For Miss Powell to end her engagement to me? In which case you have failed miserably in your quest."

Caroline's face took on an ugly expression. "I told you, Frank, that I was not to be easily dismissed, and I did achieve what I wanted. I ruined the woman who dared take my place, and caused you embarrassment in the bargain. I call that a success!"

In one stride, Frank had grasped Caroline's shoulders and pushed her against the wall. "Now you listen to me, and listen very carefully. From tomorrow onwards, if anyone mentions my name in conjunction with Miss Harding, you will feign complete ignorance and claim you saw nothing compromising in that garden. Am I making myself clear?"

She gave a derisive snort. "And what if I don't?"

Frank slid a hand to her throat. "I should wring this pretty neck of yours," he snarled. Caroline's expression changed, a touch of fear entering her eyes. "You will do as I say," he continued in a dark raspy voice, "and henceforth stay out of my business. If I ever catch you meddling in my affairs again, I will ruin you, and don't think for a moment that I can't. I have enough information on you to send your reputation to the gutter and have you shunned from the ton. Do not test me on this."

He let go of her suddenly, a look of disgust on his face, and headed to the door. Ten minutes later, he was at his own lodgings, being let in by a sleepy-looking Hudson. "Mr Stanton awaits you in the drawing room, my lord," said his valet.

"Thank you, Hudson. You may go to bed now. I shall not need you any further tonight."

With a bow, Hudson withdrew. Frank entered the dimly lit drawing room, only to find his brother dozing upon one of the settees. He approached and touched his shoulder gently. "Jasper, wake up."

Jasper sat up with a start. "Oh, you're finally back," he said, yawning.

"I was not aware you were waiting up for me. How is Charlotte?"

Jasper shrugged. "As well as can be expected. Poor thing was very shaken, terrified that the Mortons would boot her out and make her homeless."

Frank's mouth compressed to a thin line. "They would not do that. In any case, I will take care of her."

"And how do you propose to rescue her reputation, which you have now destroyed?"

Frank came to sit beside him. "I have just been to see Caroline and told her in no uncertain terms that she must deny ever having seen us in a compromising position. It will not quash all the rumours, but with my show of unity with Miss Powell this evening, it should go a long way towards extinguishing the fire."

"You do know that Charlotte will no longer be welcome in many houses of the ton after this, even if Lady Caroline denies all. She is ruined, Frank. What do you propose to do about that?"

"There is not much I can do about it," Frank retorted irritably, "but I plan to set her up as my mistress and ensure she lives in style and comfort. Once I have access to my funds after my marriage, I will settle a house on her and endow her with

225

an income for the rest of her life. She will no longer be reliant on her aunt and cousin's charity."

Jasper stared at him in disbelief. "So, having ruined her character, you will keep on dragging it through the mud? Is that it? And how does Miss Powell feel about all this?"

"Miss Powell is fine with this. We have spoken of it. And what else do you suggest I do, Jasper? I never wanted to expose Charlotte to the ton's censure, but what is done is done. At least this way, we can be together."

"Nothing you can do about it?" asked Jasper sarcastically. "How about you marry the poor girl and restore her reputation?"

"Enough!" shouted the viscount. "Marrying Charlotte is an impossibility and you know it. I am already spoken for, and besides, father would never accept her. You heard him the other night, speaking ill of her Spanish mother. He would have a seizure if he knew I was even considering marriage to such as her!"

"So be it! At least you would be doing the decent thing. To hell with father!"

Frank regarded him in shock. "You would have me go against his will? The only parent we have left? The person I have strived all my life to please? The person, moreover, who has the power to strip me of my fortune should he so wish? That is what you propose?" This last was said with a roar.

Jasper regarded him sadly. "Yes, Frank, it is what I propose, but you are too terrified to step outside those rigid confines he has drawn for you."

All of a sudden, Frank's anger drained out of him. He rested his head back on the settee and closed his eyes. In a low, ragged voice, he said, "I wish I could do as you say. I wish I could be free from all this expectation. I would marry Charlotte in a heartbeat if I could. I—I think I love her."

Jasper snorted, "I know you do, you idiot! God! I can't believe I'm your younger brother by several years. It's been obvious to me from the beginning how you feel about her. And between you and me, I think she's a splendid girl—just the person I'd like to see as my sister-in-law."

"It's not to be," Frank said bitterly.

They were quiet for a moment, then Jasper spoke, "I know I have very little money of my own, just that tiny estate mother left me in her will, which I do not have the talent to turn into a prosperous venture like you did at Hartley Court, but if it comes to the crunch, I can step into the breach and make an honest woman out of her."

Frank sat up abruptly. "What do you mean?" His voice was like whiplash.

"I mean I would do the decent thing on your behalf and marry her."

In seconds, Frank had his brother pinned down on the settee. "You will do no such thing if you value your life!"

"Alright, alright. Let me go!"

With a snarl, Frank released Jasper and got to his feet to pace up and down the room in frustration. Jasper regarded him shrewdly. "Then you marry her," he said gently. "Think on it. For now, it is late and I must get to bed. You don't mind if I stay in your spare room again?"

"Stay if you must," replied Frank. "You know my home is always open to you."

Jasper stood to go but paused to ask, "What will you do in the morning?"

Frank took a long, deep breath before replying, "First I shall go to my man of business and see what funds I can spare or borrow to buy a house for Charlotte in some respectable but less fashionable part of town. Then I shall go see her and talk her into living there."

Jasper regarded him sceptically. "She will not agree to it."

"I will make sure she does," replied the viscount in an implacable tone.

227

Over in the Powell townhouse, Helena made her way up the stairs to her bedchamber after having spent an hour trying to calm her raging mother and concerned father. The wedding was still on. She and the viscount had an understanding. All would be right. After many angry words were said, and ruffled feathers were soothed, she had finally managed to convince her parents that all was well, and they had let her get to her bed.

She opened her bedchamber door and stepped inside the room. A lone candle burned dimly on the bedside table. Over in the corner of the room, on a small pallet, slept Emma, her personal maid. On hearing the door open, Emma sat up sleepily. "I am sorry, miss, I had not meant to fall asleep," she said, getting to her feet. Quickly, she ran to her mistress and began to help her out of her dress, undoing the buttons and lifting it above her head. She placed the dress carefully on the back of a chair and returned to begin untying the tight corset that bracketed Helena's small waist.

As it was released, Helena gave a sigh of immense relief. "Thank goodness for that. It has been pinching me the whole evening." With the corset removed, all that remained was Helena's fine linen chemise, her pantalettes and stockings. Sitting on the edge of the bed, she allowed Emma to pull the pantalettes down her leg, revealing the blond curls on her mound. Another sigh issued from her.

Emma knelt at the foot of the bed and began carefully to remove her mistress's stockings one by one. As she pulled a stocking and revealed a dainty white foot, she took it in her hands and pressed her fingers into the heel, causing Helena to moan happily, "What a clever girl you are, Emma."

The young maid smiled, "I have had a lifetime to know you well, miss."

Helena smiled back, "That is true. So, knowing me as you do, what do you think I want done next?"

Emma parted Helena's legs, revealing the damp, pink folds of her tender flesh. "I think perhaps you want me to pleasure your cunt, miss."

"You think right, Emma. Go on. Do it."

Needing no further invitation, Emma settled in between Helena's thighs and dipped her face to that leaking, needy cunt. She licked and sucked and nipped, listening for Helena's sounds of bliss, until she felt the tremors that signalled the peak of her pleasure. Slowly, Emma sat back, her mouth glistening and wet. She stood and silently removed Helena's chemise, bending down to kiss each pert little breast that was revealed. Then she went away, returning a moment later with a delicate night rail which she helped her mistress into. With gentle fingers, Emma removed the pins from Helena's hair and ran a brush lovingly through it.

Finally, ready for bed, Helena stood and drew the covers back. She got under them and issued a gentle command, "Join me."

Emma blew out the candle and climbed into bed beside the mistress she had loved for years. In the dark secret of the night, they held each other and kissed for several languid minutes. When the kiss eventually drew to a close, Emma said with a sigh, "I will miss being with you like this once you are married."

"I think perhaps we shall be able to continue with our loving, dear Emma, even after my marriage."

"You think so?"

"I am nearly certain of it. Now sleep, my darling, for it is late."

Within minutes, the two entwined bodies relaxed as they both fell into a deep, dreamless sleep.

●————————————●

In the Morton household, no such harmony was to be found. Charlotte had paced the drawing room restlessly, waiting for her aunt's return. She had not long to wait. A rap on the door signalled Mrs Morton's arrival, followed by the sound of her aunt's voice. "Evening, Jones. Where is Miss Harding?"

"I believe she is in the drawing room, madam," came the reply.

A moment later, the door was opened and closed as Mrs Morton marched into the room. Charlotte stood rooted to the floor, hands clutched together, full of misgiving at what her aunt was about to say.

"Charlotte," cried Mrs Morton. "How could you? And after all I've done for you!"

"I'm so terribly sorry, Aunt Margaret. I never meant for this to happen."

Mrs Morton huffed in vexation. "A man engaged to another, of all things! And of such high standing! You must know we cannot compel him to marry you, Charlotte. You are ruined!"

Tears streamed freely down Charlotte's face. "I know," she sobbed. "What will you do now? Will you have me leave?"

Mrs Morton viewed her niece with displeasure. "That is what I ought to do, ungrateful girl. But for now, we will hasten our removal to the country. We leave for Stanbourne the day after next, and then I shall let Frederick decide what is to be done. Now I will ask you to remove yourself from my sight."

Charlotte made a hurried curtsy and with a last "I'm so sorry," went up to her room.

Chapter 33

Charlotte spent a restless night recalling the events of the previous evening, from Frank's surprising offer to their discovery in the garden, and on to Mrs Morton's fury. What would Frederick decide to do once they returned to Stanbourne? Dear lord, how was she to face him? Would Harriet turn away from her in disgust? Would she be sent back to her stepmother in disgrace? That last thought could not be borne.

Then her mind inevitably led her to Frank, as it always did. She had seen him return to Helena Powell's side just as she left the ballroom last night, a sight that had sent yet another piercing pain to her heart. All the time she had spent anxiously fretting about her fate, had he been wooing his intended and trying to make things right with her? Of course he must have. His marriage to Helena took precedence over everything else; she knew that.

A choked sob escaped her. How had it come to this? All she had meant to do was to have a short, discreet affair to furnish her with sweet sensual memories. And now she was left with her heart in pieces, her reputation in tatters and her future deeply uncertain. She wished she had a friend to turn to, but there was no one. Jasper's sweet offer of friendship she discounted. After all, what could he do? And Ruth was far away, soon to be sailing to America.

"*Oh Ruth, would that you were here with me,*" she thought mournfully.

The memory of her friend's kind, no-nonsense manner sent a pang of nostalgia through Charlotte and a yearning to be with her again. Slowly, a germ of an idea began to form in her head. Ruth and Robert would be sailing from Liverpool three days hence, off to build a fresh, new life for themselves. Why could she not go with them?

There was nothing left for her here except disgrace, heartbreak and penury. She had been frugal and had over £80 left of her annual income—enough to pay her fare and to live on for a few months until she could establish herself wherever Ruth and Robert settled. She would not be above toiling hard alongside them, for on the other side of the ocean, there could be no distinction between a gentlewoman and a farmer. In any case, she was no longer a gentlewoman. To the ton, she was now a jezebel. In America, she could start anew, even if it meant struggle and hard graft.

She scrabbled around in her mind for proverbs from her beloved philosophers. Like always, they gave her comfort and courage.

Nothing has more strength than dire necessity.

Life grants nothing to us mortals without hard work.

Seize the day.

Don't think, just do.

And what of Frank? If she left with Ruth, she would never see him again. Her heart seized once more. My how she loved him! How she ached to be with him! She did not wallow in her misery for too long though, for she had to face up to the truth. He was lost to her already. It was best that she should go. Wasn't it Byron that had once said, *the heart will break, but broken live on*? She would have memories of those three glorious weeks with Frank to sustain her.

Decision made, she settled down to a fitful sleep.

In the morning just after dawn, she awoke, barely refreshed. She dressed quietly and went down to the empty dining room, making a hasty breakfast. Then, putting on her plain brown pelisse and bonnet, she left the house, without a word to any of the servants.

232

In the early morning London bustle, she hailed a passing hackney-carriage and instructed the coachman to take her to Barings Bank on Devonshire Square. The coachman regarded her curiously, but shrugged and agreed to take her there. Upon her arrival, she entered the large, imposing building and made her way to a bank clerk. "Could you please direct me to Mr. Henry Stephenson?" she enquired as steadily as she could.

With a curious glance at the dowdy looking lone female, the clerk responded, "Up the stairs to the second floor, first door on the right."

"Thank you."

Heart pounding beneath her calm exterior, Charlotte made her way up as directed and knocked on the door in question. "Come in!" came a muffled voice.

She turned the knob on the door and entered. Inside the snug room, its walls encased in overflowing book shelves, sat behind a desk a wiry middle-aged man in spectacles, reading a document spread out before him. He looked at her in surprise. "What can I do for you Miss—"

"It's Miss Harding, daughter of Hugh Harding."

At this, Mr Stephenson rose from his desk and came to her, a pleased expression on his face. "Miss Harding, what an honour to make your acquaintance. I held your late father in great esteem. Please, do come in." He gestured towards a chair before his desk, and she sat down, her back ramrod straight. "What it is I can do for you, Miss Harding?" the gentleman asked.

"Mr Stephenson, you must be aware that on my father's passing, I was left with a small income invested in the funds, while the rest of father's estate was bequeathed to my stepmother, on the understanding that she would continue to provide a home for me. Unfortunately, a difference in opinion has meant that I had to leave my home in Alstone. I came to stay here with my Aunt Margaret, father's sister. However, for reasons I will not elaborate on, I now find myself in a situation where I must leave that home too. I have old and trusted friends, tenant farmers at Alstone, who are emigrating to start a new life in America, and I have decided to join them on that journey. They leave three days from now, on a ship sailing from Liverpool. I would like therefore to have my current balance of funds, which I believe to be in the region of £83, disbursed to me, and to make arrangements for future payment of my income to be made in America–for I understand your bank has offices over there."

Throughout this speech, Mr Stephenson regarded her with a frown, hands steepled together. Now he said, "Yes indeed, we have quite a large presence in America, and it would be a simple matter to divert payments of your yearly income to one of our offices over there. May I ask what part of America you are planning to travel to?"

"My friends have relatives already living there, in the state of Ohio. We shall be going to stay with them initially."

"I see. And are you quite sure, Miss Harding, about this proposed journey, which is not to be made lightly?"

"I have thought of little else," replied Charlotte, "and my decision is made."

"In that case, let me suggest the following. I will disburse £33 to you now, and the remainder of your funds will be written up as a letter of credit which you may present to any Barings office in America to have the funds disbursed to you over there. It will save you the trouble of having to carry with you on your person a large amount of money, and the danger of that money getting lost or stolen. I can have all these documents drawn up for you now, if you will wait a while."

"Thank you, Mr Stephenson. I would like that."

With a kindly smile, he got to his feet and left the room. She waited, hands clasped tightly in her lap, until he returned some twenty minutes later. "I am sorry to have kept you waiting, Miss Harding, but all the documents are now in order." He presented her with a leather pouch. "In there is £33 in gold sovereigns, which you may use to secure your passage and any additional expenses on your journey." From the ledger he held in his hands, he took out a sealed letter which he handed to her. "Present this letter of credit to any of our offices in America, and you shall have the remaining £50 disbursed to you in American currency should you so wish."

Then he went to sit behind his desk again, removing one final document from his ledger. "Now we come to the matter of your future disbursements. I have here a letter instructing us to credit your annual income to our bank in America. I shall need your signature right here," he said pointing to a box at the bottom of the page. He handed her a quill pen and slid the inkwell towards her. She dipped the pen in the ink, then signed her name where instructed.

"There," he said. "All done. I wish you the best of luck, Miss Harding, in this new endeavour and pray for your safe journey."

"Thank you, Mr Stephenson."

He stood again. "Let me arrange a cab to take you back home. I shall be right back." He left the room again, returning after five minutes. "The carriage awaits you at the door, Miss Harding. Let me walk you down."

"Thank you, sir. I appreciate all you have done for me today."

He smiled, "It is nothing. Now, let us go."

He walked down with her to the front entrance of the bank and helped her into the carriage. "What is your aunt's address, Miss Harding?"

"10 Grosvenor Street."

With a nod, he instructed the coachman, then stepped back, watching the carriage as it left.

Inside it, Charlotte felt dizzy with a strange mix of excitement and dread. This was it. There was no turning back now. As soon as she got to the house, she would pack up all her belongings, bid her aunt farewell and catch the earliest stagecoach to Liverpool. If she left by eleven, she should be able to make good progress towards her destination that day, and reach the sea port in good time. As for Frank... she would write him a letter of farewell and have a servant deliver it to his lodgings.

On arrival at the Mortons' townhouse, she found the household astir with preparations for their imminent departure for Stanbourne. "Where is Mrs Morton?" Charlotte asked of one of the maids.

"She is resting in her chamber, miss, and has asked not to be disturbed."

"I see. Thank you."

Charlotte headed quickly to her own bedchamber and began to pack her meagre belongings into the small trunk she had brought with her from Alstone. When it came to the ballgowns that had been crafted for her by Madame Elise, she paused. Would she need them in her new life across the ocean? Probably not. With a sigh of regret, she left them hanging in the closet, only taking with her the two new day gowns Madame Elise had sent over, as well as the older dresses she had brought with her from home.

She had very nearly finished her packing when a knock came at her door. "Come in!" she called.

A parlour maid peeped inside and curtsied. "You have a visitor, miss, waiting in the drawing room."

"Thank you."

Charlotte stood, blood rushing to her face. Could it be Frank? Hastily, she tidied her appearance then rushed down the stairs, throwing open the drawing room door. She walked in quickly then came to an abrupt stop. Standing before her was not Frank, but her uncle, Sir William Harding. The older gentleman regarded her with open derision.

She curtsied and said breathlessly, "Sir William, good day. Are you here to see Aunt Margaret?"

236

"It is you I am here to see," he intoned. "I shall come straight to the point. It has come to my attention that you have become embroiled in a shameful scandal. I am not surprised, for I told Margaret that blood will out. She did not listen to me and refused to send you away. But now…"

He made a sound of disgust, then launched into speech again, "Miss Harding, I am here to tell you, that you are to remove the scourge of your presence from this family. I am prepared to pay you, and to pay you well, to ensure you disappear from our midst and are never seen again. I give you one hour to get your belongings ready, after which I will send a coach to take you away. You may direct the coachman as to your destination, but you will need to put at least three counties' distance from us and never come anywhere near any member of this family again. Am I clear?"

Charlotte's voice was cool despite her inner turmoil, "Quite clear, sir. May I ask as to the sum you plan to pay me for this disappearance?"

He gave a dry, unamused chuckle. "Straight to money matters, as I expected from a self-serving hussy." Then he drew himself up straight and added, "I will pay you the sum of £1,000. Take it, and be careful to never set foot in our midst again. Should you break your word on this matter, you will regret it, believe me, and be dealt with harshly."

Charlotte's mind raced. She had nothing but contempt for Sir William and she was tempted to throw his offer of money in his face. Then wiser council prevailed. She was embarking on a journey to a new life and would need as many funds as possible to sustain her there. This money her uncle proposed to pay her was hers by right in any case, for it would have passed down to her father, had he not been cruelly disinherited.

Seize the day.

Don't think, just do.

Without any hesitation, she blurted, "I would need double that amount."

His brows rose at this. "Now your true nature is showing. The bad apple fallen from the tree. You think to haggle with me? Think again."

"I am not haggling, sir, merely stating. You may be happy to hear that I plan to travel very far away from here, as I shall be embarking on a ship bound for America. For this, I shall require the sum of £2,000—£100 in coins and the remainder in a letter of credit from your bank. Once I am bound on that ship, you can be sure that I will never, ever return to these shores again."

He regarded her thoughtfully, brow creased in concentration. Finally, he croaked, "Very well. I shall have that money drawn up as you say, but it will not be given to you by my man until he sees you board the ship. Be ready in an hour."

He bowed stiffly and left.

Once the door shut behind him, Charlotte dropped down to the settee, her body trembling in reaction. Had she really agreed to be paid off by her uncle like a common strumpet? Two thousand pounds! With that money, she would be able to establish herself, perhaps buy a small house and set up a school as a way to earn her keep. Her heart pounded in excitement. She had exactly one hour.

Quickly, she ran up to the study and sat down to write letters, one for Frederick, Harriet, her aunt, and finally one for Frank. The letters for the Mortons, she left on the desk. The other, she took with her. Hurrying down the stairs, she found Jones, one of the footmen.

"Jones, a carriage shall be arriving shortly for me. Please ensure that my trunk is brought down from my room. As Mrs Morton has asked not to be disturbed, I shall not be able to make my farewells in person, so I have left some letters up in Mr Morton's study. See that she receives them after I have left. Also, I do have this one letter, which I wish to have delivered to Viscount Stanton's lodgings in Wimpole Street." She passed him a shilling. "Here is money for your troubles."

He took the coin and deftly pocketed it. "Yes miss," he said. "I shall have this delivered immediately and will bring your trunk down as instructed."

"Thank you," said Charlotte. With this task complete, there was nothing further to do but wait for the carriage that was to take her to Liverpool. She put on her brown pelisse and tied her bonnet, then sat down to wait. Ten minutes later, the carriage was there and her trunk duly attached to it. Charlotte stood irresolutely in the hallway. It was time to go, but somehow, her feet could not make the journey to the door. She would never see Frank ever again. Her heart squeezed painfully in her chest. Then, with a monumental effort, she stiffened her resolve. Casting one last mournful look behind, she walked out onto the street and got into the carriage.

Chapter 34

The viscount had spent no less of a restless night in his bed. His mind thrashed, going over and over the events of the evening and his last conversation with Jasper. *"Then marry her,"* his brother had said. Marry Charlotte? Oh God what would it be like, having that precious sweet girl eternally at his side? His heart beat painfully in his chest at the thought of her, and his cock was equally painfully hard. How he wanted her.

It would take courage to stand up to his father—courage he didn't think he had. Choosing Charlotte as his wife would not only mean the loss of a colossal fortune but also the anger and disappointment of the one man he had looked up to all his life. He tried to imagine living estranged from the earl and disowned of his inheritance. He would have to live modestly with Charlotte at Hartley Court. He would lose his standing in society. He would lose his father. Hell and damnation!

But what of the other possibility? What if he went ahead with a marriage of convenience with Helena and took possession of his fortune? Then he could still have Charlotte, but this time ensure she lived a life of comfort. He could lavish gifts on her and spoil her. She would not be his wife under the law, but she would be his, and he would still get to spend time with her. All this he could have without upsetting the apple cart and losing the regard of his father. Surely this was the better plan. It would involve a loss of reputation for Charlotte in high society, but that was already the case, and did it matter so much in the grand scheme of things? She would always have his protection, and she could live a quiet life with her beloved books and their children, away from the judgement of the ton. That home would be his escape from the pressures and expectations of being the Earl of Stanton's heir. She would be his refuge. The more he thought of it, the more he liked this plan.

Amidst all the fevered thinking though, was a little, niggling doubt. His father expected him to fall into line and enter political life after his marriage. Once again, it would be hard to say no to him. The noose would tighten around his neck. He would never be free to live life on his own terms. Damnation! Why was his father such a difficult man? And why was it still so important that he please him?

Exhausted, Frank eventually fell into a deep sleep just before dawn, not awakening until late morning. Hudson had carefully laid out the day's clothes for him, and he dressed quickly, wanting to start putting his plan into action as soon as possible. He entered the dining room to find not only Jasper there, partaking of a generous breakfast, but also his friend Rupert Weston.

"Rupert," said Frank in some surprise. "I had not expected to see you this morning."

His friend cast him a stern look. "What, when all the town is agog at your affair with Miss Harding, you didn't expect me to come find you?"

Frank shrugged uncomfortably and sat down. Helping himself to some ham and eggs, he asked, "Have you come to lecture me on my sins, Rupert?"

"Never! Far be it from me to ever judge, but why did you never tell me of this? I had no clue."

At this, Jasper chortled, "Then you must have been blind, Weston, for it was immediately obvious to me the minute I met her."

"Well," said Rupert, "in my defence, I did notice that she had fallen under Frank's spell. The day he first met her, she looked as if she were about to swoon. But I never for one moment thought the interest was reciprocated."

Frank set his fork down and levelled Rupert with a stare. "Tell me again about that first time. What did you see?"

241

Rupert had the decency to look a little uncomfortable. "I don't think the good lady would like me to rehash this with you."

"Come on now, don't tantalise me with hints. Out with it. What did you see?"

"Only that she looked dumbstruck upon sight of you, and as she curtsied, she tilted dangerously in your direction before righting herself. You, of course, were totally oblivious, but the poor girl sat for several minutes with her hands clutched, trying to regain her composure."

Frank stared, struck speechless, his eyes burning bright. His poor Charlotte. Why had he not seen? The need to hold and comfort her was a raw ache in his chest. Absently, he rubbed the pain, unable to speak for several moments.

Now it was Rupert's turn to stare. "Good God! You really have fallen for her!"

"He's in love," piped in Jasper, enjoying the show.

Still, Frank did not speak.

Rupert broke the silence. "So what do you plan to do next?" he asked.

Frank gave him a cold look. "I shall marry Miss Powell, get my fortune, then set Charlotte up in the greatest of comfort and make her my mistress."

"Frank," Rupert said hesitantly. "She is a well born gentlewoman. You cannot set her up as a mistress like any common strumpet."

"Say those words again," hissed Frank, "and friendship or not, I will level you."

Rupert held up his hands. "Easy Frank. I meant no disrespect to Miss Harding. Quite the opposite. All I meant to say was that being a kept woman is not the life for a respectable person such as Miss Harding."

"It is much too late for that, Rupert," retorted Frank. "Reputation is like an egg. Once it smashes to the floor, there is little one can do to put it back together again."

"There is one thing—" began Rupert, but Frank interrupted him.

"If you are about to say marriage, then desist. I cannot marry Charlotte. Father will never allow it, and I am promised to Miss Powell. I cannot go back on my word."

Rupert looked at him doubtfully. "Then perhaps it is best for the lady to retire to the country with her family and let the whole thing blow over. In time, she may make a respectable marriage to some country squire or some such. But if you make her your mistress, then she will always be an outcast in our society."

At the mention of marriage, Frank gritted his teeth. "She will not marry anyone else. I will not allow it."

"The problem, you see," Jasper explained, "is that he wants her for himself, but he doesn't have the gumption to cross father."

"Then you are in a rare pickle!" exclaimed Rupert.

Frank finished his food, but it could have been sawdust for all he cared. Dropping his napkin on the table, he stood. "And now, gentlemen, I must go see my man of business, after which I will pay a call on Miss Harding. Excuse me."

————————•

Frank spent an interminable hour with his man of business discussing the state of his finances. All the while, he chafed at the delay in going to see Charlotte, but he had to get everything in order before he spoke to her. By the time he left the offices of Mr Eastleigh just before noon, it had been agreed that a small mortgage taken out on half of the acreage at Hartley Court would give him sufficient funds to purchase a house in town for Charlotte. Mr Eastleigh would begin the process right away. In a week, or at the most two, the purchase of a suitable house would be completed. Frank had explained what size and type of neighbourhood — respectable but not fashionable — was needed for his purposes. Mr Eastleigh had taken copious notes and assured him that all would be done as he asked.

Now, Frank eagerly hailed a cab to take him to 10 Grosvenor Street. He could not wait to see Charlotte again and tell her of his plan. He would convince her of the rightness of it. Before long, she would be his, settled in modest comfort in her new home until he had access to his fortune. They would be able to spend long nights and leisurely mornings together in bed, with no ticking clock putting an end to their pleasures. With a grin, he jumped out of the cab and tipped the driver far more than the cost of the ride. In two strides, he had crossed the road and pressed the bell.

The door did not open right away. It took a minute or two before a harried footman drew it back. Frank stepped inside. "Viscount Stanton, calling on Miss Harding," he said peremptorily.

The footman looked at him in confusion. "My lord, she has left."

"What do you mean? Has she gone out? When will she return?"

"I—I do not know sir. Perhaps it would be best to speak to Mrs Morton."

"Show me to her," the viscount commanded crisply.

The footman bowed and went to the drawing room door. Opening it, he announced, "Viscount Stanton to see you, madam."

Frank walked in, an air of determination about him. Inside, he found Mrs Morton in conference with Lady Powell, looking extremely put out. Upon hearing his name, she stood, fanning herself vigorously. "Frank," she said crossly. "What are you doing here?"

"I have come to call on Miss Harding," he replied.

244

"Well, she is not here. She has left. Oh Frank, what have you done?" cried that lady in agitation.

Frank bowed hurriedly in Lady Powell's direction then addressed Mrs Morton. "Where on earth is she?"

"That's just it. We do not know. She has left—disappeared into thin air. A carriage came for her an hour ago. She had her trunk put on it and left. All I have is this letter she wrote," said Mrs Morton in a shaky voice. She held aloft the letter in question.

"What does the letter say?" Frank demanded.

"Here, you read it," said Mrs Morton, handing it to him.

He perused it quickly, his heart sinking with each word.

Dear Aunt Margaret,

I am so incredibly sorry for all the trouble I have caused. You have been everything that is good and kind to me, and I will forever be grateful for your generosity in taking me in. I do so wish that things had turned out differently, and that I had not let my foolish heart lead me into indiscretion. I cannot undo the damage done to my name or the shame I have brought on this family. However, I can relieve you of the burden of my presence.

Please believe how sorry I am. I am leaving now and going to a place far away. Please do not worry about me, for as they say, fortune favours the brave, and I am going to be brave. I have some funds with me, and a determination to start a life afresh somewhere I am not known and where my indiscretion with the viscount can do no harm. I will always remember fondly the time I spent in 10 Grosvenor Street. Please be assured of my sincerest affection,

Yours,

Charlotte Harding

The viscount's face had turned ashen by the time he got to the end of the letter. He dropped it on the table, hands shaking in fear and fury. "Where has she gone?" he roared.

Mrs Morton threw her hands up in the air. "We do not know!"

"Have the servants been interrogated?"

Mrs Morton nodded. "Nobody seems to know. Only that an unmarked carriage drew up an hour ago and that Charlotte had been awaiting it."

"Who would send a carriage?" cried the viscount.

"Perhaps another lover of hers," suggested Lady Powell coldly. "There is no knowing what kind of alliances a hussy such as her would make."

The viscount glared at her. "Lady Powell, I would thank you to keep your insults to yourself."

She huffed in derision. "I only tell the truth of the matter. Shameful hussy, setting her cap at a man promised to another!"

"She did no such thing. It was I who was at fault; I who seduced an innocent."

Lady Powell's voice dripped in contempt, "Yes, you were at fault, but no well-bred lady would ever have succumbed to such wiles. It is clear now that as we suspected, there was bad blood in her, from that Spaniard who spawned her no doubt. I wish now that I had counselled Margaret better and prevented this shame from ever staining the good name of this family."

Frank gripped his fists tight in an effort not to show his growing rage. Turning away from Lady Powell, he addressed Mrs Morton. "I wish to speak to the servants and get to the bottom of this."

She nodded wanly and pointed in the direction of the door. Without another look, Frank strode out. He called the nervous footman to him. "You here, did you see the carriage that arrived this morning for Miss Harding?"

"Yes, my lord."

"Was there anyone in it?"

"No, my lord. Only the coachman and a groom at the front. They took Miss Harding's trunk and placed it in the undercarriage, then Miss Harding left with them."

"Did she say where she was going?"

"No, my lord."

"Did she receive any other visitors today or go out before this carriage came to take her?"

"My lord, she went out very early in the morning. I saw her hail a hackney carriage, but I do not know where it took her. She returned about an hour and a half later, and went up to her bedchamber. Not long after, there was a caller for her."

At this, Frank pricked up his ears. "Who was it?" he asked sharply.

"It was Sir William Harding, my lord. I thought he had come to call on Mrs Morton, but he asked specifically to speak to Miss Harding."

"Did you happen to hear anything they said?"

"My lord!" said the footman in a shocked tone. "I would never!"

"Oh stop. Do not pretend to have deaf ears. Surely you heard something. I will make it worth your while. Now tell me!"

The footman did not speak, looking uncertain. With a growl, the viscount dug into his pocket and took out a shilling. "Here. Now tell me what you heard."

"My lord, it was not very much. Only as Sir William was leaving, I heard him say, 'Be ready in one hour.'"

"The devil he did!" cried Frank in frustration. He returned to the drawing room, saying curtly, "It is all to do with your brother, Sir William. He paid a call on Charlotte this morning and told her to be ready in an hour. The carriage must have been his."

"But what can he mean by it?" asked Mrs Morton bewildered.

"It is quite obvious, is it not?" interjected Lady Powell. "You told me yourself that Sir William was deeply unhappy about Miss Harding's presence in your home and that he had asked you to send her away. He must have taken matters into his own hands and arranged her removal from here to save the family name."

"But where to?" Mrs Morton asked, her voice rising in agitation.

"That is what I mean to find out," promised the viscount. "Sir William's direction?"

"It is 5 Arlington Street," responded Mrs Morton.

The viscount bowed briskly, "Good day, ladies." Quickly, he strode out of the house and began to walk in the direction of Arlington Street. In the busy streets of London at this time of the day, he would sooner get there walking than by taking a cab. Ten minutes later, he was pulling the door bell and waiting impatiently for a response.

The door was opened by a stiff looking butler, who looked at him enquiringly. "Viscount Stanton, here to see Sir William," Frank stated coldly.

The butler bowed and ushered him into a richly decorated, but lugubrious looking drawing room. "I will inform Sir William of your presence, my lord," said the butler.

The viscount paced around the room impatiently as he waited. Was Charlotte here? If not, where had Sir William sent her? Nearly two hours had passed since she had left 10 Grosvenor Street. She could be miles away by now. A sound made him turn and face the door. A tall, thin gentleman with greying hair had just entered the room. "Viscount Stanton?" he enquired.

The viscount bowed. "Sir William, I believe we have met before. At White's some years ago."

"Ah yes, please, take a seat. What can I do for you, viscount?"

"I think, Sir William, that you are well aware why I am here. I come to ask after Miss Harding's whereabouts."

"Miss Harding?" Sir William looked incredulous. "Why on earth should I know the whereabouts of that unfortunate girl?"

"Let us not beat about the bush, Sir William. I am well aware of your visit to Grosvenor Street this morning, and that you later had a carriage sent for Miss Harding. What I want to know, is where it went."

Sir William shrugged, looking unconcerned. "As to that, I cannot say. I made it clear to Miss Harding that she was to remove herself from Grosvenor Street at once and go somewhere far from our midst. She agreed, in return for a hefty sum of money. I always knew there was bad blood in her."

The viscount bristled, but tried to keep his focus on the matter at hand. "Did she not say where she was going?"

"I did not care to ask," Sir William drawled.

"Surely, if you were paying her a vast sum of money, you would have wanted to ensure she did as you asked and went far away. I cannot believe that you have no inkling as to where she went."

"What matter is it to you, viscount?" asked Sir William arrogantly. "Are you not soon to be wed to that lovely Miss Powell? You can surely have no further interest in that young hussy."

"On the contrary," replied the viscount, trying his best to remain calm. "I have every interest in knowing that she is safe and well. Now let us not parry back and forth, Sir William. Where has she gone?"

Sir William chuckled darkly, "There is no point going after her, viscount. You will never catch her up. She has at least two hours' lead on you."

"Where, Sir William?"

"Let us just say, she plans to leave these gentle shores."

The viscount frowned, thinking quickly, then his face cleared. "America. The young fool is going to America."

"And good riddance, I say."

The viscount did not bother to reply. Instead, he bowed curtly, "Good day, Sir William," and strode away. Back out on the street, he hailed a passing hackney and got in. "Wimpole Street," he told the driver, "and make it quick."

The instant the cab stopped in front of his lodgings, Frank jumped out, throwing some coins carelessly in the driver's direction. He leapt up the steps two at a time and rapped on his door, which was opened promptly by his valet.

"Hudson, quick, pack a bag with enough clothes for a few days. I am leaving as soon as I possibly can."

"Yes, my lord," replied his startled valet. "Will you be needing the carriage?"

"No. It will be quicker if I ride. Send word to the stables to have Bruiser saddled and ready for me."

"Yes, my lord."

The viscount hurried into his study and unlocked the safe behind his desk. From within it, he took out a pouch of sovereigns which he always kept there for little emergencies. Pocketing that pouch, he headed out, nearly running into his brother, who it seems had been waiting for his return.

"Frank! What news have you? What is this I hear of you needing a bag packed?"

"She has left, Jasper, but I am going after her."

"Miss Harding?"

"Yes. It seems that odious uncle of hers paid her a visit this morning and compelled her to leave the Morton home. She left in his carriage not two hours ago, on her way to Liverpool, foolish, foolish girl."

"Liverpool?" queried Jasper, a puzzled expression on his face. "Why Liverpool?"

"Because she is joining that friend of hers, the one who is emigrating to America. She spoke of it once. I have been racking my brains trying to remember the details of the conversation. I believe she said her friend was leaving on the 7th of this month on the Hibernia. I must catch her up before it is too late."

"Before you go, you may want to read this. She sent you a note," said Jasper, handing it to his brother.

Frank snatched it and tore open the seal quickly. He read.

Dearest Frank,

So, this is goodbye. I am leaving to start a new life, away from the shame and scandal that I have caused. I know that you wanted me to be your mistress, but I am sure that on further reflection, you have seen how wrong that would be. I would be shaming Aunt Margaret and Frederick, my only remaining relatives, and repaying their kindness with a stain upon the family honour. I could not do that to them.

I also could not place myself in such an uncertain position, at the mercy of your whims. You say now that you would ensure I lived in comfort for the rest of my days, but consider this. A year or more down the road, once you had tired of me, you would no longer wish to be saddled with the expense of my upkeep. Knowing your kind nature, you would look for gentle ways to be rid of me, and I could not stand that.

No, it is better I leave, and start with a clean slate somewhere else. Do not worry about me, my love. I am strong and will endure. Do know, Frank, that those three weeks we spent together are the most precious weeks of my life. I shall treasure the memories of our time in Charles Street for the rest of my days. I wish you well in your marriage to Miss Powell. Be happy, my love.

Yours,

Charlotte

"Oh God!" moaned Frank. "Oh God!"

He dropped into a nearby chair and put his head in his hands. His shoulders shook as he struggled in vain to stop the tears welling in his eyes—tears of rage, frustration and heartache.

He felt a hand squeeze his shoulder. "It is not too late to make things right," said Jasper gently.

"I know." Frank sat up, pulling out a handkerchief to wipe his eyes. "I leave just as soon as my horse is saddled and Hudson has packed my bag."

"I go with you. I have already instructed Hudson, so there is no point saying nay."

Frank threw a grateful glance at his brother. "I have no intention to. I shall be glad of your support, Jasper."

Thus it was that a quarter of an hour later, the two brothers set out on their fine stallions, bags stowed away in the saddlebag by their side, on their way to catch up with Charlotte. Once they were out of the busy confines of London, they made good progress, riding at a punishing pace for a few hours before they were forced to stop at an inn to rest the horses and have something to eat. As soon as they could, they were on their way again, trying to gain as much ground on Charlotte's carriage as possible. Finally, as darkness fell towards nine o'clock in the evening, they made it as far as Bletchley, where they stopped overnight, promising to leave once more first thing in the morning.

Chapter 35

Speeding along in her carriage, Charlotte was oblivious to the frantic chase that was occurring in her wake. Her thoughts were ponderous and gloomy, yet also tinged with a hint of hope. A new life in America. One where she no longer had to apologize for her parentage or feel shame for her affair with Frank. It would be as if she were reborn. And she would have the comfort of being among loyal friends. She missed Ruth, and Robert.

The carriage was light and well sprung, the horses strong and fresh, and she made good time on her journey. By nightfall, they stopped at an inn some ten miles south of Northampton. She slept well, her exhaustion finally catching up with her. In the morning, she had the maid wake her early so that they could start their travels again as soon as it was possible. She could not afford to miss that ship, which was leaving two days hence.

The following day's travels were uneventful. They were able to reach the village of Great Haywood by nightfall, a few miles to the east of Stafford. If all went well the next day, they should be in Liverpool by early afternoon. Charlotte was not sure how to go about finding her friends in that great city. In the end, she resolved to head towards the port where she would make enquiries about the Hibernia and how to book a passage. Once at the booking office, she would make further enquiries about Ruth and Robert Ellis's whereabouts.

And thus it was that at around three o'clock on the afternoon of the 6th June, Charlotte's carriage rolled into the Liverpool dockyard. The groom jumped down and went to make enquiries about the Hibernia, returning sometime later with the information that tickets could be booked at the offices of Grayson and Butler on Castle Street. Directions to these offices were quickly supplied, and a quarter of an hour later, Charlotte was brought to a large, imposing building. She entered with trepidation and approached one of the booking clerks.

"Good day sir. I wish to buy passage on the Hibernia, leaving tomorrow for New York," she said, her decisive voice not betraying her nerves.

He glanced at her curiously, unused to lone females booking a passage across the Atlantic. "You are travelling alone?" he asked.

"No, I will be accompanying family friends who are already booked on the ship. I believe you should see a booking under the names of Robert and Ruth Ellis."

He opened a tall leather-backed ledger and leafed through the pages to find the ship manifest for the Hibernia. Running his finger down the list, he finally found their names. "Yes indeed, I can see their names here. They are both booked in steerage." He looked at Charlotte doubtfully, taking in the undoubted quality of her dowdy pelisse. "Will you be travelling in the same class, madam?"

Charlotte thought about it. She had heard tales of the dreadful conditions to be found in steerage and hoped to avoid these if she could. "What is the fare for a second class cabin?" she enquired.

"It is £20, and we have several that are available. Would you care to book one of these?"

£20 was a large chunk of the £33 she had in her pouch, but it was surely worth the price to have a private cabin rather than share a communal space in steerage. Moreover, she had yet to earn the £2,000 promised by Sir William. With that money in hand, she would not be overly out of pocket. She could even get Ruth to share the cabin with her and spare her friend the discomforts of a journey in steerage. Decision made, she said firmly, "Yes, please book me a ticket. The name is Charlotte Harding." She took out her pouch and counted twenty gold sovereigns.

"Very well, miss. Please take a seat over there while I have the ticket written out for you."

"Thank you," responded Charlotte and went to the place indicated to wait.

The clerk returned some minutes later and handed her the ticket, saying, "The ship leaves tomorrow promptly at ten o'clock in the morning, and you are advised to board at least an hour beforehand."

"I will... Would you by any chance know which inn Mr and Miss Ellis are staying at tonight? I should like to join them this evening if I can."

He shook his head regretfully. "I am afraid that is not information that I have. However, you could try making enquiries at the White Hart or the Rose and Crown. They are popular inns for travellers to America, and situated near to the docks."

"Thank you sir, you have been very helpful."

"Not at all, miss. I wish you safe travels."

Charlotte stood. "Good day, sir," she said, then headed back to her waiting carriage outside. She spoke to the coachman, "Jenkins, please enquire for directions to the White Hart and Rose and Crown inns. I am told they are near to the docks. I am hopeful my friends are staying there, but if not, I think we had better stay at one of those inns tonight, for we need to get to the ship early tomorrow morning."

"Yes miss," replied Jenkins. It was a matter of minutes for him to enquire about directions, and soon they were on their way again. They had no luck finding Ruth and Robert at the first inn, but upon making enquiries at the Rose and Crown, were told that indeed a couple going by the name of Ellis had arrived the previous day and were at this moment taking their supper in the dining room.

With huge relief, Charlotte stepped out of her carriage and went to speak to the innkeeper, requesting a room for the night and that her supper be served alongside that of her friends. A maid was dispatched to the room with Charlotte's band box, and with a surge of anticipation, Charlotte made her way to the dining room. Upon entering, she saw a scattering of people partaking of their meal at different tables, and in the far corner, Ruth's distinctive red hair, dressed neatly in a tight, no-nonsense bun. She hurried towards them, calling her name as she got near. "Ruth!"

Ruth looked up with a start, then her face transformed into a warm smile upon seeing who was calling her name. "Charlotte! What a wonderful surprise!" She stood and opened her arms to embrace her friend.

Charlotte ran to her, clutching her tight. Without volition, the tears came, and then the sobs.

"There, there," said Ruth soothingly. "Whatever it is, we shall soon sort it out with a cup of tea and some of this wonderful beef stew. Shh, Charlotte, all will be well." She held her friend for a few moments, then drew back. "Come and sit down, my dear, and we shall get to the bottom of this."

Feeling the eyes of the room on her, Charlotte sat down quickly, withdrew a handkerchief and wiped her face as best she could. Her eyes landed on Robert Ellis, who stared at her in concern.

"Mr Ellis, Robert, it is good to see you too. I am sorry for this display of emotion. I shall compose myself shortly, never fear."

"Do not apologise," he said brusquely. "Drink your tea, as Ruth said, and then I want you to tell us what this is all about."

Charlotte nodded and took a warming sip of tea. A moment later, a bowl of stew was placed before her, together with a buttered slice of crusty bread. Feeling suddenly ravenous, she set to eating while Ruth and Robert Ellis watched her discreetly.

Finally, when she could eat no more, Charlotte slid the bowl away and took a last sip of her tea. In a not quite steady voice, she said, "You are wondering, no doubt, why I am here and in such a state."

Ruth raised a brow. "Naturally," she said dryly. "Will you please now explain?"

"I have been very foolish," admitted Charlotte, "and done things which you will not approve of. However, the long and short of it is that I let myself be discovered in an indiscretion and caused a little scandal, so I am here with all my worldly belongings to join you on your journey to America. I have already been to the booking office and purchased a ticket on the Hibernia."

"Well!" exclaimed Ruth in surprise. Then after a moment, she added, "You had best tell me everything right from the beginning."

Charlotte hesitated, glancing at Robert, but he glowered at her and spoke gruffly, "Charlotte, let us dispense with formalities. I have known you since you were a babe, and I want you to tell us all, even the things you may feel shame in speaking about. You are with friends now. Speak!"

So with a deep breath, she began to speak, not omitting any important detail. Her friends listened in silence, not once passing judgement. When finally, she reached the end of her tale, Ruth asked, "Is it possible, Charlotte, that you might be in the family way?"

"I do not know. We were careful, except for one time." She glanced down at herself. "I have not increased at the waist, so perhaps not."

"It would be far too soon to show at the waist, but there are other ways of knowing." At Charlotte's blank look, she asked, "When are your menses due? Are you late?"

With a quick glance at Robert and a rosy flush forming on her cheeks, Charlotte replied, "They are usually on the 10th of the month, so I am not yet late."

"That is only a few days away," said Ruth. "In another week or so, if your menses do not come, we should know whether or not you are to have a child."

"What if I am?" asked Charlotte in alarm.

Now it was Robert who spoke, "If you are, Charlotte, then we shall find the first preacher we can in New York, and I will make you my wife. Your child will have a name and a father, and you will be under my protection. Do not worry. All will be fine."

"Oh Robert. I could not allow you to do that!"

"And why not? I like you well enough. Perhaps it is because I am of inferior social standing that you baulk at the idea."

"No!" cried Charlotte. "I detest all this snobbery, and I want well out of it once we are in America. My only thought was that you would be getting the short end of the stick — a bride that has lain with another and a child that was not your own."

"Be assured, Charlotte, that once that child bears my name, it will be mine, and I will love it regardless. Now, the matter is settled. You will come with us to America and be under my protection. It may take some time to clear the land I wish to claim and make a living from it, but I am determined to make a good life for myself, you and Ruth."

"The matter is settled," concurred Ruth, squeezing Charlotte's hand. "We will forge a new and better life together in America. You are not alone any more, my love. Now, I think it would be best to retire to our rooms and get a good night's sleep, for we have an early start tomorrow."

But barely had they stood to get to their rooms than a commotion was heard outside the dining room. The door was opened abruptly, and in swept Viscount Stanton, followed a moment later by his brother.

Chapter 36

The Stanton brothers had made good time, eating up the miles on their powerful stallions, and would have overtaken Charlotte's carriage had it not been for a small mishap. Frank's horse, Bruiser, had become hobbled, and they had been forced to stop at the nearest farrier to have it reshod. Frank chafed at the delay, but there was nothing for it but to wait until his horse was well enough to ride again.

So it was that they eventually made it to Liverpool a few hours after Charlotte, following the same trajectory of going to the docks, then to the booking office. On hearing that a young lady by the name of Miss Harding had been to purchase a ticket and that she had enquired about local inns, Frank became ever more determined to find her before the day was out and to put a stop to her wild plans of going to America.

He strode into the dining room at the Rose and Crown, uncaring of his dishevelled appearance, mud-spattered from his ride, with only one thing in mind—to find Charlotte. His eyes searched the room and landed on her. The tightness in his chest that had been his constant companion these last few days eased upon sight of her. "Charlotte!" he cried and went to her. With little consideration for formality, he gathered her to him, murmuring, "Thank God, thank God."

Charlotte went to him willingly. She had thought never to see him again, and yet here he was. She revelled in the solid feel of him, the smell of his sweat, the roughness of his whiskers. "Frank," she whispered. "What are you doing here?"

He pulled back a little to look down at her face. "What do you think? I am here for you, to stop this mad dash to America. Charlotte, my darling love, stay with me and I will make it all right. Trust me to take care of you, please."

Their reunion was interrupted by Ruth's cool voice. "Viscount Stanton, for I take it that is who you are, please let us step into the private parlour next door and continue this conversation away from prying eyes and ears."

Frank looked at her, startled. "You must be Ruth," he said.

"Indeed, viscount. Shall we?" She pointed to the door.

He nodded and let go of Charlotte. Together, the whole group, including Robert and Jasper, made their way out to the hall and into the small parlour. Jasper had the wherewithal to tell the innkeeper that they were not to be disturbed on any account before shutting the door on him.

Frank had barely waited for that door to shut before he was taking Charlotte into his arms again. "Charlotte," he now said once more. "I have come to take you back home. Trust me to make everything right."

At his words, Charlotte reluctantly pulled back, coming out of her lovesick haze and down to earth with a decisive bump. "I am sorry, Frank," she murmured, "but I cannot go back with you. My course is set; my ticket purchased. I am to go with Ruth and Robert to America."

"That you are not!" growled the viscount.

"Yes, Frank, I am. There is nothing for me to go back to except disgrace and dishonour. I was willing to be your mistress in secret for a short time, but I will not be kept by you and bring more shame to my family. That is not the life for me."

Frank's eyes were supplicating as he said roughly, "Please Charlotte, do not go. I could not bear it. I promise I will take care of everything for you, and you shall want for nothing."

"Nothing except my good name," she responded bitterly.

"Is it marriage you wish for then?" he demanded.

She shook her head sadly. "No, Frank. You would only live to regret it. Had you really wanted me for a wife, you would have asked me long before and not proposed to Miss Powell. I will not have you marry me under duress, and I will not live as your mistress, so you see, there is nothing for it but to say goodbye."

"No! Charlotte, I will not allow it!"

"You must!" she said on a sob.

"That's enough!" came a sharp voice. It was Ruth again. Now she came to stand before Frank. "Viscount Stanton, we are going around in circles here, and I think it is best we all retire for the night, for the hour is late. In the morning, you will have the chance to say your goodbyes to Charlotte and perhaps by then, you will have accepted the truth of the matter. Charlotte has made a choice, which you must respect, much as it will pain you. She will not return to London to become your mistress, and if you have even one shred of affection for her, you will not force her into a life that degrades her honour."

As the viscount made to speak, she spoke forcefully again, "Enough sir! Enough. Now I do not know what arrangements you have made for the night, but the inn is full. If, however, I were to share a room with Charlotte, than you and the gentleman could take the one allocated to me for the night."

The viscount gripped Charlotte's hand, seemingly unwilling to let her go. By the door, Robert stood with his arms crossed, a grim frown marring his face. Ruth stared the viscount down, not intimidated by his superior rank and size.

"Charlotte, please listen to me—" began Frank again, but this time it was his brother that interposed.

Jasper put a hand to his shoulder and said gently, "Let her go for tonight, Frank. Miss Ellis is right. It is late, and we are both in need of a wash. Come away. You will see her in the morning and talk again then."

Reluctantly, Frank released Charlotte's hand, but not before saying raggedly, "Charlotte, let me but obtain a license and speak to Helena to end our engagement, and I will marry you, I promise. Please, my love, do not get on that ship tomorrow."

Charlotte went still. Once upon a time, an offer of marriage from Frank would have been a dream come true. Now though,

261

it tasted bittersweet, an offer made in desperation—and possibly one he would come to regret. How many times in her most secret of hopes, had she wanted him to choose her, even in the face of his father's opposition? He never did though, and now was far too late in the day for her to believe that he had undergone a radical change of heart and genuinely wanted her for his wife. She knew Frank cared about her and that he craved the sensual pleasure of her body. It was lust that was making him speak so. It could not be anything else.

With a last residual of strength, she spoke up in a firm voice, "No, Frank. I will not marry you. Tomorrow, we must say goodbye." Standing on tiptoe, she kissed him softly on the lips then hurried to the door, which Robert opened for her. His glower made it clear to Frank that he was not to follow her, as did Jasper's squeeze of his arm. So, Frank let her go—for now.

Chapter 37

Frank lay on the bed, staring blindly up at the darkened ceiling. After some protracted discussion with the innkeeper, he and Jasper had been put up in the room that Ruth Ellis had vacated. Some hot water had been brought up for them to wash, and they had eaten a quick repast. A few minutes ago, Jasper had extinguished the candle, leaving them in pitch darkness. They were both thoroughly exhausted from riding the whole day, yet unable to sleep. Frank could tell by his brother's soft breaths next to him that he too was still wide awake.

He was proved right when a few moments later, Jasper's voice spoke quietly next to him, "So, what are you going to do now?"

For a long time, Frank did not reply. What could he do now? Charlotte was evidently set on going to America. She had refused his offer of marriage. She was with loyal friends now, who would look out for her on that long voyage. What was he to do but accept the cards fate had dealt, wish her well and go home? The fact that he would be going back to face a sterile marriage to Helena and more of living under his father's shadow was neither here nor there.

"Frank?" prompted Jasper.

Speaking so softly that his brother had to strain to hear him, Frank murmured, "I suppose I shall have to go to America as well."

Jasper shifted in the bed, turning on his side to stare at the dark form beside him. "Do you mean to follow her there to convince her to marry you, then return?"

"You may think me mad, Jasper, but I am considering burning my bridges and not returning at all."

"I do not think you mad, Frank. On the contrary, I think you are finally beginning to make perfect sense," responded Jasper softly. Then he added, "In that case, I shall come along with you too."

"You do know, Jasper, that with me gone, father would most likely make you his heir," said Frank reflectively.

"That is precisely why I have to decamp with you, Frank. I have no desire to fall into the gilded trap you've been in all these years."

Frank chuckled dryly, "Gilded trap?" Then on reflection, he added, "You are quite right to call it that." He was quiet again for a long time, eventually murmuring, "Thank you Jasper. It will mean a lot to have you with me."

Jasper snorted, "I am not just doing this for you, you know, much as I care for you, brother. This is a chance for me too. As the landless second son, my choices are the Church or the army, neither of which I feel particularly suited for. I quite like the notion of being a pioneer, seeking out new land to claim."

"It sounds romantic," remarked Frank, "but it will probably involve back-breaking work of the type we have not known in our pampered lives. Are you ready to leave the comforts of home for that?"

"I cannot wait!" Jasper said with a sigh.

Frank laughed good naturedly, "Goodnight, Jasper."

"Goodnight, Frank."

———————•———————

At the first break of dawn, the two brothers were up. They wrote letters, which were promptly dispatched. They went to the booking office and purchased tickets on the Hibernia. There were no first class cabins available, so they had to content themselves with booking the only two remaining second class ones, much to the consternation of the booking clerk, who tried very hard to convince them to sail on a later ship, for he could not imagine a viscount travelling second class.

The viscount stood firm. It had to be the Hibernia. He would not let Charlotte slip away again, and moreover, foregoing the luxuries of first class would be good preparation for the more modest lives ahead of them. Following their visit to the booking office, some extra necessities for the journey were purchased, and some haggling done with a local stable to sell their two fine stallions, earning them much needed extra sovereigns to take with them.

By the time they were done, it was already after nine o'clock, and much too late to head back to the inn. There was nothing for it but to go directly to the docks and board the Hibernia. Frank would see Charlotte again when the ship was at sea, and perhaps then, she would believe that he was serious and true in his feelings for her.

They were some of the last passengers to board the ship that day, and there was no sign of Charlotte or her friends on the deck when they did so. The brothers settled their belongings in the two side-by-side cabins allocated to them. These were located at the end of the lower deck, small but adequate, consisting of a bed with linens, a snug table with a chair, and a narrow closet. The cabins had slats on the doors for ventilation, though this in turn afforded little privacy, for Frank could hear the distinctly loud tones of the gentleman and his wife occupying the opposite cabin. The doors opened into a communal saloon with a long wooden table and benches, where passengers could socialise and dine.

Into this saloon, Frank emerged shortly after getting settled in his cabin. His brother, like a shadow, soon followed. There was still no sign of Charlotte's presence, though he knew from speaking to one of the ship mates on arrival that a Miss Harding had boarded the Hibernia some several hours previously. Unless she was ensconced in her cabin, there was only one other place she could be—on the top deck to have a last view of England as it receded into the distance.

After a short discussion, the brothers decided to find their way up there. This took longer than they anticipated, as they were waylaid by other passengers in the saloon wanting to make their acquaintance. With the minimum of civility, Frank introduced himself to the couple occupying the cabin opposite, Mr and Mrs Stanhope, a merchant banker and his wife. He also said his greetings to a Mr Trombley, a railway engineer, and finally to a Mr Brookes, an American gentleman from New York, returning home after an extended visit to his relatives in England. With the civilities over, he excused himself and hastened with his brother up the steps to the upper deck.

He was greeted with a gust of wind as he stepped on to the swaying deck; the ship had cast off its anchor and was on its way to America. Eagerly, he looked about, not for a last sight of England, but for a diminutive figure in a drab brown pelisse.

"Over there," said Jasper quietly by his side, pointing with his eyes.

And there she was. Charlotte stood in profile from him, holding on to the deck rail as she stared ahead at the last traces of England's shores. Her face looked pale, with shadows under eyes from which tears were streaming down. Frank felt that now familiar tightening of his chest on seeing her in such pain. Oh dear Lord, this was all his fault, but he would make it right. He had been such a fool and blind for much too long. That would stop now. From this day forth, he would make it his life's mission to put a smile on that precious face, plain to him no more.

He stepped determinedly towards her until he stood mere inches away. "Charlotte," he spoke. She froze, unable to believe her senses, then whipped around, her streaming eyes wide with shock.

"Frank?" she croaked.

"Yes, darling. You did not think I would let you go so easily, did you?"

"I—I," she stammered, unable to say more.

Gently, he wiped the tears away with his thumb. "No more of these, my love. From today, we start a new life, one in which I will strive every day to bring you the happiness you deserve. I love you, Charlotte. Marry me, please."

Poor Charlotte was still too incoherent to answer. Was this a dream? A delusion?

Frank smiled, "You do not need to answer me now, but know this. I shall ask you to be my wife every single day until you say yes. Now come here." He drew her to him, letting her burrow her face into his chest, feeling her soak the fabric of his waistcoat with yet more tears—happy ones he hoped.

"About time you came to your senses, viscount," said a dry voice beside him.

He turned his head to see Ruth Ellis watching him in satisfaction. "Yes," he agreed, "it is well past time I stopped being such a fool."

She smiled then, "Good."

Jasper came round to his other side. "I do not have champagne to make a toast with," he proclaimed happily, "but here's to a fresh start for all of us in America. May God let us prosper!"

"Amen!" responded Ruth.

Charlotte pulled back in surprise. "You mean to stay in America?"

"I mean to follow you wherever you go, sweet Charlotte. And I think it is well for us all to make a fresh start, as Jasper says. Don't you think?"

She nodded, her eyes welling again.

"Oh my love, what did I say about no more tears?" remonstrated Frank.

"It is only because I am so happy," Charlotte said with a sob.

For this, she was rewarded with another tight hug.

Letters dispatched on 7th June, 1835

To: Mr Eastleigh
Offices of Eastleigh, Bridges & Co.
Chancery Lane, London

Dear Mr Eastleigh,

I write to you with a change of plan. I no longer wish to purchase a house for Miss Harding, as had been previously instructed, for the lady is journeying to America on the Hibernia today, and I plan to join her in the sincere hope that she will consent to become my wife. I also plan to establish myself in America permanently, with no view to returning to England in the foreseeable future. With this in mind, I would kindly request the following.

First, that the funds released from the mortgage I have taken on my land be deposited in an account with the banking firm Barings & Co in New York.

Second, that the income from my investments and the tenancies on my estate at Hartley Court be used to repay this mortgage according to the agreed schedule. The remainder of the income is to be accrued and deposited in said bank account in New York on a quarterly basis, minus all required expenses — wages of my estate manager and servants for keeping the house and estate in good order, as well as the fees for your firm's services.

Third, that my lodgings in Wimpole Street be vacated and my tenancy there be brought to an end. All personal belongings to be packed and shipped to me in New York, care of the offices of Barings & Co. My valet, Mr Hudson, to be paid three months' worth of wages and given the appropriate references.

I shall write again once I am fixed in my new home in America, but for the time being, please send all correspondence to me via the offices of Barings & Co in New York.

Respectfully yours,
Viscount Stanton

To: Miss Helena Powell
27 Berkeley Square, London

Dear Helena,

By now, I am sure you will have heard of my having left London to chase after Charlotte. I have finally caught up with her in Liverpool, where she is set to sail to America today, intent on starting a new life away from the scandals of the ton. She is with some close childhood friends, who are also emigrating.

Helena, I have made the decision to go with her. I cannot bear to let Charlotte go, for I am deeply in love with her. I am therefore releasing you from our engagement. Please accept my most sincere apologies for the hurt and embarrassment I have caused you. I am so terribly sorry and wish I could have known my feelings sooner and spared you this. My only consolation is the knowledge that your affections were not deeply engaged, and that there has yet to be an official announcement of our betrothal in the Times or the need to retract it.

It was an honour to have known you, Helena. I have nothing but warm regard and admiration for you. I wish you well and hope you will find it in your heart one day to forgive me.

Yours,

Frank Stanton

To: Earl Stanton
Stanton Hall, Stanton Harcourt, Oxfordshire

Dear Sir,

I write to let you know that I am leaving for America to be with Miss Charlotte Harding, who I plan to marry just as soon as she accepts my proposal. I have already written to Miss Powell breaking off our engagement and offering her my sincere apologies. I know that my decision will cause you pain and disappointment. I am sorry for this, but I have lived too long according to your wishes with little regard for my own wants. Father, I have never wished for a political career, and I had no desire to marry Helena Powell. Those were things you wanted and imposed on me in the misguided conviction that they would bring me fulfilment, but that is not the case.

What I wish for is to live a quiet life, managing my own lands and investments, raising a family with the lady I love, and that lady is Charlotte Harding. We sail today, bound for New York, where I hope to celebrate our nuptials. From there, we will travel to the state of Ohio where I have plans to settle and establish myself. It is my wish, as much as it is possible, to build a prosperous life based on my own labours rather than on an inherited fortune that I have not earned or deserved.

I know that this decision will leave you without an heir to pass the Stanton estate to — as Jasper too comes with me — and I am sorry for this. But as my brother rightly says, that patrimony is a gilded trap. I need to be free of it to live life on my own terms. I have seen with my own eyes what little happiness the massive Stanton fortune has brought to your life, father, and it is not an example I wish to follow. Please know that I continue to hold you in the greatest affection and esteem.

Your loving son,
Frank Stanton

To: Earl Stanton
Stanton Hall, Stanton Harcourt, Oxfordshire

Dear Sir,

I am leaving for America to accompany Frank on his next adventure and to see if I can make my own fortune. Doubtless you know that the Church and the army are better off without my bumbling presence. All my life, I have been a sad disappointment to you, so one more disappointment should not matter greatly.

Perhaps sir, had you shown us more warmth, loving affection and less rigid enforcement of your rules, your two sons might not now be going to live so far from you. While I may have been a disappointing son, let me take this one opportunity to say that you, father, have been a most disappointing parent too. Perhaps had mother lived, things would have been different. By all accounts, she had a warm and loving nature, though of course I cannot remember her at all since I was but a babe when we lost her.

I wish you well, for despite the disappointment mentioned above, I do still hold you in great affection. Wish me luck, father!

Your errant son,

Jasper Stanton

P.S. Please could you arrange for my belongings to be boxed and shipped to New York, care of the offices of Barings & Co. I would mourn the loss of that splendid maroon waistcoat which so offended you last I wore it.

Epilogue

Five years later

"Repeat after me. *Five or more, let it soar. Four or less, let it rest.*" The dozen children in the schoolroom chanted the little rhyme that Charlotte had taught them to help with the rounding of numbers. It was a late June morning, and already the warm breeze coming in through the open windows signalled yet another hot day to come.

Charlotte rubbed her lower back, which ached a little from standing on her feet for so long and from the growing child in her belly. There were still another two and half months to go before this child, her third, would make an appearance. Perhaps this time, it would be a girl. She hoped so, and so did Frank.

"Now children, you have five minutes to complete the questions on the board. Working quietly." Charlotte walked around her classroom, checking on her pupils' efforts and correcting when needed. She had set up this small school a year after her arrival here from England. And what a year that was! There had been great happiness as can only be found when two people in love come together, but there had also been intense struggle, and long days of industrious work to clear the forested land the two Stanton brothers had claimed, close to the Ellis family holdings.

Frank and Jasper had spent those days in hard physical labour, aided by two young farm workers they had hired. It was a far cry from the snobbery, pomp and idleness of the life they had left behind in England. Their daily work outdoors had changed them too. They had been tall and muscular before, but now their muscles were honed even stronger and their skin browned by the sun—handsomer than ever in Charlotte's eyes.

Using logs from the trees they had felled, the two brothers oversaw the erection of a new house, a graceful and spacious building overlooking their thousand acres of corn and wheat fields. That project took another year to complete, during which time the Stantons lived in a rented cottage in the village of Saybrook, which lay just over a mile away from their land. There it was that Charlotte came up with the idea of starting a small school to educate the local children. At first, her pupils had numbered only three, rising over the years to the dozen in her classroom now.

"Alright children, class over. Wipe your boards and put them away neatly please." With a clatter, the boards were put away. The children stood, and one by one, filed out of the classroom to make their way home. With a sigh, Charlotte tidied away and set up the large blackboard for the following day's learning. Then she too made her way out, locking the school's door securely. She walked the few paces to the stable building where her mare was munching placidly on some straw, then tethered it to the compact buggy parked nearby and climbed aboard. With a light flick of the reins and a "Come on, girl", she began her short journey home. First, she stopped at her friend Ruth's house to collect her two young boys, Daniel and Benjamin.

"Have you been good for Auntie Ruth?" she asked four-year-old Daniel as she saw him.

"Yes mama! We helped feed the chickens and cleaned out the barn, didn't we auntie?"

Ruth smiled, "They did indeed." Her eyes settled on Charlotte with concern. "You look tired. Is your back paining you again?"

Charlotte rubbed at it wearily. "Only a little. I shall rest once I am back home, and it will be fine."

"Do not push yourself so. Perhaps you could shorten your school sessions and reduce the time you spend on your feet there."

"I will consider it. I do feel so heavy on my feet these days."

"Then do it," said Ruth firmly.

Both boys were helped on to the buggy, and a box with a dozen fresh eggs placed inside. "Goodbye Ruth," Charlotte called out. "Give my regards to Robert."

"Goodbye Charlotte. Don't forget to rest. Let Ruby run after these two little hellcats for a while."

"I will." With that, Charlotte set the buggy moving again. It took only a few minutes to reach home. As ever when she crossed the gravelled path and saw the large, white-trimmed house ahead with its shingled roof and long, inviting porch, she felt a sense of pride at what the two Stanton brothers had achieved, working in harmony side-by-side. To her eyes, this house was more beautiful than any of the imposing mansions she had seen in London.

With quick, efficient movements, she brought the buggy to the stable, untethered her mare and gave her a rub down, ensuring there was plenty of water and fresh straw for her to munch on. With the two boys in tow, she walked to the house, stepping inside to the delicious aroma of baking bread. Right on cue, Daniel whimpered, "Mama, I'm hungry!"

"Well, pa and Uncle Jasper should be in very soon. Take Benjamin with you and go wash your face and hands, then you can help set the table for dinner."

"Alright. Come on Ben," said Daniel.

As they headed to the downstairs washroom, Charlotte went into the spacious kitchen and pantry, bearing the fresh eggs that Ruth had just given her. "Hello, Ruby. How is dinner coming along? The boys are famished, and I expect the men will be too when they arrive shortly."

Ruby was both their housemaid and cook, and an absolute godsend. She was married to Davy, who was in charge of the growing number of cattle at the Stanton farm. She was a warm-hearted country lass from Yorkshire who had come to America on the Hibernia as a newlywed with her husband Davy five years ago. On that journey, they had met and befriended Robert Ellis, who had been travelling in steerage along with them. On arrival in New York, Davy had, with very little hesitation, ditched his original plans and decided to join Robert Ellis and the Stantons on their journey to Ohio. He had elected not to claim his own parcel of land, but to work with the Stantons on theirs in return for a percentage share of their enterprise. Davy and Ruby lived in a cottage he had built, some yards further along on the acreage he had helped to clear away. The arrangement worked well for everyone.

Now Ruby replied, "It's a chicken pot roast today, with a side of buttery mash and beans. And for pudding I've made a spiced carrot cake." While she spoke, she took out the large loaf of freshly baked bread and began to slice it up.

Charlotte raised a brow. "Carrot in a cake? I had not thought to see that."

Ruby chuckled, "Neither had I, but I overheard talk of it at the village store the other day, and I thought to myself it would be worth a try."

"I am sure as with everything you bake, Ruby, that it will be delectable," said Charlotte taking out the butter dish from the pantry.

"Ah, well we shall see."

Charlotte took the basket of bread and the butter to the dining room and set them on the table. Just as she did so, she heard the back door opening and the distinctive sound of boots on the stone floor. There was a gruff sigh as the boots were removed and placed on the boot rack. A moment later, Frank padded into the hallway and caught sight of his wife. His tired face broke into a warm, happy smile on sight of her as it always did. Incongruous to think that he had once thought her plain.

Two strides and he was at her side, taking her into his arms for a long, hungry kiss. He would never tire of the taste and feel of her soft, plump lips. When they emerged from the kiss, he saw with satisfaction that her breaths were ragged and her face flushed a rosy pink. "Madam wife," he growled low. "I do believe you are in urgent need of your husband's cock."

"There is no time," she panted. "We are about to serve dinner."

"Then we shall have to be quick. Upstairs, now," he gritted. Taking her hand, he pulled her up the stairs with him, just as the sound of the back door opening again heralded Jasper's arrival. Quickly, they flew up the steps and down the long hall to their bedchamber. As soon as the door shut behind them, he locked it and glanced feverishly at her. "You have one minute, sweet hussy, to bare that cunt and spread it for me." Saying this, he began to rip at his own clothing, pulling his shirt over his head and taking down his pants and drawers in one go. In moments, he stood before her in his naked glory, the muscles in his abdomen rippling and glistening with a hint of sweat, his large cock jutting out from the nest of dark hair at his groin.

Charlotte's mouth went dry at the sight of him, as she paused her undressing to admire him. *My husband is a beautiful man,* she thought, not for the first time.

"I gave you one minute, hussy. Are you looking for a spanking?" demanded Frank.

"Maybe?"

He lunged at her then, twisting her around and pushing her onto the bed so she landed on her elbows and knees. Hiking up the skirt of her dress, he took hold of her pantalettes and tore them off, exposing her lush bottom. With a ragged breath, he drew her legs apart and brought his mouth to her moist cunt. He licked and sucked at her, relishing the sweet musky flavour of her. She writhed under his touch, making little moans of pleasure. Without warning, his hand came to land a loud smack on one bottom cheek. She squealed. He repeated the action, this time on the other cheek. "That, madam wife, was for failing to follow your husband's instructions. Now are you going to be a good hussy and take this cock in your cunt?"

"Yes, yes," Charlotte said breathlessly.

276

Barely had she spoken than he slammed into her, burying his long length all the way inside her tight passage. "Ah," she cried.

In response, he plunged into her again, and again. Soon, he was setting a punishing rhythm, chasing his pleasure and hers. One of his hands held her hip firmly in place as he hammered his cock into her. The other crept up to the juncture of her legs, finding the firm little nub of flesh that brought her so much joy. "Yes!" she panted, wanting more.

"Are you going to come when I say so, lady wife?" he grunted.

"Yes!" she cried.

He thrust forcefully again, pounding her with his cock. "Then come now!"

With a cry, she gave herself over to pleasure, her cunt tightening around him in blissful convulsions. A second later, his shaft swelled, and he spilled his seed deep inside her, groaning in satisfaction. He stilled, staying buried in her heat for a few moments more before reluctantly pulling out. Without a word, he got a wet cloth and wiped her clean, admiring the pink handprints he had left on her flesh. He kissed her there, then bent to retrieve her discarded undergarment from the floor.

She turned around slowly, her swollen belly hampering her efforts. He kissed her there, murmuring, "Hello daughter. If you are as wanton as your mama, then I predict trouble."

Charlotte huffed, but smiled as Frank helped her pull on the pantalettes again. Just as she finished readjusting her dress, the door handle moved as someone outside tried to get in the room. "Ma, pa," came Daniel's voice. "Come down for dinner. We are waiting for you. Why is the door locked?"

With a laugh, Frank called out, "Never you mind, son. Go back down. We shall be with you shortly."

With quick strokes, he wiped his body clean from the cum and the sweat of the day, then put on the fresh clothes Charlotte

277

had taken out of the drawer for him. In moments, he was ready, and taking her hand, walked her down the stairs to the dining room where Jasper sat with the boys, an amused expression on his handsome face.

"Poor Daniel is wondering why ma and pa's door was locked," he mocked. "I could not for the life of me explain."

"Then don't," came Frank's reply as he took his seat. "Let us say grace and eat. I for one cannot wait a minute longer." And so, they did.

Another year later

Frank and Charlotte stepped out into a bright, sunny June morning as they emerged from the church at the end of Sunday service. They were followed by Robert Ellis and his new bride, Felicity. At the rear came Ruth, and with her, Jasper Stanton.

Aged twenty-six, Jasper had finally come into his own. He was a man in his prime, though he still had a tendency for jokes and merriment. He hoped now he had finished the building of his own house on a plot beside Frank's place, that Ruth would finally see fit to accepting his offer of marriage.

He had proposed to her at least once every single year since they had come to America. The answer had always been no. She was too old for him. Pah, nonsense! They came from a different class. Again, not an issue now they were in the land of the free. He had no home to offer her. This, he had taken seriously. With meticulous care, he had built what he hoped was the house of her dreams. Now all he had to do was ask again. Perhaps after lunch, which was a large gathering at Frank's house, he would take her out for a walk to the edge of the creek, then get down on one knee.

The Stantons and the Ellises climbed aboard their various buggies and began the ten-minute journey home. As they drew up in front of the large, white-trimmed house, they saw a carriage drawn by four fine horses stopped out front. Five-year old Daniel echoed everyone's thoughts when he asked out loud, "Who is that?"

Frank frowned, not recognising the carriage as belonging to anyone he knew. "I do not know, son." He jumped down and walked towards it. As he did so, the carriage door opened, and an older gentleman made his way cautiously down.

Frank stopped in his tracks, not believing his eyes. "Father?" he asked doubtfully.

"Well, are you not going to invite me in?" countered the Earl of Stanton gruffly.

"Yes, of course. Come on in, father." He flew up the porch steps to open the door.

With a regal air, the earl followed him, looking about curiously. He stepped into the large, wood-panelled hallway, then into the front parlour. Turning around, he inspected the airy room, decorated tastefully, with little in the way of ostentatiousness. "So, this is what you turned your back on Stanton Hall for," he remarked.

"This and a lot more besides," replied Frank.

By now, Jasper had entered the room. With far less reserve than his brother, he strode forward. "By Jove, father, you are here!"

"As you can see," responded the earl drily.

A moment later, his younger son had him in a warm embrace. Startled, the earl froze, then clapped his son awkwardly on the shoulder in return. "Jasper, you are grown at least an inch taller since last I saw you."

Jasper grinned, "And broader too!" He inspected his father from top to toe. "I am glad to see you hale and hearty, sir."

The earl waved an impatient hand. "You know that I never get sick." His eyes looked over Jasper's shoulder and took in Charlotte, holding her baby daughter in her arms. He bowed curtly in greeting, then peered at the baby. "I take it this is Isabella," he said.

279

"Yes, it is," she replied softly.

Frank had kept up a steady, one-sided correspondence with his father, sending a letter at least once a month, though never receiving anything in return. He had often wondered if his letters had been received and whether they had been read. Now he knew.

The earl ran a finger down the baby's soft cheek, then looked over at Daniel and Benjamin, both of whom were gawping at him, their eyes like saucers. "Well," he said. "Aren't you going to greet your grandpa?"

Daniel stepped forward then and bowed, the way he had seen his father do. "How do you do?" he asked in a very proper manner, eliciting a proud smile from both of his parents.

"I am well, thank you Daniel. It is good to finally meet you after hearing so much about you from your father's letters." The earl bent down to greet his other grandson. "And you must be Benjamin."

The boy nodded shyly, then hid his face behind his father's leg.

Frank laid a reassuring hand on Benjamin's head, all the while saying, "Please, father, do sit down. Would you like a cup of tea? Or perhaps something stronger."

"I would not mind a small glass of sherry, Francis."

"Of course. I shall join you in one."

Jasper placed a hand on Frank's shoulder. "Stay, I shall get them."

They all settled themselves on the various settees and armchairs in the room. A ponderous silence ensued, broken only when Frank blurted out, "Why are you here, father?"

The earl glared at his son. "Do I need a reason to want to see my only living family, especially since not a single one of them has the decency to come see me?"

"I was not sure I would be welcome. You never answered any of my letters."

The earl huffed, "Francis, what did you think I would do if you came to me? Turn you away?" He glanced at Charlotte, sitting with her dozing daughter in her lap. "No disrespect to your wife, but I was not going to be blindly foolish like that old Sir Edward Harding and disown my own flesh and blood! I had hoped you would realise this in time and come visit. When you did not, I decided it was time to take matters into my own hands. The crossing on the steam ship was quick and fairly painless. Then the steam train very conveniently took me the rest of the way. No doubt my journey was a lot easier than yours was six years ago."

Frank smiled, "No doubt."

Jasper handed his father the glass of sherry and said jovially, "Well I'm jolly glad you did. It is good to see you, father."

The earl took the sherry and sipped it appreciatively. "And it is good to see you, son. I take it the grey painted house next door is yours?"

"It is," said Jasper proudly. Then he added, "Father, there is someone I would like you to meet. I hope one day she will agree to be my wife."

The earl fixed his steely gaze on his younger son. "Then send Miss Ellis in, for I am just as curious to meet the person who inspires such devotion in you."

"How did you know?" asked Jasper, surprised. "I am sure I never said as much in any of my letters to you."

The earl snorted, "You said plenty, believe me! Now bring her in, for I fancy she is the young lady that was in the carriage with you just now."

Jasper jumped to his feet and went to the dining room, where Robert, his wife and Ruth waited, not wanting to intrude on the family reunion. "Ruth, he wants to meet you. Please, all of you come in. I promise he doesn't bite."

The Ellises rose to their feet and followed Jasper into the parlour. The earl stood, bowing stiffly to Robert and Felicity.

Then his attention fixed on Ruth. "When are you going to put my boy out of his misery?" he barked.

Ruth curtsied, then eyed him coolly. "Earl Stanton, a pleasure to make your acquaintance."

"You have not answered my question."

"That is because it is not yours to ask." Her eyes searched for Jasper's.

"Then for the love of God, Jasper, ask it!" demanded the earl.

All eyes turned expectantly on Jasper. He stood, frozen in surprise. Then quickly regrouping, he smiled at Ruth, "I had hoped to do this a little more privately, but here goes." He dropped to one knee in front of her. "Ruth, love of my life, will you do me the great honour of becoming my wife?"

She did not respond at once, seemingly thinking his offer through. Then, in a calm voice, she spoke, "Yes Jasper, I will."

"Thank the Lord!"

Jasper drew her to him and placed a chaste kiss on her lips, promising himself that first opportunity he got, he would kiss her again, a lot less chastely.

That day, Sunday lunch was a merry affair, with the double joy of the earl's arrival and Jasper's engagement. After much insisting from Frank, who did not want his father to put up in the dubious accommodation of the village inn, the earl agreed to stay with them. His trunk was duly brought down from the carriage and unpacked by his faithful valet.

The earl's sojourn in America lasted long enough to see his younger son wed a month later. And then the day of his departure finally dawned. Frank rode beside his father to the train station and waited with him on the platform. Some minutes later, the train chuffed in and came to a stop before them. The earl's trunk was loaded on, and he now prepared to board. He turned to Frank in a final farewell. No embrace, for this was not his style. He placed a hand on his son's arm and said, "Goodbye Francis. Please keep writing."

Frank nodded, a lump in his throat. "I will."

"And Francis. You have done well for yourself here. I am proud of you."

Not waiting for an answer, the earl turned on his heel and climbed aboard the train. Frank watched, his eyes glazed with tears he refused to shed, as the train chugged on, taking away the father whose approval he had always craved.

Afterword

About the author

M.M. Wakeford writes romance in many genres including contemporary, sci-fi and historical. All her stories strive to capture that heady feeling of falling in love, with authentic characters whose journey to a happily ever after is lined with dilemmas to overcome. If you're looking for a page turning romance with high emotion and a good dose of spice, you've come to the right place.

The Vixen's Unlikely Marriage

A Historical Marriage of Convenience Romance
(An Excerpt)

Book 2
THE STANTON LEGACY

M.M. Wakeford

Chapter 1

Ohio, September 1860

She nudged open the stable door and stepped inside. All was quiet except for the occasional snuffle of the horses. It was over an hour since they had been brought back into their stalls for the night. They had been rubbed down and fed, their water trough filled. Nobody would be coming back in here until morning.

Shutting the door quietly behind her, she carefully struck a match and lit the small oil lamp she had brought along, setting it atop an empty shelf so that it cast a dim orange glow throughout the stable. Then, very carefully, she stepped up the ladder to the hayloft. A brown woollen rug had been spread above the hay bales in anticipation of her arrival. She smiled. *Good old Jimmy.*

She began to undress methodically, unbuttoning her dress and pulling it above her head. Beneath it, she wore only a shift and a pair of stockings held up by a garter. These she removed too, leaving her pale naked body gleaming like an alabaster sculpture in the dull light. It was a pert body, its youthful curves subtle yet noticeable. Her breasts were tipped by dusky pink nipples that tightened and pebbled in the slight chill of the evening. Dark blond curls nestled upon her mound, only a fraction darker than the curls on her head.

She lowered herself to the rug, leaning upon her elbows, and waited. Not two minutes later, she heard the stable door open and gently shut. "Grace!" whispered Jimmy's voice.

"Up here," she responded quietly.

She heard his boots cross the stable floor to the hayloft ladder and his quick steps climbing up. He paused as he reached the top, his eyes finding her spread naked on the rug. For a long moment, he simply stared at the wondrous sight.

"Oh my great Lord!" he declared in absolute awe. "How beautiful you are."

"Are you just going to stand there and gawp?" enquired Grace with an amused and pleased smile.

"No ma'am." In one bound, he was over the ladder and at her feet. His eyes stayed fixed on her luscious beauty while he hastily disrobed. The shirt flew over his head, revealing a wiry, muscular frame. Work boots were kicked off and his pants pushed to the floor together with his undergarments. He stood above her, powerful thighs from years of training and riding horses, freckled skin tanned by hours spent under the sun, and a thick cock jutting from a nest of sandy coloured curls.

She gazed at him appreciatively. *"Men are such interesting looking creatures,"* she thought, *"especially down there."* She noted the drop of cum that oozed from the dark-fleshed tip of his cock and the two plump sacs behind it that dropped down like low-hanging, succulent fruit.

A moment later, his body came down on top of hers and she felt that hardened shaft press into her abdomen as he sought her mouth for a kiss. She opened her lips to him, letting her tongue tangle with his. He tasted like Jimmy, an earthy male tang, with a hint of the beef stew he had just eaten for his dinner.

They kissed hungrily as hands explored whatever was within reach. He squeezed a breast with a palm, then brought his fingers to play with the pebbled texture of her nipples. They kissed some more.

Grace was familiar with his kisses. They had been fumbling around in darkened corners, snatching stolen moments to lock their lips together ever since she had turned fifteen—he a year older. Over time, their fumbles had become more intense, more curious, until two months ago, when, just shy over her eighteenth birthday, she had stumbled upon him swimming in the tree-sheltered shore of the creek lake. It had been a blisteringly hot day, and he had badly needed to cool off in the water. She too, had come armed with a towel for exactly the same purpose.

"Jimmy!" she called. "You have stolen a march on me. I came here to bathe. Now what am I to do?"

He swam towards her and stood in the shallow end of the lake up to his waist. "Why don't you join me?" he suggested with a cheeky grin.

At first, she hesitated. Should she? Ma and pa would definitely not approve, but there again, they would not approve of those delightful stolen kisses she had indulged in for the past three years either. What could a little more sinfulness matter in the grand scheme of things? She shrugged and called out to Jimmy, "Alright."

With hands that shook ever so slightly, she undid the fastenings of her dress and slipped it over her head. Quickly, before she lost her nerve, she took off her undergarments, and fully bare, ran into the cool, welcoming embrace of the water.

Jimmy watched her in astonished awe, not quite believing that she would follow through with his suggestion. For a while, they circled each other, splashing about in delight at the wonderfully soothing caress of the water on their naked skin. Soon though, they began to swim a little closer to each other until Jimmy took his courage between his hands and grabbed her.

That afternoon had ended with Grace giving away her maiden head, the blood of which was washed away in the calm waters of the lake. When finally she had dressed to go home, she had known that this one time would never be enough, and that she would seek every opportunity to lie with Jimmy again. In the past few weeks, the hayloft in the stable had become the place where they met in secret for their lovemaking. Each time, Grace grew more hungry for the ache and release that Jimmy's body gave her. She could no longer imagine going through life without this.

Now, Jimmy's hand crept down her body to stroke the soft, hidden flesh at the pinnacle of her thighs. It was sticky and wet with her desire. He knew that a few more strokes would have her convulsing in sweet relief, but he wanted to feel those heavenly contractions on his cock. "Gracie," he said roughly. "I need to be inside you."

In answer, she guided his shaft to her opening. Taking this as his cue, he pushed forward, thrusting himself into her all the way to the hilt. They both sighed in pleasurable relief at the sensation of being joined so intimately. "Oh Jimmy, you feel so good inside me," Grace breathed.

"Not half so good as you feel to me." He began to thrust deep into her, slowly at first but soon building up a rapid rhythm as they both chased their climax. His cock was thick and long enough to hit a spot deep inside her tight passage, rubbing it pleasurably until she cried, reaching that state of bliss. As he felt her contracting tightly around his cock, he remembered just in time to pull out and shoot his seed on her abdomen. He had been careful, apart from that first time by the lake, not to come inside her, and so far, they had been lucky.

Having grown up on a farm, both knew well the reproductive facts of life, and neither relished the prospect of producing a child outside of wedlock. Jimmy also knew that Grace would never be more than a secret fling. Her father, Jasper Stanton, and her uncle, Francis Stanton—who back in England was a viscount—owned the extensive farm on which he worked as a stable boy, and they would hardly be likely to approve a match between Grace and himself. He didn't mind. Of course, he was very fond of Gracie, but their relationship was built on camaraderie and lust rather than love.

Gently, he rolled over until he lay on his back beside her, basking in the afterglow of pleasure. After a while, he murmured, "You had best be getting back, Gracie, before you are missed."

She stretched her arms luxuriously over her head and gave a sigh, followed by a yawn. "I know. Help clean me up."

He sat up and reached into the pocket of his pants for his handkerchief, using it to mop up the sticky cum that coated Grace's belly. Once she was clean, they both stood and silently dressed.

"You go first," Jimmy whispered. "Leave the lamp here. I'll take care of it."

"Goodnight," she whispered back, then climbed down the ladder and slipped out the door.

Chapter 2

The following morning, which was a Sunday, saw Grace and her family attend service at their local village church. Sitting with a bowed head, Grace spent most of the time daydreaming about her next encounter with Jimmy and what she would like to do with him. Perhaps he would allow her to explore his cock with her mouth as she had been longing to do. There was no delicate way of asking for such a wicked thing, so she determined to come right out with it and ask anyway. Of the sermon, she heard very little—something to do with fire and brimstone, no doubt.

Finally, service was over, and they filed out of the church into the breezy autumnal sunshine. "Well, thank God that's done!" muttered Jasper Stanton, Grace's father. "I vow the reverend gets worse every time. Can he not lighten up just once in a while? There are only so many dire warnings about hellfire that I can take!"

Ruth, his wife, put her arm through his. "Never mind now, it is done, and we may go home. Beth has baked a pumpkin pie specially for you."

Jasper smiled fondly at his youngest daughter, "Anything made by your hands, Beth, is sure to be perfection."

"That's what you say every time," laughed Beth, "but may I remind you, pa, of the blackberry cobbler from two summers ago that I managed to char in the oven."

Jasper waved a dismissive hand. "The exception that proves the rule, my dear."

"I see the reverend looking our way, pa," warned John, the middle child in the family—now at sixteen, more of a young man than a child.

Jasper shuddered. "Then let us go quick, for I have no wish to converse with him."

They headed towards their buggies, which were tethered to a post, the horses munching placidly on some straw. Ahead of them, his brother Frank and his wife Charlotte, were climbing aboard their own vehicles together with their two sons and daughter. It was a tradition among the Stantons that Sunday lunch was an extended family affair, with the location alternating between each brother's house every week. Today, it was Jasper's turn to play host at the large, grey-painted home he had built for Ruth all those years ago as a way to convince her to marry him. It had worked! They would soon be celebrating nineteen years of wedded bliss, though who was counting?

●————————————————●

Much later, after the pumpkin pie was demolished with many a word of praise, Grace stood to help clear the dishes from the table, together with the other womenfolk in the house. Sunday was a day off for their housemaid, Rose, so they all stepped in to do the household chores. The girls may have had an earl for a grandfather back in England, but over here, nobody was considered too good to do honest manual labour. With so many helping hands, it was quick work anyway.

Grace dried her hands on a dish towel and prepared to leave the kitchen to join everyone in the main parlour. She was stopped, however, by her aunt Charlotte, who was married to her uncle Frank. "Grace, if I may have a word with you?"

Startled, Grace replied, "Yes, of course."

"Let us go sit at the table in the corner there by the back door, so we are not overheard."

Now even more curious than ever, Grace did as she was told. Charlotte got straight to the point. "Grace, you know of course that the stable building is within view of my bedroom window. Last night, I had gone to draw the curtains when I noticed some movement outside. On closer inspection, I saw that it was you, coming out of the stable. Strange, I thought. Then lo and behold, the stable door opened again, and this time I discerned the familiar form of Jimmy walking out, looking very furtive indeed."

She paused and waited for Grace to respond. When Grace said nothing, Charlotte continued, "I can only assume, Grace, that you were meeting him there for some kind of assignation."

Grace nodded, but still did not speak.

Charlotte sighed, "How far has it got?" At Grace's questioning look, she added, "Have you lain with him, Grace?"

"Yes," mumbled Grace.

"Oh my dear Lord. I take it Ruth does not know of this?"

Grace shook her head vehemently. "No, Aunt Charlotte and please, she must not know."

"Ruth is my best friend. I do not keep secrets from her."

"Please, just this once. It would upset her terribly to find out."

"Yes, it would," Charlotte agreed. "A shotgun wedding to Jimmy is not what she has envisaged for your future."

"There won't be a need for that to happen, Aunt Charlotte, if we keep things between ourselves."

"And what if this results in you being with child? Have you considered, Grace, the risks you are taking?"

"We are being very careful."

At this, Charlotte snorted. They were quiet for a moment, then she said with a wistful smile, "Grace, I do not believe I have ever told you this, but your uncle Frank and I had an affair in London, before we came to America and got married. It caused a small scandal at the time, because you see we were caught in an embrace at a society ball. It was why I decided to leave England and come here with your mother and uncle Robert. Then Frank followed me of course, and the rest is history."

Grace was staring at her aunt in surprise. "I never knew!" she breathed.

294

Charlotte chuckled, "Well, it is not something we go around talking about. The reason I am telling you now is because I want you to know that I understand, but also that you need to be very, very careful. If I discovered you, then who is to say someone else might not do so too? You heard the sermon in the church today. People here would not be understanding and you would be branded a jezebel. It would cause an even greater stir than my scandal did back in London."

"I shall be very careful," Grace promised.

"What steps are you taking to ensure you do not become with child?"

Grace flushed. "We, erm, he does not complete inside me."

"Well, that is a start, but not enough. You still run too high a risk of becoming an unwed mother unless you do something more."

"What else can we do?" enquired Grace.

"You need to be very aware of your menses and note down the details of your cycle. On some days, when you are very fertile, you must avoid being with Jimmy altogether. The first eight days after you start bleeding should be safe, and the week before you are due as well, but the time in between is when you must be very careful."

Grace listened attentively, making a mental note of this extraordinary advice from Aunt Charlotte. "I will be," she promised again.

Her aunt observed her closely then sighed, "Very well, let us go back before we are missed."

Chapter 3

Life continued as normal over the course of the following month. Grace, ever the fast learner, heeded her aunt's advice and redoubled her efforts not to have her dalliance with Jimmy discovered. It seemed she was successful, for there were no further difficult conversations to be had with any member of her family, and her monthly bleeding came reliably on time.

One late October morning, she was in the main parlour, in the company of her mother and sister, engaged in the never-ending needlework that was required to maintain all their clothing in good order. Through the window, they heard the sound of a horse clattering over the gravelled path to their house. A few moments later, there came a knock on the door, which was answered by Rose, who then hurried into the parlour holding a folded slip of paper in her hand. "This came for Mr Stanton, ma'am."

"Thank you, Rose." Ruth took the folded slip of paper. "It looks like a telegram," she mused.

They had never received a telegram before, but had heard of the much vaunted new invention that facilitated communication across great distances.

"Who could it be from?" wondered Beth.

Ruth's mouth formed into a tight line. "I am very much afraid that it can only be news from England, and not anything good." She pondered a moment then came to a decision. "Grace, will you be a dear and go fetch your father. He said he would be in the outer west fields, supervising the mending of fences there. Hop on your mare and get him quick."

"Yes, ma."

Grace hurried out, stopping only to put on a warm riding coat and boots. Then she was out like an arrow, running to the stable. She found Jimmy there, cleaning out a stall with a broom. "Help me saddle Willow, quick," she called out. "I must get to pa at once."

He put the broom down, startled, but rushed to do her bidding. "What's the matter?" he asked.

"A telegram has arrived. Probably from England."

Jimmy brought the horse round and, with quick, efficient movements, attached the saddle and reins. Grace went to stand on the block and lowered herself into the side-saddle position, placing her right leg bent in front and tucking her left leg behind. Once secured into position, she urged her mare forward. As soon as she had crossed the gravelled entrance to her house and was out on the narrow mud road, she bid her horse to speed up, galloping at a brisk pace towards the outer west fields.

She slowed down as she approached her destination, her eyes searching for her father in the distance. She finally spotted a group of men further down to her right, of which one had the distinctive, tall gait of Jasper Stanton. She nudged her horse to move at a canter towards them.

Hearing the sound of hooves, Jasper turned his head to observe her approach with a frown. As she stopped her horse beside him, he called out worriedly, "Grace, what is it?"

"Pa, you need to come home now. We have received a telegram for you."

Jasper reacted instantly. He turned to his foreman, Tom Shaw, giving him quick instructions, then strode over to his horse, tethered nearby. In a thrice, he had mounted it and was urging it into a gallop. Grace followed, matching her father's pace on her own mare. Within minutes, they were both dismounting and handing over the reins to Jimmy before hurrying up to the house.

Ruth waited for them inside, the sealed telegram clasped in her hand. On seeing her husband, she went over to him. "It's addressed to you and Frank," she said, handing it over. With a frown, Jasper took it and quickly unfolded the sealed sheet of paper. He read it, then silently held the sheet out to his wife.

"What does it say?" asked Grace, impatient to know.

In a voice laced with worry, Jasper replied, "Father is gravely ill. He wishes us to return home as soon as possible."

"What will you do?"

Jasper stood still, thinking, his eyes on Ruth. She came to him, placing a soothing hand on his chest. "Ruthie, can you get us all packed and ready to leave by tomorrow?" he asked very softly.

"Yes." Ruth was firm, decisive.

Jasper inhaled deeply. "Very well. Let me go make the arrangements." Thinking things over as he spoke, he continued, "Tom can take over the running of the farm while we are away. He practically does it already. Frank's overseeing the transport of a grain consignment in Ashtabula today. I'll need to ride over and find him. While there, I'll see about booking our train passage to New York."

"I'll send word to Robert," said Ruth, speaking of her brother, who owned a large tract of neighbouring land. "He can help keep an eye on things here while we are away."

"Yes, good idea," murmured Jasper, running an agitated hand through his mussed hair.

Ruth held his eyes. "We could be at Stanton Hall within two weeks, at most three. We will do all we can to get there as quickly as it is possible. Beyond that, there is nothing more we can do except pray. What will be will be."

Jasper exhaled deeply, then drew his wife to him, finding comfort in the embrace. He dropped a kiss to her forehead then pulled back reluctantly. "I had better get going," he sighed.

The Vixen's Unlikely Marriage
Out on 19th February, 2024
Kindle Unlimited & Paperback

Also by this author

LOVE AGAINST THE ODDS: THE COMPLETE SERIES

A series of standalone novels which feature star-crossed lovers who have to fight the odds in order to be together.

Book 1 - Liberation

A steamy contemporary multicultural romance

Two people meet one day in a coffee shop and bond over their love of cinnamon rolls. On paper, they're nothing alike. Different backgrounds, different lifestyles, different life experiences. Yet they click...

The odds are stacked against them. Can they overcome them to be together?

Book 2 - Duplication

A sci-fi erotic romance

What are the odds that two people, from two separate universes should meet and fall in love? Will they overcome the odds to be together? This is a romance like you've never read before, partly set in a fictional universe with a very different moral code to ours.

As always with works by M.M. Wakeford, there is a guaranteed HEA and plenty of steam!

Book 3 - Determination

A steamy contemporary romance

Two people, living miles away from each other, from very different walks of life. Circumstances bring Audrey and Jacob briefly together. Sparks fly, but the odds are stacked against them. Can they overcome them to be together?

Book 4 - Infatuation

A steamy friends-to-lovers multicultural romance

Two people meet on a plane and begin a close friendship. They're from very different backgrounds – Kamal a devout Muslim and Liv, a chef whose friendship with her two male best friends includes "benefits".

Can Kamal and Liv overcome the odds and become more than just friends?

What people say about Love Against the Odds:

"Great Boxset… Each story is well written. I loved the story lines." 5* Amazon review

"Not your ordinary romance novels! … I'd highly recommend them. They show very accurately what love is like 'against the odds' and how when you meet the right person, there's no getting around it. Somehow love always finds a way." 5* Amazon review

KRANTOR'S MATE

One day, on a planet far from Earth, I meet my fated mate. The only problem is, he's in love with someone else.

Martha has enrolled on a six-month exchange program to the planet Ven, whose people have recently made first contact with Earth. Newly single and broke, Martha looks forward to this once-in-a-lifetime opportunity to find out more about the Venorians, an intriguing humanoid race of massive bronze-skinned people.

As the son and heir of the Kran, planet Ven's ruler, Krantor has four somars—men who are his lifelong bodyguards and companions. He loves them all dearly, but one of them, Prilor, he loves best of all. Krantor knows he's destined to meet his fated mate one day, but it's Prilor he wants to spend his days and nights with. And he certainly hadn't banked on his fated mate being a human!

Will Martha give up her life on Earth for a fated mate who already loves another? And what of the feelings she has developed for Shanbri, another of Krantor's somars?

Author's note: this is a standalone sci-fi romance with steam and spice aplenty, featuring FM, MM, and MFM relationships, and a guaranteed HEA for all.

What people say about Krantor's Mate:

"What a phenomenal read. The worlds, culture, and species created were diverse and detailed… I went on such an emotional ride with this book." 5* Amazon review

"I found this an interesting and original approach to the reverse harem and fated mate tropes... Thought-provoking and provocative, with high heat throughout." 5* Amazon review

"M.M. Wakeford offers a completely new take on fated mates. With all the expectations that are set with a trope, the author blows it out of the water with her fabulous storytelling." 5* Amazon review

"This is a fantastic sci-fi romance... I loved the characters and I highly recommend this book." 5* Amazon review

"Not what I expected, it's refreshing! This book takes a unique twist on polyamorous relationships AND fated mates." 5* Booksprout review

MELINDA'S CHOICE

Two very different men, and yet I want them both. I can't have my cake and eat it though. I have to make a choice.

Melinda Garcia, recently appointed Earth Federation's ambassador to the planet Krovatia, is a career woman going places... and leaving behind a broken marriage to the man she still loves.

For the last two decades, there has only been one woman in Wyatt's life. Yet his inability to get on a spaceship and leave Earth has cost him. Is there any way to win Melinda back?

Kirimor, a powerful male with five lovely drashas—concubines that service his needs as the most senior priest of Krovatia—has fallen for the lovely Earth female, but will she accept him as he is?

Two different men who love her. One difficult choice to make.

Author's note: Melinda's Choice is a steamy science-fiction romance featuring a love triangle between a strong, determined woman, the man she loves and the sexy alien with a tail that sweeps her off her feet.

What people say about Melinda's Choice:

"This has become one of my favorite all-time sci-fi novels... Melinda's Choice has many reasons for me to love it." 5* Amazon review

"A great alien romance/fated mates... This book will have you feeling all the emotions as you journey with Melinda throughout the story...

I definitely recommend this book for my fellow alien romance lovers!" 5* Amazon review

"This is a fabulous book. The way the author carefully created different cultures and species was masterful." 5* Amazon review

"O.M.F.G! This was my first sci-fi romance and let me tell you... I'm forever obsessed!" 5* Amazon review

Milton Keynes UK
Ingram Content Group UK Ltd.
UKHW020749090924
448088UK00012B/743